THE INHERITANCE

The Inheritance

E. V. Morgan

Author's Note

This novel contains references to self-harm, suicide, and sexual abuse. It explores themes related to intergenerational trauma.

This is a work of fiction. Unless otherwise indicated, all the names, characters, places, events, and incidents in this book are either the product of the author's imagination or used in a fictitious manner. Any resemblance to actual persons, living or dead, or actual events is purely coincidental.

1

Even before I saw her broken body, I knew she was dead. The wind had carried the putrid stench of death ahead of her, filling my nostrils with the odor of rot and decay. I crested the hill, my eyes swimming with tears and sweat as she came into focus.

The mountain lion had curled up to die at the base of a gnarled pine tree. Its ancient roots jutted from the soil, gently cradling her corpse. Three crows perched on the lion's body, talons piercing her flesh, poised to dismantle her.

Squawking in protest, the birds scattered at my approach, landing on a branch where they grumbled to each other like gossiping teenagers. I glared at them as though they'd measured out the lion's life on a string and snipped it short.

My heart was still racing from the two-mile hike through the Montana wilderness, complemented by a stitch in my side. I keeled over, resting my hands on my knees, struggling to breathe through the pain. Sweat trickled down my face and into my open mouth, salty and warm.

Falling to my knees, I clenched my hands into fists, fingernails biting into the tender flesh of my palms, as I examined the lion's mangled, lifeless body. Her muzzle and whiskers were covered in blood. Flies crawled through her matted fur and across her glassy green eyes, filling the air with their incessant buzzing. A few landed on me, sipping my sweat and tears, their legs stained scarlet with blood. I swatted them away, furious at their insatiable appetite for death.

She'd limped up here after being shot, with milk and blood speckling her engorged teats, perhaps in some vain attempt to reach her litter of cubs. They'd die without her. Starve to death in a dark den, for no reason other than because someone decided to kill their mother.

When the radio-tracking signal indicated the lion had stopped moving a few days ago, I'd assumed the battery was low, triggering the tracking collar to release and freeing her from the bulky necklace she'd worn for the past three years. Despite following her blood trail through the canyon, I refused to believe she was dead, desperately hoping that the scarlet stains smeared on rocks and leaves were from one of her kills.

I should've known better.

This wasn't the first of my study animals to perish at human hands, but this one hurt the most. She was the first lion I'd ever collared. I remembered how my hands shook as I secured the collar around her neck, my heart fluttering with anticipation and excitement. She'd barely been more than a teenager, still finding her way through the world after leaving her own mother. Since then, I'd been her shadow, following her life from afar, reveling in her beauty and her struggles. I'd watched her grow up, take a mate, become a mother herself.

Now she was dead, her light snuffed out, her offspring doomed. And I was sick of the waste.

Wiping tears from my eyes, I removed the radio-tracking collar and placed it reverently into my backpack. I spent a few silent moments beside the lion's body, my hand clenched in her thick, matted fur as I marveled at the sheer size and power of this elusive creature — of the muscles that had once rippled under her skin, the curved claws protruding from her paws, the sharp incisor peeking out from between blood-speckled lips. My heart ached as I thought of her being ravaged by crows and coyotes and beetles before succumbing to decay, though I knew her body would sustain those creatures and nourish the roots of this pine. A kind of blood sacrifice.

I whispered a final goodbye, then headed down the canyon, the stitch in my side screaming in protest. When I reached the road, I got inside my truck and pulled out my cell phone to check if I had a signal. As if in confirmation, it greeted me with a barrage of notifications of missed calls and messages from my mother.

My chest tightened as I skimmed her first few messages. I resisted the urge to respond, knowing it would only make things worse. Nevertheless, guilt lodged deep in my gut, like a half-digested meal, as I ignored the remaining notifications.

Instead, I dialed Doug Whitcomb, the local game warden with the state fish and wildlife department. Though most people called him Dougie, I'd been met with scorn the one time I'd tried using that nickname with him. Doug had made it clear that I could expect a base level of tolerance from him. Nothing more. He seemed personally offended by the fact that a twenty-five-year-old female like me could dare to work in this male-dominated field.

After a few rings, Doug's gruff voice rumbled through the phone. He didn't seem surprised to hear from me. I should've realized what that meant.

"One of my study animals was shot," I said. "Probably by the Heart Ranch folks. They're known to be trigger-happy. I've tried talking to them but they won't listen to me. You need to make sure they're fined."

He sighed. I could practically see the strained expression he adopted during our meetings. "The ranch had a depredation permit, Laurel. A mountain lion's been getting into their sheep flock and tearing them to pieces."

I closed my eyes and pinched the bridge of my nose. "Did they even try to protect their sheep?"

"They don't have the resources. This was the only option."

"Then they only have themselves to blame. The lion was acting in her nature. And now her cubs will die too."

"What do you want me to do, Laurel? My hands are tied."

"Killing animals should be the last resort. Figure out non-lethal options first. And if that doesn't work, you need to warn me before you issue kill permits for animals in my study area."

He scoffed. "It's not that simple. There're procedures I need to follow—"

"It is simple. Your job is to protect these animals. Do your goddamn job," I said, ending the call before he could protest. My phone immediately started vibrating again. Rather than answer, I clenched the phone tight in my palm, bolstering the courage to answer, certain it was Doug calling to chew me out or my mother trying to reach me again.

When I finally checked the screen, I realized it was Chris Demos, my mother's closest friend and my childhood nanny. She rarely called me. Perhaps my mother had asked her to intervene in our latest struggle. Steeling myself for an argument, I answered the phone.

"What's up?" I said, not bothering to hide my irritation.

There was a slight pause before she spoke, her voice thick. "Laurel, it's... it's about your mom."

"I can't deal with her anymore, Chris. She can't expect me to drop everything and take care of her whenever she has an episode. I've tried. It's too much."

"Laurel—"

"I know she put you up to this, but we can't keep enabling her. She needs real help. And it wouldn't kill Maura to call her now and then. I'm not her only daughter."

She muffled a sob. The sound made my flesh prick with goosebumps. "Chris, what's going on?"

A pregnant pause filled the air before she spoke again, and my world shattered.

"There's been an accident. Your mother is dead."

2

A week later, I found myself sitting on a pew at my mother's funeral. Chris sat beside me, her shoulders hunched, fingers clutching her short black hair. Though the service was about to begin, the seat on the other side of me remained empty. There was still no sign of my sister.

The sound of the door slamming shut echoed through the space. Heart lurching, I whirled around, but the narthex was empty. Fresh-cut flowers and incense cloaked the church in a suffocating stench. I struggled to breathe. My eyes blurred and turned downwards towards the floor. There was no point in staring at the closed coffin. I'd never gaze upon my mother's face again.

The priest droned on for what seemed like hours. He spoke of my mother in vague terms, as though all mothers were interchangeable. Chris spoke, but her words slipped past me, too quick to catch, like fireflies at dusk. I was so lost in my own thoughts and memories of my mother that I struggled to listen to hers.

Though Chris asked me to give a eulogy, I refused. Funerals painted a picture of the deceased that were often closer to fiction than reality, and I was never one to lie. My relationship with my mother was complicated, the early years filled with longing for her affection; the later years filled with fierce closeness and even fiercer fights.

Instead, I wrote my mother a letter, the pages brimming with angst and grief and longing and loss. Prior to the service, I knelt beside my mother's coffin, gripping the lid with white knuckles as tears streamed down my cheeks, and slid the letter inside.

Maybe I'd write her another letter, years later, once the pain lessened and time had coated my memories of her with honey.

Stirring me from my catatonic state, Chris grasped my elbow and coaxed me to my feet, guiding me outside. I blinked in the harsh sunlight, transfixed by the sight of tombstones peeking through the church gate. My feet rooted to the ground, paralyzed. I wasn't ready for what came next.

Chris murmured in my ear, urging me forward into the cemetery. When we reached the gaping hole in the ground, she wrapped her arm around my shoulder, pulling me tight against her. I watched, numb, as they lowered Mom's casket into the earth. Next to Dad.

I thought I would howl and shake with grief, but I felt empty, untethered from reality, like I was observing the burial of someone else's mother rather than my own. Despite Chris's presence beside me, I never felt more alone. My sister's absence, though not unexpected, made my heart seize, like falling through broken ice into the dark water below. I reached into my pocket instinctively, rubbing the smooth talisman stone between my fingertips, seeking comfort from memories of better times.

After bidding farewell to the remaining guests, I saw her. I didn't believe my eyes at first. Sweat and tears blurred my vision. I squinted, trying to bring the woman into focus, but she shimmered like a mirage on the horizon.

I made my way towards her, past tombstones and mausoleums, through fresh cut grass that clung to my bare legs. One of my feet, slick with sweat, slipped out of its high heel. I kicked the other shoe off, picked them up, and continued walking, eyes never once straying from the figure ahead of me. With each step, my heart expanded in my chest, until it felt as though it would burst through my rib cage. I willed myself back to stillness, knowing that allowing hope to bloom within me would bring only disappointment.

As I neared the edge of the cemetery, I realized with a shock that it wasn't a fever dream borne of grief and despair. It was her.

Maura stood beneath the canopy of a weeping willow, catkins gently nudging her arms in the breeze. Our eyes locked. We stood there, rooted to the ground, captive in the gravity of the other's orbit. Clouds hung heavy in the sky, the air quiet and pregnant with potential. My breath caught in my throat. I inched closer; worried she might bolt like a spooked deer if I moved too quickly. She straightened, piercing me with inquisitive brown eyes beneath arched eyebrows.

"Good of you to show up." Bitterness leached through my voice.

"I'm sorry for your loss," Maura said. "I know how much she meant to you. And how much you meant to her."

I stared at her in disbelief. "She was your mother, too, for fuck's sake. She died thinking you hated her."

"We had our issues, but I didn't hate her, Laurel. It was just easier for us to be apart. She wasn't a mother to me the way she was to you."

"She could've been if you'd given her half a chance. But you ran away instead. I was just a kid when you left."

"I left in order to protect myself."

"Protect yourself from what?!"

Maura pressed her lips tight together, as if to stop the truth from spilling out. But I knew she wouldn't tell me why she left. Neither had my parents, no matter how many times I'd asked.

Holding in a groan of frustration, I turned my back to her, unwilling to gaze upon my sister, the stranger. I wanted to shake her until she spit out an apology for abandoning our parents and me. Until she admitted why she'd left us to begin with.

After taking a few deep breaths, I faced her again. She met my gaze with a mixture of calmness and pity that only infuriated me further.

"I needed you growing up, you know," I said. "I still need you. Now, more than ever. Our parents are both dead. There's nobody left, except us. So help me understand why you left me. Please."

She looked taken aback. Confused, almost, as though she'd never considered how much her absence hurt me. Her ignorance shouldn't have come as a surprise. She'd always been self-absorbed, seemingly unaware of how her actions affected those around her. How her actions affected me. I fought back tears as

I thought of all the times in our childhood when she'd pushed me away when I'd craved her closeness.

"My choice to leave was never about you. I can't change what happened in the past, but I'm here now, Laurel. Isn't that enough? Can't we just move on?"

A small tendril of hope unfurled deep within me. I felt myself soften, overcome with the urge to wrap her in my arms, to give in and let go of the past.

In the corner of my eye, a flicker of movement caught my attention. I turned in the direction of our parents' graves. Soil cascaded into the gaping maw, obscuring our mother forever. Our mother, who'd been so consumed with Maura's emotional problems that she'd spent most of my childhood neglecting me, until the day Maura finally walked out the door and abandoned us both. When confronted with those memories, my urge to reconcile dissolved.

"We can't move on until you tell me what really happened. Why you left," I said, a challenge in my voice, willing her to respond.

Maura set her jaw, transforming her porcelain face to cold marble. Her eyes flickered with familiar rage. I braced myself for a fight, but instead of lashing out, she closed her eyes and took a deep breath. When she spoke, her voice was full of sorrow and regret.

"This was a mistake. I shouldn't have come. Take care of yourself, Laurel."

Head held high, my sister turned and walked away. Despite thinking there was nothing left within me that could break, my fractured heart splintered, the jagged pieces shredding me from the inside out.

I realized I never asked her why she'd bothered to come.

After leaving the cemetery, I felt gutted, raw, and hollow, and not just because of my mother's death. Maura always had this effect on me, stirring up buried thoughts and feelings, reminding me of nagging questions long left unanswered.

The thought of attending the reception Chris was hosting made my stomach churn. I couldn't sit there picking at a plate of food while people cast pitying glances my way, whispering about my sister's absence and our mother's tragic end. Besides, a dull ache radiated through my lower pelvis, harmonizing with the stitch in my side that had been plaguing me since I found the dead mountain lion.

Seeking answers and reassurance I suspected I'd never find, I drove through the familiar streets of my childhood neighborhood. I slowed to a stop at the intersection of Sussex and Keeler. My eyes brimmed with tears as I stared, captivated, at the crooked telephone pole and the plastic-wrapped bouquets of flowers and flickering candles at its base. Broken glass still littered the cement, glittering in the candlelight.

This is where my mother had drawn her last breath. Her car had folded around that pole, killing her on impact, leaving her body a bloody, twisted mess.

I wrenched my gaze from the morbid scene and drew a shaking breath before resuming the drive, past row after row of cookie-cutter houses, before turning into the driveway of the home I'd grown up in.

Entering the front door filled my heart with warmth. Being inside my childhood home felt like relaxing into a soft bed at the end of a long day. Part of me expected Mom or Dad to emerge from the kitchen, faces alight with joy.

When my gaze settled on Mom's empty armchair, the illusion shattered, the warmth I'd felt moments ago drained from my body. Her favorite knit blanket was nestled in the chair's well-worn crevices. An old mug of tea rested beside a creased paperback on the adjacent table, the stale scent of chamomile and lavender the last vestiges of her presence.

Eyes blurring, I instinctively rushed towards the safety of my parents' bedroom. I turned on the light, illuminating the four-poster bed that dominated the space. My stomach lurched as I stared at the rumpled pillows and the pale blue comforter scrunched at the foot of the bed. I imagined my mother tangled in the sheets, writhing as she struggled through another sleepless night that would be her last, my harsh words echoing through her diseased mind. Unease crept through my body, like spiders crawling through my veins. Still, I felt myself drawn towards the bed. Towards her.

My muscles trembled and ached, grief transforming my usually strong body into a quivering mess of limbs. I sank onto the bed and ran my hands over the sheet, searching for comfort in the memories from my childhood it evoked. Of nights spent curled in this bed between my parents, immersed in a bedtime story or seeking safety after a nightmare. A scab on my palm snagged on the pilling fabric, the flash of pain jarring me back to the present.

My mother was dead, gone in an instant, caught in a tumult of shrieking metal and shattered glass. And it was my fault.

When she'd called me the night before her death, I'd lost my temper and pushed her away, rather than helping her when she needed me the most.

I thought I was making a stand. Instead, I'd been digging her grave. The next morning, she stumbled into her car, blood swimming with a dangerous cocktail of anti-anxiety meds, antidepressants, and alcohol.

Mom's depression had always lurked beneath the surface, but the past few years had been especially hard. I'd shouldered the weight of my mom's clinging dependence ever since my dad died a few years ago. She'd treated me like an emotional safety blanket, smothering me while I struggled through a rigorous PhD program at Hildegard University, where my father had taught for decades. The more I tried to free myself from her grasp, the tighter she held on, until her desperation threatened to drown me.

Despite my familiarity with Hildegard and its campus, my choice to attend the school had nothing to do with my own ambitions, and everything to do with my mother. I needed to be close, to care for her. It meant sacrificing my dream of attending a more prestigious graduate program, like Yale or Stanford, somewhere with the prestige, resources, opportunities, and connections to catapult me out of stagnation and launch me into my career.

It would be easy to resent my mother for the choices I'd made. But it was easier still to blame my sister. Maura refused to support our parents, leaving me responsible for their well-being. She hadn't visited after Dad's lung cancer diagnosis and didn't attend his funeral. I couldn't remember the last time she'd spoken to Mom. After leaving home at age eighteen, Maura limited her contact that first year to a few short, tense phone calls and holiday cards addressed only to me. Then, nothing.

Until today.

I dragged myself out of bed and padded down the hall towards Maura's old room, as though the answers I sought might lurk within its walls. As I peeked inside, musty air rushed out, a relic from years of abandonment.

Though my parents had sterilized all signs of Maura's existence from the room, I still felt a twinge of unease in violating her old space. Gone were the posters, the belongings carpeting every available surface, and the blare of angry music, replaced with a neatly made bed, a pink dresser, and the faint forgotten smell of cheap incense. My parents had erased her presence from our home.

Fingers curled tight around the doorframe, my mind flooded with memories — of Maura's screams as she raged at Mom, the familiar sound of the door slamming, her muffled sobs. My parents had locked the echoes of those moments deep inside this room, where they'd been waiting escape, like the evils from Pandora's box.

Tears cascaded down my cheeks. I stumbled backwards, breath hitching in my chest. I squeezed my eyes shut, willing myself to stop from spiraling into the dark place I'd worked so hard to forget.

It was too late. In the darkness of my eyelids, I saw Maura sprawled across the carpet, blood pooling from her arms, surrounding her like grotesque angel's wings.

I wandered the rooms and halls of my childhood home like a wraith, as long-forgotten memories collided with the harsh reality of my mother's rapid decline. The signs of her illness were all around me: wine bottles overflowing from the recycling bin; bread rotting on the counter; prescription medication bottles spilling their pills across the kitchen table; unwashed dishes cluttering the sink, their porcelain surfaces crusted with old food.

My chest tightened, breath shallow. Grabbing the trash can, I threw my arm over the table counters, like a criminal trying to erase evidence at a crime scene. I rushed to the sink and filled the basin, ignoring the sharp stab of pain as I immersed my hands in the scalding water, vigorously scrubbing pots and plates until their surfaces gleamed. As the sink emptied, the noose strangling my chest loosened and my breath slowed.

The doorbell rang, the noise so jarring that I nearly sliced my finger on the butcher's knife I was cleaning. When I opened the door, I found Chris standing there. She charged inside and wrapped me into a tight hug. I buried my face in her neck, inhaling her familiar scent of saddle soap and lilac. I allowed my eyes to close. Tension drained from my body.

Chris pulled away, scrutinizing me. Lines etched her face, her skin reminding me of a crumpled sheet of paper that had been smoothed out again. I wondered with alarm when she'd grown old.

"How'd you find me?" I asked.

"You weren't at the reception. I figured you'd be here."

"I couldn't deal with being around all those people. And it felt wrong to go back to my own place."

"Do you want me to leave?"

"No, no, it's fine. Come in. Please."

Though Chris had been inside my parents' home countless times, she moved tentatively, as though inside a stranger's house. She clutched her elbows as she studied the photos on the wall and the stack of paperback books on the coffee table, as if noticing these details for the first time.

"It's so strange that she's gone," she finally said. "I keep thinking she's only popped out to the store, or she's in the yard, and that I'll turn around and find her standing there."

A lump formed in my throat. "Yeah, I know what you mean."

Chris drifted over to the piano and ran her fingers over the keys. "She used to play so beautifully. It's so quiet in here without her music." She turned to me. "Didn't you play piano growing up?"

I nodded, not trusting myself to speak, awash in memories. Growing up, Mom practiced piano each evening after reading me a bedtime story. I'd fall asleep listening to the soothing sound of her music. After Maura left home, I requested piano lessons so I could spend more time with my mom, despite having little interest in music. Mom was delighted.

One year later, when I was around ten years old, she found me banging my head against the keyboard. I couldn't master a particularly difficult section of a Bach minuet and was finding it harder and harder to pretend I enjoyed practicing piano.

"Having trouble with the new piece?" Mom asked, sitting beside me on the piano bench. I didn't respond. Instead I emitted a low groan of frustration muffled by the keyboard. She laughed and coaxed me into an upright position. "How are you liking your lessons?"

I squirmed and stalled, preparing to lie. Before I could respond, Mom gave me a knowing smile, though there was sadness in her eyes. "You asked for lessons because of my interest in music, not yours." It was a statement, not a question.

My face flushed as I nodded in agreement. Tears gathered at the corners of my eyes. I turned away, not wanting her to see how upset I was, worried that without this interest tying us together, we'd drift apart. Seeing my distress, Mom grabbed my hands and squeezed them, searching my eyes with hers.

"Don't ever do anything solely because you think it's what others want or expect of you. Be true to yourself. Forge your own path. If that means digging in the mud for bugs instead of practicing your etudes and scales, so be it. Don't let my life dictate how you live yours."

I never played the piano again.

"You okay, Laurel?"

The sound of Chris's voice forced me back into the present. I shook my head to clear it and forced a smile. "Yeah. Just... remembering. And you're right. It doesn't feel like home without her music."

"Let's fix that."

Chris headed into the kitchen and turned on the old CD player that sat above the sink. The joyous tones of Saint-Saëns's "The Carnival of the Animals" filled the room. She sighed and closed her eyes, nodding her head to the music. My cheeks flushed as I surveyed the stained kitchen floor and grimy countertops I hadn't yet cleaned, but Chris seemed oblivious to the mess.

I rummaged through the cabinets for the herbal tea my mom kept on hand for Chris's visits. A few minutes later, we sat down at the kitchen table, mugs in hand. Chris stirred sugar into her tea and blew on the hot liquid before taking a sip.

"I saw Maura at the cemetery," she said.

"Yeah, after sixteen years of silence."

"At least she showed up. That's something, right?"

"Do you know why Maura cut off contact?" I asked. "She still won't tell me."

Chris sat back and ran a hand through her hair, brow furrowed, though she didn't seem surprised by the question. I leaned forward, hungry for answers. She opened and closed her mouth a few times before speaking.

"Maura experienced a lot of pain growing up. She struggled with depression, anxiety, self-harm. Your mom wanted to help, but didn't quite know how." Chris hesitated, eyes flicking away from mine. "I don't want to speak ill of your mom, but she might have made things... harder, for Maura.

"She loved Maura and felt her pain so deeply it almost debilitated her, too. But Maura didn't need your mom's empathy. She needed her strength and resilience. Your mom couldn't give Maura what she needed, not because she didn't want to, but because she didn't know how. Maura's choice to keep her distance from your family had nothing to do with you."

A lump formed in my throat as I absorbed Chris's words. Its elements were familiar, grounded in my own experiences in childhood and the story my parents had told me about Maura's emotional struggles. But it still didn't explain why Maura's mental health had declined so rapidly during her adolescence.

Had something triggered it? Something my parents and Maura wanted to keep from me, even at the expense of me having a relationship with my sister? Why didn't Maura trust me with the truth now that our parents were dead?

"Maura's the only family I have left." My lower lip trembled and my gaze moved down to the table, struggling against the surge of tears threatening to overwhelm me. "I want her in my life, but whenever I try to get close, she runs away."

Chris reached for my hand. "Oh, honey. I know you're feeling alone right now. But there's more to family than shared blood. You might not have Maura in your life, but you have me. Remember that."

I nodded, sniffling, and pulled my hand away from hers. It was easier to agree with Chris than admit how deeply hurt I was by Maura's continued estrangement. Despite what Chris said about family, both inherited and chosen, the bonds of sisterhood still tugged at me, my blood calling out to Maura's, yearning for acknowledgment I feared I might never receive.

As though sensing my discomfort, Chris shot me a sympathetic smile. "I know today's been hard. I'm around if you ever need to talk, okay? I mean it when I say you're family."

"I know. Thanks, Chris."

We headed towards the door and exchanged another hug. Before I could pull away, she gripped my shoulders and stared into my eyes.

"Remember what I said about your sister. Focus your energy on the future, and on people who choose to be in your life. You've experienced enough pain. I don't want to see you hurt."

I smiled tightly and ushered her outside, refusing to acknowledge the unwanted advice.

My family had been running from our history for too long. Something happened to Maura that drove her away. Now that our parents were dead, losing my sister wasn't an option.

It was long past time for Maura and me to have honest reckoning about our past.

3

The pain started about a week after my mother's funeral. What had been an annoying, but manageable, twinge on the left side of my abdomen was now a full-blow cramp, announcing itself whenever I moved too quickly or reached for a glass on a high shelf. It was accompanied by a dull, throbbing pain in my pelvis, my gut distended and full, as though I had overindulged in a rich meal. Ibuprofen helped, a little. So did heating pads, applied gingerly across my belly as I lay splayed across my bed, cocooned in misery.

Attending to the physical pain was a distraction I was all too eager to indulge. It was easier to lose myself in the complaints of my body than sink further into despair and grief, haunted by thoughts of how I might have prevented my mother's untimely death. Not usually one to worry about aches and pains, which were ever-present during long days in the field, I now found myself spending hours googling symptoms and identifying outlandish diagnoses.

But it was thoughts of my mother that rescued me from the black hole of medical forums and message boards, where the anxious denizens of the internet reacted with shock and existential dread at more common malaises, like the sight of red blood in the toilet (hemorrhoids) or stabbing pain in their skulls (chronic migraines). I could hear my mother's voice in my mind, so clear that tears sprung to my eyes. "You're in graduate school. Health insurance is covered through your tuition. Just go to the doctor, Laurel."

Though grateful to learn that I carried my mother within me, I couldn't imagine living the rest of my life with her whispering in my ear, reminding me of her absence.

But my phantom-mother was right. The pain constantly demanded my attention. I needed to get actual help, if only to snap me out of this self-inflicted fugue state of self-pity. I made an appointment with a general practitioner at Hildegard's student medical center. Maybe the return to campus would be enough to jolt me out of grief and force me to confront my looming responsibilities as a graduate student.

The next day, I traded in pajamas for rumpled jeans and a t-shirt and headed back to Hildegard's campus for my appointment. With its sleek exterior and gleaming metal walls, the health center clashed with the historical red-bricked buildings characteristic of the rest of campus. After checking in with the receptionist, I was called back into an exam room, where I perched atop the exam table, my leg jiggling with nervous energy while the paper sheet beneath me crinkled.

A few minutes later, an older man in a lab coat entered the room, his wispy white hair ruffling as the door swung shut behind him. Taking a seat on a wheeled stool, he cocked his head and flicked his rheumy blue eyes over me, then consulted a clipboard. "I'm Dr. Harris. What seems to be the problem, Laurie?"

"It's Laurel," I corrected, then explained my symptoms.

"Any chance you're pregnant?"

Panic jolted through me as I wracked my brain, trying to remember the timing. About a month ago, I picked up a man in some backwater Montana town during my research. Exhausted from hours spent in the field, I was content listening to him describe, in grandiose detail, the perils of working in the logging industry. After a few drinks and a few laughs, we spent the night together. The next morning, he asked about my work. After learning about my fascination with mountain lions, he laughed and shared his predilection for trapping bobcats and poisoning coyotes. The mood soured, and I left, fuming.

With a tangible sense of relief, I remembered that I'd had my period since then. I was in the clear.

"Not a chance," I replied firmly.

He nodded, then rattled off a series of questions I'd already answered on the intake forms — about my menstrual cycle, birth control methods, alcohol consumption. My irritation grew with each wasted breath. I wanted critical thought and expert opinion, not boilerplate questions with little relevance to my actual issues.

After exhausting the questions, he poked and prodded my abdomen, my flesh tingling at the touch of his ice-cold hands. He checked my heart and lungs next, muttering inaudibly as anxiety rolled through me in waves. I'd expected easy answers and quick results that would put my mind at ease, not this prolonged process of humiliation, forced to surrender my body's inner workings to this stranger.

Dr. Harris's stool creaked as he leaned back and pushed away from the exam table, removing the stethoscope from his ears, and studied me, brow furrowed. "Have you been under any stress lately?" he asked finally. "More so than usual?"

I stifled the laughter rising in my chest, which transformed into a croaking sob halfway up my trachea. The doctor smiled patiently, waiting for me to respond.

"Well, my mother just died, and I'm a graduate student. So yes. But if I wanted to talk about my feelings, I'd have called the mental health department."

"Sometimes stress can show up in unexpected ways. I see it all the time. Chronic stomachaches, headaches, muscle cramps. They're common among students dealing with the pressures of the academy. Especially among girls. Mix in the death of a parent, and it's no wonder you're suffering."

"You're saying this is psychological," I said, bristling. "That I'm making it all up."

"On the contrary. What you're feeling is quite real. We can run some tests, make sure you don't have an infection, but I suspect this is stress-related. Try meditation, exercise, make sure you're sleeping enough. Limit alcohol consumption. Some people find reducing or eliminating certain foods can provide relief. In fact, with the bloating and stomach pains you're experiencing, I'd recommend taking a food sensitivity test. There's one test in particular I think would be useful. We sell it in the pharmacy. It uses your DNA to screen you for hereditary diseases, like certain cancers, in addition to food allergies. Yes, I think you'll find the results illuminating. I'm sure you'll feel better mentally once your stomach flattens back down, too."

I glowered at him, incredulous, as the waistband of my jeans pressed uncomfortably against my distended stomach, the now-familiar dull ache radiating through my pelvis.

The doctor cleared his throat, made a show of looking at his watch, and glanced towards the door. Turning to face me, he said, "You'll be fine, Laurie." He patted my knee paternalistically and breezed out of the room, leaving me alone as another twinge of discomfort radiated through my lower pelvis.

I left the doctor's office fuming, baffled at how wrong it had all gone. Despite the urge to storm out of the health center with my middle finger raised, I followed the doctor's instructions, though I was skeptical that the tests would reveal anything useful. I had my blood drawn to test for infections, then picked up the DNA testing kit from the pharmacy. After swabbing the inside of my cheek, I filled out the testing kit's form, which promised to provide me with insight into food allergies, genetic disease, and other important information about my health and heritage.

As I read more about the test, I found my initial reluctance fading somewhat, replaced by growing interest. If nothing else, the test promised to reveal more about my family's lineage through a data-sharing agreement with another company specializing in family trees. I reflected on how remarkably little I knew about my extended family and ancestors. Even my grandparents were nothing more than names to me. With my mother dead and my sister estranged, I longed for some sort of connection with my bloodline. Perhaps this genetic test could help ease that longing.

Rather than return home, I headed towards the Wallace Hall of Science, determined to use my studies as a distraction from my ailing health and unsettled grief. Wallace Hall stood sentry over Hildegard University's campus, with imposing monolithic stone walls and floor-to-ceiling windows that glinted in the early morning sun.

I entered the building and made my way towards the lab space I shared with Luis and Petra, two other doctoral candidates in the Ecology program. When I opened the door, my nostrils filled with the earthy scent of chrysanthemums, a bouquet of which was perched on my desk. I opened the card at the base of the vase. A condolences gift from the other members of my lab. A flush of gratitude washed over me at the gesture.

Though my desk was remarkably organized, especially relative to my lab-mates, I automatically brushed aside a few stray petals, straightened a stack of textbooks, and arranged my pens and pencils in a neat row before sitting down and pulling out my laptop and datasheets. I opened a notebook and started creating a list of tasks I needed to accomplish to get back on track. There were samples to process, datasheets to enter, data to analyze, articles to read, lectures to attend. As the list grew, my chest tightened, an invisible rope pulling me beneath the tide.

I thought returning to the lab would be reinvigorating. I thought if I pretended things were normal, I'd be able to transition back to my studies like nothing had happened. Instead, my once sharp mind felt sluggish, and it seemed impossible to break through the shroud of grief wrapped around me.

Losing my mother was hard enough, but her death had also ripped open the old wound between me and my sister, which had never fully healed. Chris insisted that Maura's issues had been with our parents, but it didn't explain why Maura chose to sever her relationship with me, too.

I was determined to get answers about my family's history, but there wasn't a clear path forward to get them. Maura refused to answer my calls, and Chris claimed she'd told me everything she knew. While I craved closure with my past, part of me realized my singular focus on Maura's estrangement was preventing me from processing my grief and moving forward.

A sharp rap sounded at the door. I jolted upwards and saw my PhD advisor, Richard, looming in the doorway. My thesis research was part of a long-term study on mountain lions Richard had started decades before.

"Laurel. Good of you to show up." Richard strode over to my desk and studied the bouquet. "I see you got our flowers, then? It was my idea. The whole lab chipped in."

"Yep, thank you."

Richard smiled and sat down at Luis's workspace, his lanky legs bent at awkward angles as he perched atop the short chair. He grimaced and kicked his feet onto my desk, nearly upending the vase. I winced as dried mud sloughed off his worn hiking boots and landed on my data sheets.

"First off, how are you?" he asked.

"Oh, you know." I shrugged, forcing a smile.

"It's a shame about your mother. Such a shame. But if you keep moping around, you'll risk falling behind even more. Use her loss as a motivation, okay? Once you get back to your usual routine, you'll forget all about her."

I gaped at him, shocked at his callousness. As though losing a parent was like getting a flu you could recover from, rather than a permanent wound I would carry forever.

Behind Richard, I glimpsed Luis in the doorway, clutching a coffee cup, his eyes wide. Richard craned his neck over his shoulder, then clapped his hands together and said, "Ah, Luis. Come in, come in."

"No, no, you look so comfortable. I would hate to intrude. I'll come back later."

Richard laughed and waved him in, oblivious to Luis's sarcasm. "That's alright, come in, please. Tell Laurel our big news."

Luis trudged inside and deposited his messenger bag and coffee on the desk, inches from Richard, who appeared unfazed. "Well, after wrapping things up in Mexico, I completed all of my analyses, and it looks like the vaquita population could recover if they're managed differently," Luis said.

"That's great! Congratulations," I said, though I couldn't help but compare his progress on this highly endangered porpoise species to my own. My research on mountain lions had been stumbling along, even before my mother's death.

"Not that part," Richard said, rolling his eyes. "Tell her the rest."

"I've been invited—"

"We've been invited to Mexico to present our results to the government. I just hope I don't get mugged or kidnapped by gangs."

An awkward silence filled the room. Luis closed his eyes and took a deep breath while his cheeks flushed a dark red. Richard smiled at me, his eyes glinting, as if in challenge. Though I was used to Richard's inappropriate and offensive sense of humor, it didn't make his comments any less hurtful. I wanted to say something, but Richard was a walking troll, hungry for an argument. It was better to ignore him.

"I'm sure you don't need to worry about that," I replied, refusing to take his bait. He responded as if I had.

"I'm only joking. Lay off, for fuck's sake. You're too sensitive, the both of you." Richard's expression sobered, and he turned to face me. "Laurel, there's something I want to talk to you about. I can't get into it now. Come by next Monday at 9am. We'll talk then, ok?"

"Sure."

"Excellent, excellent." Richard glanced at his watch. "Well, I'd better be going. I have a lecture to get to."

Luis pressed his lips together as Richard loped out the door. Once Richard's footsteps faded, Luis pulled me into a tight hug. The crown of his head brushed against my chin. After releasing me, his eyes met mine, full of pity.

"Laurel, I'm so sorry about your mom. How are you holding up?"

I hesitated, unsure of whether the question was genuine, uncertain of whether he wanted the truth. As I struggled to find the right words to express my grief, I found my tongue heavy and unyielding.

"Dumb question," he said, raising his hands and shaking his head. "Forget I asked."

"It's fine. I'm... I'm okay. I honestly thought Richard would go easier on me. The flowers are a nice gesture, but he also told me to use my mom's death as a burst of inspiration. So that wasn't great."

"These flowers?" Luis gestured to the bouquet, and I nodded. "I bought those with contributions from the other lab members. Richard didn't put in a dime."

"And here I was, thinking Richard was a changed man, full of generosity and compassion."

"Don't hold your breath."

"Maybe we'll get lucky and he will get kidnapped by gangs."

Luis snorted. "If they ask for a ransom, I'm not chipping in. He still owes me $5 for last month's department lunch."

4

The rest of the morning, Luis and I fell into a comfortable silence, working at our respective desks. With him for company, it was easier to return to my studies. I'd been living in virtual isolation for the past few weeks while grappling with my mother's death and my sister's intentional absence from my life. Being around Luis made me realize how much I needed the comfort of a familiar face to keep me grounded.

Around noon, Luis ripped off his headphones and tossed them aside. "I need a break. Want to grab lunch?"

Tapping a pen against my lips, I assessed the progress I'd made. Despite being deep in data entry, I'd barely dented the stack of datasheets beside me. My eyes were fatigued from staring at my laptop for the past few hours, but I was reluctant to interrupt my progress. The decision was made for me when my stomach emitted a loud growl.

"It's settled then," Luis said, grinning. "I'm buying."

We headed to the university gym parking lot, where food trucks parked during the week. A few minutes later, tacos in hand, we settled beneath an oak tree on the quad, which was crowded with students lounging on picnic blankets and benches, enjoying the warm, early days of the fall semester.

Luis took a bite of his taco and groaned in pleasure, salsa dribbling down his chin. He wiped his mouth with a napkin and said, "I have a confession to make."

"What's that?" I asked between bites.

"I prepped some lunches for the week but intentionally forgot to bring one today. Sometimes you just want a taco, you know?"

"Yeah, I know."

"Have you seen Petra since being back?"

I shook my head. Petra was another doctoral candidate in our lab, on track to defend her thesis and graduate this spring. Luis, Petra, and I were farther ahead in our studies than other students in Richard's lab, so we'd gravitated to each other.

"She's putting together a post-doc application to work with Veronica Hall over at Michigan, but Richard has some sort of vendetta against Hall and told Petra he wouldn't give her a reference."

My eyebrows shot up. "Come on. There's no way he's that petty." Without a reference from her PhD advisor, Petra's odds of securing the position were slim to none. Her career would be over before it even started.

"He is, though. My theory is that he wants Petra here as long as possible, since she's managing most of his projects."

I shuddered, my mind conjuring an image of Petra, ten years into her PhD, still toiling away in the lab as Richard drank wine on the porch of his lakeside cottage.

Luis's gaze flicked to mine, a muscle in his jaw working. "I'm starting to wonder if Petra might have... pissed Richard off. Maybe she did something that made him look bad. That's all

Richard cares about, you know. His reputation, his image, his ego. Petra's been acting strangely the past few weeks. I thought it was just stress, but I'm beginning to suspect it's something more."

"We're PhD candidates with a demanding advisor. Plus Petra's long-distance with her husband right now. That's enough to make anyone stressed. What more could there be?"

Luis was about to reply when a stray Frisbee collided with me, upending my agua fresca over my jeans. I muttered a curse and began blotting the growing stain with a napkin. A shadow fell across me.

"I'm so sorry!"

The voice sounded familiar. I looked up and forced myself not to groan at the spindly sophomore cowering above me, clutching his Frisbee to his chest.

"Oh. Laurel. I didn't realize—I mean, your drink? Should I get you another one?"

"It's fine, Ray. Don't worry about it."

Luis shot me a quizzical look while Ray stood awkwardly beside us, gaping at me. Ray's friends started hollering at him to come back. He gave a slight shake of his head, muttered something unintelligible, and loped away like a skittish horse.

"What the hell was that about?" Luis asked. The cadence of the earlier moment was lost, forgotten in the shuffle of spilled beverages and unwanted memories. Luis seemed to realize it, too, his face softening as though relieved by the distraction. His wagged his finger at me. "I think that young one might have a crush on you."

"Don't be ridiculous." Ray was still a teenager, at least six years younger than me. Certainly not an age that sparked my romantic interest. Even if he were older, I doubted he'd ever be my type. He was too scrawny and insecure.

"Well, something's got him worked up," Luis said.

"It's a long story."

"Spill, woman."

I smiled, recalling what had happened. Enough time had passed that I could laugh about it rather than grimace. "Ray was in one of my freshman lecture sections last year. Interested in field biology. He approached Richard, asking about summer internship opportunities."

"No chance of that."

"Nope. But he was persistent. Richard got annoyed and offloaded him onto me. Said I should let him join me in the field, since his family vacations in Montana each summer."

"Oh, God, no."

"I know. It's horrible."

Like me, Luis understood that the appeal of field biology was the opportunity for solitude. The work often required an extra set of hands, but you could choose with whom you worked. Having a competent field crew with good chemistry was essential; otherwise, those long hours in harsh conditions could lead to catastrophic meltdowns. My own field technician this past summer quit after a month, unable to handle the demands of the work.

"Anyway, I take Ray out to a field site," I continue, "it's swelteringly hot. The terrain is steep and rocky, and he's wearing some horrid, trendy sneakers with no grip. We barely get half a mile out before he's panting and near delirious. We stop by a rock outcrop for a drink. Then I hear a rattling sound."

"Tell me it's not a rattlesnake."

"It's a rattlesnake. He's pretty much on top of it and makes a comment about how he can hear my cellphone vibrating. I tell him to back away. He freaks out, starts jumping around like he's walking on hot coals, and steps on the damn thing. It bites him right on the ankle."

Luis made a strangled groan, clutching his hair and squirming theatrically.

"Ray hyperventilates and passes out. I drop our gear and carry him out like a goddamn firefighter. At the hospital, they examine him and discover it was a dry bite. No venom injected. Turns out he'd fainted from anxiety and heat exhaustion."

I hid a smile as Luis doubled over, shaking with laughter. Ray was busy playing Frisbee with his friends, studiously avoiding us, as if he knew he was the topic of our conversation.

"Let me guess. He's an English major now?" Luis asked.

"Yeah, that sounds about right."

"The university should give you a medal."

"Nah," I said, grinning. "Everyone has their fair share of bad field days. Like when I used a plant identification book to figure out the three-leaved plant I found on a hike. Turns out it was poison ivy. I had to throw away the book afterwards, since I stored the leaves in it so I could study them later. It took several rounds of steroids for the rash to go down."

Luis struggled to keep a straight face, but a snicker escaped his lips. "I mean, it's awful, but also kind of hilarious. Not as bad as the rattlesnake thing, but still pretty bad."

"Yeah. Only this happened when I was eight not eighteen."

We both erupted in laughter. For the first time since my mother's funeral, I felt like myself.

I didn't realize that it would also be the last time.

Over the next week, I threw myself headlong into my work, determined to make progress before meeting with Richard on Monday. When Friday evening arrived, I was still in the lab, hunched over my laptop as the last rays of sunlight winked out over the horizon. The murmurs and echoes of students walking through the corridors dissipated, and Wallace Hall settled into stillness, its rooms dark and quiet.

An empty coffee mug and granola bar wrappers sat atop my desk, the only sustenance I'd consumed all day. Though my stomach ached with hunger, I ignored it, forcing myself to concentrate. My chair creaked as I sought a comfortable position, trying in vain to relieve the dull ache radiating through my pelvis.

A bright red error message popped up on my computer screen. I groaned. I'd spent the entire afternoon debugging the statistical code for my research data, but whenever I fixed one problem, another seemed to pop up, like a never-ending game of whack-a-mole. If this kept up, I'd need to spend the weekend locked in the lab until I generated some useable results. I couldn't risk showing up to Richard empty-handed.

Richard was an excellent mentor and scientist, but his exceedingly high expectations for his students, combined with his impatience and lack of emotional regulation, meant that any signs of weakness or failure were met with his disapproval, if not outright hostility. I had my own high standards, too, and hadn't allowed myself to lessen them, despite my current state of grief. Richard appreciated my drive. I'd managed to stay on his good side thus far and wanted to keep it that way. It seemed Petra was bearing the brunt of his disapproval these days, anyway.

My eyes were bleary and fatigued from hours spent staring at lines of code. I missed being in the field, tracking mountain lions through rugged forests and rocky crags, sleeping beneath the Milky Way, miles from the nearest person. When I started this program, I hadn't anticipated how much of ecology involved sitting in front of a computer. My dad, who'd taught biology at Hildegard for decades, never warned me about it, either. Probably on purpose. He knew how much I hated being inside.

My gaze settled on a framed photo of my dad atop my desk. In it, he was perched in his canoe, mussed silver hair sticking out from beneath his rumpled fishing hat. He grinned at the camera. I reached into my pocket and pulled out a smooth river stone, its dark blue surface painted with an image of a bird in flight. My fingers closed around the stone, allowing warmth to seep inside it, losing myself in the bittersweet memories it evoked.

Growing up, Maura was filled with inexplicable rage and despair, most of which was directed at Mom. Their fights occurred behind closed doors, leaving me clueless as to what the issues were. I'd always blamed Maura for the rift between her and our parents. But these past few years had taught me that mothers could fail daughters, too, and I wondered if I'd gotten it all wrong.

Whenever things between Maura and Mom reached a boiling point, Dad whisked me off on hikes or camping trips, just the two of us. I adored our time together. It seemed Maura and I gravitated towards the parent with whom we shared a surname. I was a Lane, while Maura was a Ryder. Our parents had wanted to make sure each of their family names were passed on, since neither of them had siblings. In Maura's case, her intimacy with our mother was characterized by conflict rather than coexistence. But I suppose hate is its own type of closeness.

An avid fisher, Dad was eager to impart his knowledge and love of the pastime to me. Though I relished spending time outside with my dad, I disliked most everything about fishing. My stomach twisted in distress whenever I saw fish wriggling on hooks, their gills gasping for water and eyes wide with panic. I hated the needless suffering, and started pretending to secure bait to my hook, casting an empty line into the water.

I think Dad figured out the real reason I never seemed to catch any fish. On our first trip to the Indiana Dunes, where this photo was taken, he conveniently "forgot" our fishing equipment and handed me my first pair of binoculars. We spent the trip birdwatching along the Little Calumet River. That's when I realized I wanted to devote my life to the natural world and its inhabitants.

Dad gave me the river stone to commemorate the trip. He'd caught me eyeing it at a kitschy roadside gift shop, my pockets brimming with sweets from the candy store next door. Tracing my finger across the bird painted atop the stone, he explained how birds used the sun, the stars, and the magnetic pull of the earth to navigate during their migration, allowing them to return home year after year. He told me the stone was a talisman that would guide me home, too. It would serve as a compass and a guide when I needed help finding the right path.

I'd carried it with me ever since.

Turning my attention back to my work, I squinted at the glowing monitor through the deepening twilight, searching for the innocuous phrase or misplaced comma that was derailing my code. But I soon resigned myself to approaching the problem with fresh eyes tomorrow morning.

The sound of an email notification caught my attention, reminding me of all the unread emails I'd neglected the past week. I opened my inbox, relieved to see that the results from the DNA testing kit had come through. Since my blood sample had tested negative for infection, I hoped that a food allergy or sensitivity might be responsible for my symptoms. I opened the website and clicked on my results.

My heart sank as I reviewed the results. No obvious food allergies, but potentially a weak sensitivity to dairy. I so rarely ate animal products that I doubted my occasional indulgence in ice cream was responsible for my chronic discomfort. Though disappointed that the results didn't point to a clear answer, I wasn't particularly surprised. But my experience with Dr. Harris had been so negative that I was reluctant to return. Perhaps he was right. My mother's death and Maura's brief reemergence at the funeral could have taken a deeper psychological toll than I originally realized.

Rather than dwell on my disappointment, I turned my attention to the heritage results. It was a welcome distraction, and one that I'd been looking forward to. My brow furrowed as I reviewed my ethnicity estimates. Though my dad's family had Scottish roots, the results showed I was mostly French and German, with only a sliver of Scottish ancestry. I frowned, wondering why the results were so different from my expectations.

A message on the webpage caught my attention. The subject was "SmartMatch with April Bennett." Though I'd paid extra for the service, which promised to connect me with any other relatives in their system that shared my genetic code, I hadn't expected a match to show up. My parents had said so little about my family that I'd long ago accepted that we didn't have any. It seemed I'd been wrong. My heart began racing at the prospect of connecting with someone who shared my blood. I clicked on the message.

> *Laurel, you have no idea what it means to me to have found you. Please get in touch. I'm in Chicago and would love to meet up.*

I navigated to the SmartMatch page on the BloodlineDNA website and stared at the results, dazed.

April Bennett and I had matched as first cousins.

The results made no sense. I blinked and rubbed my eyes, certain they were playing tricks on me. Neither of my parents had siblings, which meant I couldn't have any first cousins. When I studied the results again, I found them unchanged. The realization knocked the air from my lungs. For a moment, I couldn't breathe. Panic flooded through my chest.

The company had made a mistake. It was the simplest explanation. The lab technicians must have mixed up my test tube with someone else's, or contaminated my sample with another person's DNA.

But April's location nagged at me. She lived in Chicago. The city where my parents met. The city where they'd raised Maura before relocating to Grenadier after my birth. The city where Maura had lived since leaving home at eighteen.

I forced myself to consider the possibility that April was my cousin. That would mean I had an aunt or uncle unknown to me. Perhaps there'd been an adoption in the family — one of my parents, or a sibling of theirs.

Once the thought wormed its way into my mind, I couldn't shake it loose. It would explain why my parents had been so tight-lipped about our family. It would explain why I'd had little to no contact with other family members, save my father's parents, who were long since dead. It would explain why my mother refused to talk about her parents, no matter how many times I'd tried to learn more about them.

What had she been afraid of?

5

Two days later, I found myself in a Chicago café, waiting for my cousin to arrive. When I messaged April back, she'd replied almost immediately and suggested we meet. Eager for answers, I agreed, despite all the work I needed to do before meeting with Richard the next day.

I wrapped my fingers around a steaming mug of coffee and scanned the bustling café, wondering whether April would recognize me from the photo I'd sent her last night. The café was near Loyola University, where April was a sophomore, and was filled with students engrossed in their laptops and textbooks. My jittering knee banged against the underside of the table, sending a shock of pain through my leg.

A shadow fell across my table. I looked up to find a young woman staring at me. She had warm, brown eyes above sharp cheekbones and golden brown skin that glowed in the early afternoon sunlight, with hair shorn close to her scalp. I frowned as she set a mug down on my table. Her lips quirked before splitting into a grin that threatened to tear her face in two.

"I've waited so long for this moment," she said.

Before I could respond, she pulled me out of my chair and into a tight hug. Her body was tall, strong, lean. Like mine.

The muscles of her back flexed beneath my hands as she rocked us back and forth, squealing with delight. She released me, her face beaming, and sat down. I sank into my chair, stunned, unable to wrench my gaze from her.

"I can't believe you're here. This's so crazy. I freaked out when I got the notification. I submitted my DNA forever ago but never matched with anyone. Not until you." April's words sprinted from her mouth, tumbling one after the other. But then she paused, frowning. I realized I was gaping and slammed my mouth shut.

"I'm not what you were expecting, am I?" she said.

"No, no. This's just a lot to take in."

"Because I'm Black, you mean."

Warmth spread across my cheeks. I sipped my coffee to avoid her prying gaze. Race wasn't something I was used to discussing so openly.

"You can say it, you know," she said calmly. "I'm Black. Biracial, actually. Black mom, white dad. Only I never knew him. I've been looking for him, like, forever, basically. That's why I was so excited to match with you."

I exhaled and set my mug down, realizing we'd both come here seeking answers. Only I didn't have any.

"April, I'm sorry, but I don't know who your father is. Neither of my parents had any siblings. I'm not sure how we matched. There might've been a mistake with our test results."

"DNA doesn't lie. We're cousins," she insisted. "Did you mention me to your parents? They must know something, right?"

"No. They're both… dead."

April's face fell and her posture sagged, her bottom lip trembling. This clearly wasn't the answer she'd been hoping for. After a moment, she took a breath, regained her composure, and said, "I'm sorry to hear that. Losing your parents must've been hard, especially since you're so, well, young."

"Thanks. It was hard, but I'm doing okay. I'm grateful for the time I had with them."

Reaching into my pocket, I pulled out my talisman stone and held it in my palm. My dad had been such an important part of my life. I couldn't imagine who I might have become without his guidance. Only, parents were a gamble. It was hard to know whether April's life would've been better or worse with her father in it.

"Do you have any siblings? Grandparents? Anyone else in your family who might know something?" she asked.

Maura flashed through my mind, but I pushed thoughts of her aside and shook my head. Asking Maura about our family was a waste of time.

"What about your mom?" I asked. "What's she told you about your dad?"

"She met him at a bar when she was twenty-nine. They had a one-night stand, and here I am! She never even got his name."

"Well, she'd know what he looks like, at least. That's something."

She shook her head. "No. Every time I ask her about him, she shuts me down. I can't talk to her about this. Trust me, I've tried."

"Why? I mean, it's clear this is important to you."

"Because she's selfish, that's why," April replied, her eyes downcast. "She thinks finding my dad would disrupt our perfect little family. Only it's not perfect. Martin and Rochelle don't care about me, not really. That's my stepfather and half-sister," she added. "I don't fit with them. I'm just extra baggage." April slumped into her seat, her face crumpling. Tears began trickling down her cheeks.

It was obvious how important connecting with a new family member was for her. My heart ached as I realized that the hopes and dreams she'd carried were shattering before my eyes, yet I didn't know how to comfort her.

"I need your help. Please," she begged. "There must be something you can do."

"I'm sorry, April, I don't see how."

"But you came all this way, so I know you're curious about our family. You want to figure this out, too. What's holding you back now?"

Maura's words from the cemetery pushed their way up from my subconscious.

She wasn't a mother to me.

I hadn't considered the possibility that Maura and I might be adopted.

Blood drained from my head, leaving me dizzy and nauseous. The café suddenly seemed too small, too packed with people. My ears rang from the cacophony of sounds around me: voices rising and falling, music blaring from loudspeakers, the shriek of the elevated train. Each sound rattled through my head, setting my nerves aflame.

It couldn't be true. It just couldn't.

Desperate to get outside, away from the chaos around me, I lurched up from the table. The ever-present stitch in my side intensified, causing me to wince in pain. April rose to her feet, concern etched across her forehead. "Wait, where are you going?"

"This was a mistake. It's all a mistake. I shouldn't've come."

"No. Please don't go," April pleaded. "We need to work this out."

"There's nothing to figure out." My hands shook as I shoved my wallet and phone into my bag. "We aren't related. The company made a mistake. I hope you find your dad, I really do, but you'll have to do it on your own."

Her body sagged. For a moment, I saw glimmers of myself within her: the shape of her face, the long lines of her body. But I couldn't allow myself to accept that.

Because if I did, it meant everything I understood about my family and my place in it was a lie.

6

I spent the three-hour drive home oscillating between denial and panic. Questions I never before thought to ask raced through my mind, along with answers I'd never considered. If Maura and I had been adopted, it would help explain her hostility towards our parents. Why she fought with them. Why she broke off contact.

It wasn't until I turned into the cul-de-sac that I realized where I'd navigated, and the questions plaguing my mind reverted to a low murmur. A pang of grief and loneliness struck me, like a fist wrapped around my heart, as I stared up at my childhood home.

The once cheerful red door looked like a gaping mouth, the shuttered windows staring at me like glassy eyes. Without my mother's care, the lawn sprawled, unkempt, the tall grass brown and wilted.

This home had once been my sanctuary, a tether linking me to my parents, my childhood. Now I wondered how much of my upbringing had been a lie. Whether my entire family had been a lie.

Secrets never stayed hidden, though. I just needed to find them.

I parked the car and made my way up the path. The front door shuddered open, its stiff joints groaning in protest. The house had settled into the stillness of abandonment and neglect. Yellow streetlights cast distorted shadows through the living room. For a moment, I thought I saw a black shape rising to meet me. Bile rose in my throat. I fumbled for the light switch, bathing the room in brightness. The shadows dissipated. I exhaled.

Determined to bring some life into this home that reeked of disuse, I flicked on the rest of the lights and yanked open the windows. Though this house was once my home, I felt like an intruder, searching out secrets in its dark corners. I hadn't been here since my mother's funeral, and the space now felt unfamiliar and uninviting.

As I padded down the hallway, memories awoke from deep within me. Memories of creeping towards my bedroom in the dead of night after being out late with friends, the corners of my lips and tongue sticky with the sickly-sweet taste of soda laced with cheap vodka.

Mom had been overprotective, convinced I'd be raped if I was out past 10pm or wore anything that ended above the knee or below the collarbone. It hadn't dissuaded me, though. I'd lurch through the hallway well past curfew, heart thudding, certain she'd catch me, only to find her snoring with the lamp on, a cheap paperback resting on her stomach, Dad asleep on the couch.

When I neared the bedroom, I half expected to find the lamp lit and hear Mom's gentle snores wafting through the open door. Instead, I was greeted by darkness and silence. After switching on the light, I focused my attention on the sturdy wooden chest at the base of the bed. Anything important to my parents made its way inside this chest, where it was safe behind a metal lock. Once polished and gleaming, the lock was now dull, with rust creeping along its edges.

If there were secrets hidden in this home, I'd find them there.

I knelt in front of the chest and tried opening it. The lid didn't budge, dashing my hopes that my mother had foregone use of the lock in her later years. Unsure of where the key might be hidden and impatient to start my search, I headed to the garage and grabbed a screwdriver. Upon returning, I jimmied the tool behind the lock and applied pressure. My muscles strained against the stubborn latch until it finally gave way, splitting the wood trim in the process. A momentary pang of guilt flitted through me at the sight of the mangled chest. In my minds' eye, I saw my mother's disapproving frown. I sent her a mental apology, promising I'd have it repaired.

After tossing aside the screwdriver, I heaved open the lid. The stale scent of lavender and pine rushed out. I started removing and sorting through the items. Old birthday and Christmas cards. An embroidered quilt. A child-sized pair of black patent shoes. Mom's wedding dress. And beneath them all, a stack of children's artwork and one of Maura's old sketchbooks.

Smiling, I flipped through the drawings and paintings, recalling lazy afternoons making art with my sister. Whenever Maura pulled out her sketchbook, the world around her disappeared. She'd grow so consumed with the act of creating that I often went unnoticed. I was her silent shadow. Despite hours spent mimicking her confident strokes, I was unable to produce anything matching her talent.

My drawings were pitiful attempts to recreate the precise taxonomic illustrations of plants and butterflies that lined the walls of my father's office. Maura tended towards the abstract, weaving splashes of color into rich tapestries, with muted suggestions of birds and vines creeping across the pages.

Discovering one of Maura's sketchbooks inside my parents' chest felt like uncovering long-forgotten treasure. I traced my fingertips over the cover and ran my thumb across the pages, but didn't dare open it. This sketchbook was as personal as a diary. Combing through her illustrations without Maura's permission felt like a violation. Even so, it didn't feel right leaving the sketchbook here to rot. Mind made up, I placed it beside my bag to take home. I'd figure out what to do with it later.

The rest of the chest contained a jumble of binders and file folders, which I stacked on the floor beside me. Resting my back against the chest, I began the painstaking process of combing through their contents for anything that might point towards adoption records or an alternative explanation for my newly acquired cousin.

Most of the papers were financial records and tax documents. I set those aside, reminding myself to hand them over to Chris, who'd been named executor in my mother's will. I knew the estate would be split between Maura and me, but I wasn't sure what Maura would do with her share. After Dad died, Maura donated her portion of his estate to charities.

Dad's folders were stuffed with article pre-prints from his research and official documents from Hildegard University. I paused when I came across a faded manila folder with my advisor's name, Richard Sandberg, scrawled across it. My dad had taught at Hildegard with Richard, so it wasn't unusual that he had some files about Richard in his possession. All the same, my curiosity won out, and I placed the folder in my bag to peruse once I returned home.

After what felt like hours of fruitless effort, Maura's sketchbook and Richard's folder remained the only interesting items I'd discovered. The nagging feeling of unease I'd carried since receiving my DNA test results dissipated, leaving me with a newfound lightness. I hadn't unearthed any adoption records or incongruous documents about our family's history. There wasn't anything to suggest I'd been adopted. Perhaps matching with April had been a mistake, after all.

April. I groaned and clutched my head, recalling how I'd rushed out of the café, leaving her hurt and confused in my wake. I'd call her tomorrow morning and apologize. Explain that my reaction was driven by my own fears, rather than anything about her or her search for her father.

As I began putting the items away, I paused, peering into the chest's bottomless depths. Nestled on the floor was a small photo album, its black cover camouflaged against the dark-stained wood. I frowned at it. Why would this be hidden? Why hadn't I seen this before?

Family portraits lined the walls and shelves of my childhood home, and photo albums cluttered the bookshelves and coffee table. Photos of Maura, however, were absent. Had our parents buried her here?

Despite the deepening twilight and my desire to return home, I grabbed the album and curled up on the bed, stifling a yawn. I opened the cover, exposing the first page.

Maura stared back at me.

She stood outside this very house, a book bag slung over her shoulder. Her body was hunched inwards on itself. Even under the baggy clothes, I could tell her muscles were taut, limbs prepared to lash out. Her eyelids were smudged with charcoal eyeliner, brown eyes glinting beneath overgrown bangs. She glared at the camera.

I extracted the image from its protective plastic cover and read the caption on the back. *Maura, first day of high school, 2001.* A smile tugged at my lips as I recalled how much I idolized her growing up, convinced she was versed in some special, esoteric knowledge of the world that she alone possessed. Now I realized she'd been another stereotypical teenager rebelling against a cookie-cutter suburban lifestyle.

My mood soured as I skimmed through more photos. Maura's sixteenth birthday, her face grim even from behind a table piled high with presents. Maura's high school graduation, scowling as she held up her diploma. Me, perched in Maura's lap when I was only three or four years old, grinning up at her while she stared into the distance with dull, blank eyes. In this collection of photos, joy and delight were clear on everyone's faces but Maura's. These disappointing moments now lay buried in a chest to fade over time.

I closed my eyes, lost in memories from childhood. The joy of swimming in Lake Michigan, despite the sand in my swimsuit. Sweltering days at Six Flags, nauseous and giddy from riding rollercoasters with Dad. Summer getaways to quaint cabins in sleepy villages along Michigan's shoreline, where mice scrabbled under the floorboards and spiders spun webs in the cabinets.

In each of those memories, Maura sulked in the background, while Mom and Dad fought behind closed doors, Maura's name uttered in low tones. When it became too much, I'd run into the woods or onto the beach, intent on escaping the rage and despair that followed Maura like a shadow.

Once Maura moved out, things changed. Life with my parents grew easier. Before her departure, my parents constantly argued about how to manage her rage, her declining mental state. After she left, our lives softened, replaced instead with arguments about how full the dishwasher should be before running it and whether we should have pasta or tacos for dinner.

My eyelids fluttered open. I flipped through the remaining pages, more out of boredom than curiosity. During this period of waning attention, I nearly missed the photo. Almost slammed the album shut and returned it to the chest. But it grabbed and held my attention, sending chills up my spine, and I found myself unable to look away.

In the photo, my mother sat in a lawn chair, her face cast in shadows, her arms crossed over her chest. A man I didn't recognize loomed behind her. He was as thick as a tree trunk, with ink-black eyebrows and a scowl on his face. Though the intimacy between them leapt from the page, I knew he wasn't a boyfriend. Couldn't be. Judging by my mother's age in the photo, my parents would have been married at the time it was taken.

Frowning, I pulled it out and turned it over, seeking more information. My mother's familiar sloping cursive was scrawled on the back. *Joan and Garrett, 4th of July, 1990.* The name didn't sound familiar. If he'd been close to my parents, they hadn't spoken of him with me.

Garrett appeared in several more photos. In one, a young Maura perched, lopsided, on Garrett's lap. His face was twisted into a smile as he tugged at her ponytail. Even then, Maura had a penchant for furrowed brows and pursed lips. I extracted the photo from its protective covering and studied the caption. The words reverberated in my chest. I struggled to process what they meant.

Maura with Uncle Garrett, 6th birthday party, 1993.

My hands trembled as I stared down at the photo of Garrett and Maura.

My uncle.

April's father.

My parents had kept him a secret from me, chosen to pretend he didn't exist. But why?

Even as Dad languished through the last months of his life, lungs rebelling against his body, he remained silent about our secret family history. I wondered if Mom would have told me about Garrett, if she'd perished from some long-lingering disease, rather than the sharp, sudden impact of her car against that telephone pole.

One thing was certain: my parents had carved out Garrett from our history like a malignant tumor. The only evidence of his existence was a few photos rotting away in a wooden chest. Like Maura.

Maura and Garrett were absent from the family portraits glimmering on the walls and the photos cycling through the digital picture frame I'd given my parents for their thirtieth wedding anniversary. It was as though acknowledging Maura and Garrett's existence was akin to blasphemy.

My parents had cast them both out. But why?

I set the photo aside, grabbed my cellphone, and dialed Maura's number. She didn't answer. Instead, I sent her a snapshot of the photo with the message:

I found out about Garrett. Call me.

Each moment of silence was agonizing. I chewed on my thumbnail, willing her to respond. When the phone vibrated, I nearly dropped it before answering, my palms slick with sweat. There was a slight pause before Maura's voice, quiet and raw, cut through the stillness.

"Where'd you find that photo?" she asked.

"In Mom's old chest. It says Uncle Garrett on the back. Who is he?"

"Christ... I thought... when I saw your message..."

"What?"

She hesitated, as though weighing her words. It only made me more certain she was preparing to lie.

"Nothing. He was a friend of Joan's, that's all. They fell out of touch."

"So it has nothing to do with the girl I met today who claims she's our cousin?"

Though I hadn't planned on telling Maura about April, the words spilled from my mouth before I could help myself. Discovering Garrett had changed things. Two variables, supporting the same hypothesis. I needed answers.

Maura's ragged breathing pulsed through the phone. "What are you talking about?"

"I took one of those BloodlineDNA tests and matched with this girl, April Bennett. She's looking for her father, wants my help finding him. I didn't believe her at first, but then I found this photo. So stop shitting me and tell me the truth."

Maura hesitated for a moment. When she spoke, her voice was laced with defeat.

"He's Joan's brother. They had a falling out and lost touch decades ago. I don't know why, or what happened to him."

Her words shocked me into stillness, until outrage propelled me forward again.

"Why didn't anyone tell me?"

"Joan didn't like talking about him, and it wasn't my place to tell you. I hardly knew him to begin with. That's all I know."

I tightened my grip on the phone, imagining I was throttling Maura. "Stop playing games with me. You know more than you're letting on, I know it. What happened to him? Does he have something to do with why you left?"

Maura's voice lashed out, sharp enough to cut. "Leave this alone, Laurel. I mean it."

"I can't do that. I won't. This isn't about us, or your un-resolved issues with our parents. This is about April. She de-serves to know her father. Don't you get that? Wouldn't you want to know your dad, if you grew up without him?"

"You have no idea what you're talking about," she hissed. "Joan cut him off — must have cut him off — for good reason. April's better off not knowing him."

"But why? Why are you being so secretive? Just tell me the truth for once in your fucking life."

"I can't get into this. I won't," she shot back, then paused. Her voice grew quiet. "Please, let this go. Don't ask me about this again."

Before I could ask her why, the line went dead.

7

The next morning, I awoke to a bright stream of sunlight pouring in through the window, my skin prickling from the sudden flush of warmth. Eyelids leaden, I blinked as the room melted into focus.

My gaze snagged on the empty merlot bottle perched on the bedside table. The blood red liquid had oozed down its side and pooled atop the surface. The taste of stale wine lingered on my lips, and my mouth felt stuffed with cotton. I reeked of sweat and booze.

The events of the previous day slammed into me again: meeting with April, discovering Garrett, the disastrous call with Maura. Afterwards, I'd polished off a bottle of wine and wallowed in self-pity before falling into a deep, dreamless sleep nestled atop my mother's bed, legs tangled among the soft, wrinkled sheets.

Resisting the temptation to crawl back under the covers, I rolled over and fumbled for my cell phone to check the time. It was 8:45am. My eyes widened. I had a meeting with Richard in fifteen minutes.

I bolted out of bed, gathered my belongings, and raced to my truck. The tires squealed as I careened down the street, though I knew I wouldn't arrive on time. My fingers tapped on the steering wheel as the clock inched up to, and past, 9am.

When I finally made it to campus, I grabbed a metered parking spot a few blocks from Wallace Hall. I scrounged inside sticky cup holders and pawed through my glove compartment until I unearthed enough money for an hour of parking.

After feeding the meter, I sprinted down the sidewalk, my bag jostling against my shoulders as my pelvis seized in protest. Sweat trickled down my forehead and pooled into the small of my back. When I arrived outside Richard's office, I didn't bother to knock, choosing instead to throw the door open.

"Richard, I am so sorry—"

"These allegations—"

My mouth clammed up. Selena Young, the dean of the science department, swiveled around in her chair and glanced at me through red-framed glasses. Across from her, Richard gripped the arms of his leather chair, face stony as he glared at me.

"I didn't know you were expecting a student, Richard," Dean Young said, scrutinizing me.

"I was, but she's thirty minutes late, and usually not this rude."

"I'm so sorry," I said, my face flushing. "I didn't mean to interrupt."

I scurried out and closed the door behind me. Though my muscles ached and my head was pounding, I resisted the urge to sink to the ground. Instead, I made my way to an armchair and dropped into it like a lead weight.

My knee jittered at a staccato pace as I reflected on my mishap. I strained to recall what Dean Young had been saying. Something about allegations, though I didn't know whether they were against Richard or someone else. I'd puzzle it out later.

I forced myself to concentrate on my upcoming meeting, for which I was wholly unprepared. Though I intended to work on my research last night, it felt impossible, my mind brimming with unanswered questions about Garrett and April. I couldn't focus on anything except my fractured family.

"I don't think we've met yet."

Startled, I looked up and found Dean Young studying me, wearing a polite smile. I flashed her a weak one in return.

"I'm Laurel. Laurel Lane. I'm a PhD candidate in Richard's lab."

"Hm. That name sounds familiar. Perhaps we have met already. It's hard to keep track of everyone."

"We haven't, but you may have known my father. Howard Lane. He taught biology here until he passed away a few years ago. That's... that's actually his old office," I said, gesturing towards the door. The sight of Richard sitting behind my father's old desk still felt jarring, even years after his death.

"Yes, that's right," she said, snapping her fingers. "Before my time, but I've heard wonderful things about your father. Seems he was a devoted and talented educator, and a real advocate for his students."

A lump formed in my throat. "That's kind of you to say. Sorry for barging into your meeting."

"It's fine, these things happen." She peered down the hall, then leaned closer and lowered her voice. "But please keep whatever you may have heard to yourself. It was meant to be a private conversation. Your discretion can help keep it that way."

I hesitated, then said, "Of course. No problem."

"Thank you, Laurel." She flashed me an assured smile before striding down the corridor, heels clicking against the tile. I frowned as I watched her depart. Promising her my silence filled me with unease. What were they trying to hide?

The sound of a door creaking open caught my attention. All thoughts of the overheard conversation dissolved as I glimpsed Richard emerging from his office, his mouth a thin gash across his red face. I shrank into the chair, trying to make myself invisible. Dean Young may have forgiven my transgression, but Richard wouldn't let me go that easily.

"Laurel. My office. Now."

Richard's office had the well-worn, decorous feeling of a library in an old estate house. A lustrous oriental rug sprawled across the floor, while towering bookshelves stuffed with old books lined the walls and exotic potted plants perched atop the windowsill. Though I knew he thought his taste was refined, it came across as pretentious. The books were clearly for show, their spines never cracked. There wasn't a watering can in sight, leading me to suspect that the janitorial staff were charged with keeping his plants alive.

Once a familiar and comforting space, the office was now unrecognizable from the memories I held from childhood.

When this office had been my father's, I'd visited him regularly, entertaining myself for hours scrounging through his collection of curios; animal skulls and bones, taxidermy butterflies, pinecones, yellowing maps, naturalist illustrations of wildflowers, well-loved books with dried plants stuffed between their pages. Dad always managed to find time to answer my never-ending questions about my discoveries, even if it interfered with our ability to complete our respective homework.

My eyes instinctively gravitated towards the place on the wall where my father had once hung a family portrait. It was gone now, replaced by a framed cover of a National Geographic issue featuring Richard grinning beside a tranquilized mountain lion. Now Richard settled into the leather armchair that had once been my father's, his fists clenched, a pinched expression upon his narrow face. I buried myself in the seat opposite him, cringing under his disapproving glare.

"What the fuck's going on? You can't show up late and barge in here like that."

I winced, trembling at his fury-filled voice, willing myself not to crumble. "I'm so sorry, I overslept, and there was traffic, and—"

"Whatever. I don't have time for your excuses," he said, waving a hand. "We need to talk about what happened between you and Dougie Whitcomb."

My heart sank as I realized where this was going.

"Dougie called me a few weeks ago," Richard said. "Sounds like you got into an altercation with him? And he's had complaints from Heart Ranch about you, too. Care to explain what the fuck that's all about?"

His use of Doug's nickname wasn't lost on me. Richard was in the boys' club. Not me. It wasn't surprising that Dougie complained about me, but it seemed ridiculous to describe our phone conversation as an altercation.

I took a deep breath, steeling myself for an argument. "Someone shot one of our study animals. I thought it was poachers, so I called Doug. He'd issued a depredation permit to the folks at Heart Ranch. I'd told them to protect their sheep, but they wouldn't listen. It's a waste, Richard. The lion had cubs."

Richard tossed his glasses onto a legal pad and rubbed a hand over his sun-spotted bald patch.

"Look, I get it, I do. I don't like losing animals, either," he said. "I've lost them over the years, and it hurts each time. But you were way out of line. We can't get involved in these kinds of issues. It's too politically fraught. We could've lost our research permit."

"But aren't we doing this work to improve how those lions are treated?"

He sighed. "Of course we want that, of course. I've been working on these issues with people like Dougie for longer than you've been alive, but it takes time."

"Time's running out. The population's declining. You know that better than anyone."

Richard's face deepened into the same shade of red as the rug beneath our feet. "Don't lecture me about my research. I've built this work from the ground up over decades, but your behavior might have jeopardized the entire project. It makes us both look bad. I can't cover for you when you overstep your bounds. It's embarrassing. A fucking disgrace."

I stared at him with incredulity. The double standard was absurd. Richard and Dougie behaved however they liked, but labeled me a troublemaker for voicing my opinions. To make matters worse, hot tears pooled in my eyes as I realized I couldn't handle this — not here, not today. I instinctively reached into my pocket, cupping the talisman stone in my palm.

"Oh, come on, pull yourself together," Richard said, tossing his hands up. "I am so sick of all you girls with your fucking crying. You'll never make it in this field if you don't toughen up."

I flinched, willing my tears to stop, but they only flowed harder.

"Now get back to work. Stick to the science and keep your agenda to yourself. We'll meet again this time next month, and I expect to see results."

Forcing myself to stand tall, I nodded and walked towards the door. Though I wanted to appear composed and confident, my body betrayed me, legs wobbling. Then Richard called out behind me.

"Oh, and Laurel, you look like shit. Wouldn't kill you to shower and comb your hair once in a while."

I managed to make it to the bathroom before throwing up.

8

I crouched in a cramped bathroom stall, gripping the toilet bowl, the taste of vomit on my tongue, hot tears running down my cheeks. The events of the past few days were hitting me. Hard. Richard's belligerence had finally pushed me over into a state of complete overwhelm.

Once, while hiking with my father, I ambled off the trail and stumbled into a swamp. My foot sank deep into the mire. As I struggled to free myself, my leg submerged deeper and deeper until the cold muck crept around my waist, suctioning me in place. I started hyperventilating, convinced the earth would swallow me whole, like quicksand. But then my dad wrapped his arms around me and pulled me to safety.

That's how I felt now — stuck and sinking fast. Unable to extricate myself from the messes surrounding me: with Richard, with Maura, with April. Only this time, my father couldn't rescue me. I was on my own.

After my tears subsided, I trudged over to the sink and peered into the mirror, wincing at my bloodshot eyes, limp hair, and rumpled clothing. I sniffed my shirt and wrinkled my nose at the stale stench of old sweat emanating from me.

Richard was right about one thing. I did look like shit.

I washed my face, rinsed out my mouth, and ran a hand through my tangled hair. As I patted my face dry with a paper towel, the bathroom door swung open. I looked up, startled, to find Petra staring back at me through the mirror. Though she shared lab space with me and Luis, I hadn't seen her since before my mother's funeral.

She looked almost as bad as me. Her face was haggard and drawn, with purple rings encircling her green eyes, and her normally pristine pixie cut was overgrown and mussed.

"I saw you run in here after leaving Richard's office," Petra said. "I figured you wanted some privacy, so I stood sentry outside and scared away some undergrads. But then I got worried and decided to check on you."

"I'm fine, just having a bad morning."

"Richard giving you a hard time?"

I threw the paper towel away and nodded. Agreeing with her seemed easier than explaining everything that had transpired over the past day. She didn't need to know about my newly discovered cousin. Or uncle, for that matter.

"I'm meeting Luis for coffee. Join us."

Not bothering to wait for a response, she walked out the door. My stomach growled, and I followed her, desperate for a proper breakfast, coffee, and distance from Richard.

On the walk over, Petra riddled me with questions, which I responded with one-word answers, if saying anything at all. My mind was racing, trying to process everything that had happened since receiving April's fateful message. Petra eventually got the hint and fell silent, though I caught her sneaking sidelong glances at me as we strode through the quad and into town.

Despite my internal state of turmoil, I smiled when Petra ushered me inside Gretchen's Cup, a rinky-dink cafe that had been in Grenadier for ages. After Maura moved out, my parents brought me here almost every weekend for egg sandwiches, hot chocolate, and games of Scrabble.

Gretchen's stood in sharp contrast to the other cafes that had popped up over the past few years, with their sleek wooden tables, chrome countertops, and lattes laced with delicate swirls of espresso and oat milk. Gretchen's looked like a thrift shop had puked inside of it.

A menagerie of armchairs of different shapes, sizes, colors, and various states of decay were crammed around wooden tables with rickety legs. Next to the counter laid a stack of board games and puzzles in moldering cardboard boxes. The soft sounds of an acoustic guitar floated through the air.

Luis waved to us from his perch in a horrid orange armchair that looked like it had been reupholstered with old carpet. After placing our orders, Petra and I sank into armchairs across from Luis. I blew on my steaming cup of coffee, the scent a salve to my aching head and tense muscles, and nibbled on a muffin. The pounding headache that had plagued me all morning started to dissipate.

"Richard's done a number on Laurel," Petra said.

"What happened?" Luis asked.

I gulped down some coffee and wiped my face with a napkin before responding. "Someone shot one of my study animals. I thought it was poachers, so I told off the game warden. He got pissed off and complained about me to Richard, who wasn't happy."

"Don't take it personally. Richard is easily displeased by his underlings," Petra said.

"Doesn't mean he should treat us like shit," Luis said from behind a mug the size of a cereal bowl. "You should know better, Petra."

She frowned, twirling a plain gold wedding band around her finger.

"I don't understand why Richard refuses to stick up to the game and fish people. Their go-to solution is always to kill more lions. You're trying to change management with the vaquitas, right, Luis?"

He snorted. "Yeah. Richard has no problem telling Brown folks in Mexico how to manage their wildlife. But telling his fellow white men the same thing? Not so much."

My lips quirked upwards at Luis's apt assessment.

"How's the rest of your research going?" Petra asked me.

"Not great. I'm pretty far behind."

"You need to triage," Luis said, his tone becoming business-like. "What's the most critical task on your list?"

I chewed my thumbnail as I collected my thoughts, desperate to distract myself from ruminating over my family's lies. For once, my research seemed like the least of my problems, and the easiest to address. "Processing my samples and data from this past field season. I hate doing it. The lab work is so tedious and takes forever."

"I have some undergrad research assistants working for me this semester. I'm running out of things for them to do. You can borrow them," he said.

Shock radiated through me. "Oh no, I couldn't. You might still need their help later on."

"I don't, though. I'm just writing up my dissertation. They'd appreciate the extra hours."

"No, it's fine, really. I should do the work myself, anyway."

Petra grasped the arm of my chair. "Laurel, let him do this for you. If we're going to survive this program—"

"Survive Richard," Luis said.

"We've got to help each other," said Petra.

I hesitated, loathe to admit that I was struggling, but the offer of help was too tempting to dismiss. "That would incredible. Thank you."

"She's finally come to her senses," Petra said, rolling her eyes at Luis, who grinned back.

Relief flooded through me, and the knot in the pit of my stomach lessened, replaced with gratitude for my fellow classmates. I allowed myself to think that things might be okay. That things might go back to normal.

But then I remembered Garrett towering over my mother like her jailor, and I realized the normalcy I longed for may have been nothing but an illusion.

After leaving the cafe, I headed home. I couldn't focus on my research. Not today. Between family drama, too much wine, stale clothes, and a run-in with Richard, I was emotionally and mentally drained.

While most Hildegard graduate students lived in shared apartments downtown, I'd opted for a more isolated, and serene, existence in a rental cottage straddling acres of old farmland. The long-abandoned fields were slowly being reclaimed by the woods, with saplings sprouting from the lush soil and wildflowers blanketing the ground each spring. Every evening, small critters scurried through the underbrush, desperate to avoid the shrewd eyes and sharp claws of barn owls.

The cottage was modest, featuring a cheerless gray exterior and off-white accents along the windowsills. The paint cracked and peeled a little more each season, scattering paint chips across the porch like broken eggshells. Despite its flaws, this was my home, and I took pride in caring for it.

Once inside, I showered and changed into fresh clothes, then spent a few minutes tidying up. My cottage was nearly spotless, but the chores served as a valuable distraction from the storm of emotions whirling within me. Only after the cottage was gleaming did I allow myself to sink onto the couch and turn my attention to the questions ricocheting through my mind.

My thoughts immediately drifted towards my mother, triggering a wave of heartache. I longed for one last moment with her to demand answers to questions I'd never known to ask.

What led to the estrangement between her and her brother?

Why hadn't she told me about him?

And why had Maura insisted that April and I stay away from him?

I realized my parents had failed me. Rather than trusting me with the truth, they'd chosen to lie about our family history. And now that they were dead, Maura had taken up their mantle of obfuscation.

What were they trying to protect me from?

I resented being coddled, resented others deciding what I should and shouldn't know about my history. I deserved to make those decisions for myself. April deserved that, too. She deserved to know her father, despite Maura's insistence to the contrary. We both deserved to learn the truth about our families, to understand where we came from.

If we wanted answers, we'd need to work together.

Taking a deep breath, I called April. Upon answering, she said, "You found something out, didn't you?"

"Yeah. I went to my parents' house and found a photo of a man with my older sister, Maura. It said Uncle Garrett on the back. I asked her about it, and she admitted he's our uncle. He had a falling out with my mom. They lost touch years ago."

April exhaled, her soft breath brushing against my ear. "I knew it. I knew the minute I saw you, it wasn't a mistake."

"Apparently not."

"You didn't tell me about your sister," she said accusingly. "Why didn't you ask her to begin with?"

"It's... complicated. We aren't close."

"Where's Garrett now? What happened to him?"

"I don't know. Maura said... well, she said we should forget about him."

"Why?"

I sighed and shook my head. That question had been plaguing me, but I didn't have an answer. All I could do was speculate. "I don't know, April. Maybe he isn't a good person. I mean, my mom cut her brother out of her life and pretended he never existed. There has to be a good reason why."

"That's not fair. You don't know that. Maybe your mom did something that pushed him away."

"You need to know what you're getting into here, April. Garrett might not be what you're hoping for," I said, thinking of Maura's warning.

"It's not like he abandoned me or something. He doesn't even know I exist." She paused, breath hitching. "I'd rather know him and be disappointed than not know him at all."

"Yeah, I figured as much."

We lapsed into silence for a moment, then April's voice, tentative and hopeful, broke through.

"Does this mean you're going to help me find him?"

Maura's face surfaced in my mind's eye. Our relationship, if you could call it that, hung by a thread. If I went down this path, the thread holding us together might snap. But relationships were built on trust. I couldn't trust her if she chose lies over the truth.

My parents had excised Garrett from our family, either by choice or by force. Maura had excised herself. She refused to tell me why, but maybe Garrett could. This was my chance to get answers.

"Yes. I'll help you," I said. "I'll help you find your father."

9

April and I arranged to meet again the following weekend to scour the internet in search of Garrett Ryder. It meant losing another day of work on my research, but I didn't care; any sense of loyalty towards Richard had dissolved during our last meeting. My thesis research could wait. This was more important.

The rest of the week crawled by. I handed over the mountain lion blood samples I'd collected this past summer to Luis's lab assistants before burying myself in the library, avoiding the shared lab space out of concern I might encounter Richard. Despite my attempts to focus on my work, all I could think about was Garrett and April and the secrets pulsing through our shared blood.

When Saturday rolled around, I woke early, my muscles thrumming with nervous energy, and arrived at April's apartment by mid-morning. After ringing the doorbell, I heard the patter of racing feet. April barreled through the door, clad in sweatpants and a tank top. She grabbed hold of me, breathless and grinning, her hand warm against my skin.

"About time you showed up. Come in."

I followed her up the stairs and into a cramped studio apartment, brimming with belongings. You could traverse the entire space using furniture as stepping-stones, never once touching the ground. An air conditioner perched on her windowsill, its groans and hums soon joined by the screech of a cheery red teapot. April bustled over to the kitchenette and turned off the stove. The kettle stopped singing.

"I'm making a coffee. Do you want one?" she asked. "Or tea, water?"

"Coffee would be great, thanks."

April hummed to herself as she prepared our drinks. I sat down on the couch, examining the college textbooks and homework assignments splayed across the coffee table, resisting the urge to answer the questions on her biology lab assignment. After a moment, April handed me a steaming mug and curled atop the bed, cradling her drink to her belly. I thanked her and took a sip before setting the coffee on the table.

"I brought you something." I rummaged in my bag and handed her the photo of Garrett and Maura. "It's him. Garrett. The man who might be your father."

April's face paled. She put down her mug and plucked the photo from my hand, being careful not to smudge or crease it. Rather than examine it, she placed the photo face down on the comforter, a muscle in her jaw twitching.

I tucked my head down and picked at a fraying thread hanging from the couch cushion, trying to give her some privacy. When I snuck another glance at her, April was examining the photo, her bright eyes wet.

"Well, he's tall, like me. Like us," she said. "But the resemblance ends there. I think I take more after my mom. Maybe that's a good thing." She forced out a laugh as she handed me the photo, fingers quivering.

"Keep it." I reached out and folded her hands over the fading image.

April nodded and brushed at her eyes. "Thank you. Now we just have to find him."

We spent the next few hours scouring social media accounts, vital records, genealogical records, and background check databases for Garrett Ryder. The work was tedious and slow, but we soon compiled a hefty list of potential leads, almost overwhelming in its extent.

April had since migrated to the floor, where she sat cross-legged, laptop on her knees, fingers tapping on the keyboard. She exhaled and closed the screen.

"This is pointless," she said. "How're we gonna figure out which one's him? If he's listed here at all."

"I'll start reaching out to people, explain who I am, and tell them about my mom's death. If he's on this list, he'll respond. I'm sure of it."

April walked over to the kitchenette and pulled out a packet of ramen. She held it up towards me, eyebrow raised. I shook my head.

"Okay. Say you find him. What then?" she asked as she boiled some water.

"I set up a meeting. On my own."

Her eyes narrowed, and she opened her mouth to argue, brandishing a fork in my general direction. I lifted a hand to stop her.

"It'll give me the chance to scope him out, make sure he's not dangerous or mentally unstable. My parents cut him out for a reason. I don't want to put you at risk or jeopardize your chance at connecting with him."

Speaking with Garrett first could help me get answers of my own, too. About why he wasn't part of my parents' lives. Whether he knew the reason for Maura's estrangement. Gauge how he might react to learning about his daughter.

I wanted April to meet her father, but I couldn't shake the feeling that there was something... off about Garrett. I felt obligated to make sure he was safe before facilitating an introduction.

April crossed her arms, glowering, but relented. "Fine. You can reach out first. But you need to share everything you find out with me. No secrets."

"Agreed. Just don't contact anyone on your own. I'm our best bet, at least for now."

April sighed and nodded. We were startled by a sharp rap on the door.

"If that's Norman, I'm going to lose my shit," she muttered.

"Who's Norman?"

Instead of responding, April turned off the stove and yanked open the door. She gaped when she saw the other person.

"Mom! What are you doing here?"

My stomach lurched. I craned my neck and glimpsed a petite Black woman through the gap in the doorjamb. She grinned at April.

"I was in the neighborhood and thought I'd stop by."

"You can't just walk into the building like that, Mom. Norman has called the police for far less."

"You can't let people like him stop you from living your life, April."

"I know, but—"

"Oh! I didn't realize you had company." She squeezed past April and shut the door. Before her mom could reach me, April lunged for my laptop and slammed down the screen. Then she snatched up the photo of Garrett and tucked it into the band of her sweatpants. Face flushed, she whirled around to confront her mother.

"You can't barge in here like that."

Her mom raised an eyebrow and cast a sidelong look at her daughter, who squirmed beneath her gaze, then turned towards me. "I'm Simone."

"Laurel. Nice to meet you."

April was right; she did take after her mother. They shared the same almond-shaped eyes and high cheekbones, and though Simone's body had softened with age and motherhood, she still moved with April's strength and grace. She radiated a contagious brightness, with an amiable smile that crinkled the corners of her mouth and eyes, and a calm demeanor that immediately put me at ease.

The sensation didn't extend to April, however. She hovered behind her mother, hopping from foot to foot as if in urgent need of the bathroom. "Mom, this isn't a good time." Grabbing Simone by the crook of her elbow, April pulled her towards the door. Simone laughed and shrugged easily out of April's grasp.

"You should've told me you had an older girlfriend," Simone teased. "I didn't even know you were gay."

"She's not my girlfriend! And I'm not. B-but it would be fine if I was!"

"Of course it would be, dear. But there's still the matter of why you're so embarrassed." She snapped her fingers, the gesture jangling the gold bracelets on her wrist. "Oh, I know. I listened to a program on NPR about how college students are making money nowadays. They call themselves cam-girls, I think?"

"Oh my God! I'm not webcamming!" April clutched her head, eyes wide with horror.

I stifled a laugh, then realized I should intervene and save April from further embarrassment. Thinking of the lab assignment, I said, "I'm a tutor, helping April with her biology class."

Simone's face fell, and she turned towards April. "You didn't tell me you were struggling with your coursework. This isn't like you, honey."

April's eyebrows shot straight up as she glanced from her mother to me, lips moving wordlessly. I gave her an encouraging nod, hoping she'd run with the story.

"Yeah... yes. That's it. We, uh, Laurel's been helping me with my lab assignments. I didn't want to tell you... because..."

"It's okay, it's okay. We all need a little help sometimes. I just wish you'd told me sooner." A crease burrowed across Simone's forehead as she leaned towards April, voice low. "I know I haven't been able to help much with your tuition, but I can certainly afford a tutor."

The two of them carried on with their discussion, soon oblivious to my presence. Even as they bickered, their shared affection was obvious: the playful manner by which they sparred back and forth, how Simone pulled her daughter into a begrudging hug, their laughter soaking the room like warm light on a summer's day.

But as I watched them, my stomach churned uneasily. Finding Garrett wouldn't just affect me and April, I realized. It would ripple outward, touching everyone around us, too.

Simone didn't want April to find her father, perhaps to protect her from potential heartbreak. Regardless of the reason, April and I were heading down a path that could forever transform their relationship.

Simone eventually departed, but not before shoving a fistful of cash at me to cover my fictional tutoring costs. When I refused, her face hardened, and behind her, April shook her head, coaxing me to accept the money. I relented, pocketing the cash, and thanked Simone for her generosity. She shot me another dazzling smile and hugged April goodbye.

Once Simone left, I handed April the crumpled bills as she apologized profusely for the intrusion. I assured her it was fine, though deceiving her mother filled me with a nagging sense of unease. Finding Garrett would impact April's relationship with her mom, in ways she probably had yet to contemplate, and my attempts to talk about it were shut down. I wondered if their bond was strong enough to weather what came next.

April was determined to find her father, no matter what. Thanks to me, she knew his name. She'd track him down with or without my help. The damage was done. There was no turning back.

We spent the rest of the afternoon getting to know one another. April confided in me about her struggles to make ends meet while attending university, where she was majoring in psychology. Though she began as a dance major, she'd bowed under pressure from her mom and stepdad to switch to something more 'secure.' She said performing in her college's dance troupe was enough for her, but I could tell it wasn't. Like me, she didn't seem capable of doing anything halfway.

I learned, too, about the fraught relationship between her and her stepfather, Martin. He married Simone when April was three. A few years later, they had a daughter, Rochelle. Martin doted on his biological daughter, barely acknowledging April's existence.

Throughout our conversation, April's family and her place in it gradually emerged, like wiping condensation from a windowpane. She felt like an outsider, convinced Martin and Rochelle viewed her as a nuisance at best, and an interloper at worse. In response, she'd turned inward, building up a narrative about her biological father as the one person who would truly understand and accept her.

I wondered if Garrett would live up to her expectations.

Though April's hopes and regrets spilled easily from her mouth, I clammed up when her attention focused on me. My heart was a messy, raw thing, and that pain was for me alone.

We parted ways in the late afternoon. Shortly after I left, April texted me a photo of her mom, urging me to share it with whomever I contacted. The hope in her words made my stomach churn. I was sick with worry that we'd uncover some unpleasant truths about her father. About our family.

Over the next week, I fell into a predictable rhythm. I spent my days in the lab, plugging away at my research. My evenings were spent working through the records we'd compiled from social media accounts and online databases. To make the task more manageable, I first compared each individual's photo, when available, to the photos of Garrett I'd found in my mother's album. Of course, those photos were taken around thirty years ago, making it difficult to identify any sort of resemblance to profiles found online. To address that, I also filtered accounts by age, based on the assumption that he was at least Joan's age, if not older. I sent emails, called phone numbers, and sent social media messages to these Garrett Ryders explaining who I was and telling them about my mother's death.

Days passed. No response.

Though I knew the odds of finding him were slim, my stomach sank each time I checked my phone and found no new notifications. He could go by a different name, lack an online presence, or be deceased. I forced myself to consider the possibility we might never find him. Finding that too depressing to contemplate, I tried to remain positive.

When Friday evening arrived, I left campus before dusk, exhausted from hours spent in front of the computer. The sky was streaked with brilliant reds and oranges, though dark storm clouds loomed in the distance.

Once at home, I examined the contents of the fridge, decided I was too tired to cook, and microwaved a bowl of canned chili. After finishing my meal, I glanced at my phone out of habit. My heart skipped a beat when I saw a voicemail alert from an unfamiliar number.

Might be spam. Might not.

Holding my breath, I dialed my voice mailbox. A deep, gravelly voice filled my ears. "This's Garrett Ryder. I received your message about my sister's passing."

I bolted upright, heart racing, and almost dropped the phone.

"You probably don't remember me," Garrett continued. "You were just a baby the last time I visited. Joan, well, she didn't want me coming 'round anymore, after everything that happened. Anyway. Call me back if you want to talk more. Okay, bye now."

The phone went silent as the message ended. I replayed it over and over until I was stunned into stillness.

I'm not sure how long I sat there, paralyzed and catatonic, blood roaring in my ears, eyes vacant and unseeing. A gust of wind battered the window blinds against the open frame and raindrops pattered against the roof. Soon the rain picked up, pummeling the cottage in a sudden downpour. The earthy scent of rain filled the room.

I lurched to standing, stubbing my toe. Cursing, I hobbled over to the windows and pulled them shut. Despite the pain blooming in my foot, I couldn't keep still. I paced around the living room, gnawing at my thumbnail, my mind a jumbled mess of disjointed thoughts. Whenever I'd grasp one, it would slip away, or morph into something else. But I kept circling back to that one simple, devastating word.

Sister. He called Mom his sister. I hadn't wanted to believe it, but it was true.

This man was Mom's brother. My uncle. April's father.

What had driven our family apart?

I stumbled like a drunk back towards the couch. Before I could second-guess my decision, I set my jaw and dialed Garrett's number.

The space between each ring sent shivers of anticipation up my spine. What if he didn't answer? What if —

"Hello?"

The blood drained from my head at the sound of his now familiar voice.

"Anyone there?" he prodded.

"This is Laurel Lane. Is-is this—?" I choked on the words.

"This's Garrett. God, Laurel. Never thought I'd talk to you again. As for Joan…" He sighed. "Never got the chance to say goodbye. I suppose she's in the ground already?"

"Yeah, the funeral was weeks ago. I would've reached out sooner, but… I didn't even know you existed until recently."

Garrett chuckled. It morphed into a hacking cough. "When that woman cuts someone out, she commits, huh? I take it Maura finally told you about me, then."

I hesitated, thinking of April, but decided to leave her out of this. At least for now. Instead, I explained about the photo album, the call with Maura, my internet searches.

"Humph. I would've hoped Maura'd be honest with you once Joan passed. Though I suppose I'm not too surprised she wasn't," he said, almost to himself.

"Why's that?"

"Because of all that shit with Brandon. Joan wanted nothing to do with the family after that. She poisoned you'n Maura against us."

Goosebumps pricked my skin, unease settling deep within me. "What are you talking about? Who's Brandon? What happened?"

My breath caught in my throat as silence radiated through the phone for an agonizing beat before Garrett spoke again.

"Ah, for fuck's sake. You don't know anything, do you?"

10

G arrett lived in the small town of Winters, just south of the Indiana-Michigan border. We agreed to meet at his place the following afternoon.

I tossed and turned all night, every nerve ablaze, each neuron firing in nauseating anticipation of Garrett's story, knowing it would forever shift my understanding of my family and my place in it.

Despite my promise, I hadn't told April that I'd contacted Garrett. Not yet, anyway. My mother had severed her relationship with him for a reason. I wanted to learn why before dumping April into a potentially volatile situation.

But there was another reason for my silence, one I was loath to admit. Part of me wanted to protect April from whatever secrets my parents had worked so hard to shield me from, despite my initial conviction that she needed to make the choice for herself.

One thing was certain: I couldn't tell Garrett about his daughter during this initial meeting. I wanted to gauge his character, build our relationship, earn his trust. From there, we could move on to bigger revelations.

The next day, I left early, reaching Garrett's town a full hour before our scheduled meeting time. Vacant storefronts sprouted like weeds along the crumbling road, while factories loomed on the horizon, their intricate smokestacks jutting towards the sky.

The landscape soon opened up into a patchwork quilt of farm fields and housing developments with abundant faded For Sale signs that reeked of desperation. I slowed, my eyes darting from street signs to the scrawled directions clutched in my hand, which Garrett had dictated to me last night.

There it was. Garrett's street. Willow Lane.

A crow swooped in front of me and landed on the street sign, studying me with its beady black eyes. My hands slackened against the wheel. I slowed to a stop, staring at the bird, suddenly struck with helpless, unexpected panic.

What was I doing?

I was about to plunge headfirst and blindfolded into frigid, murky waters, with no one to rescue me if it all went wrong. Despite our shared blood, Garrett was a complete stranger, one who might be dangerous. I'd been so focused on protecting April that I neglected to think of my own safety.

I rested my forehead on the steering wheel and squeezed my eyes shut, straining to recall details from our initial phone call, any clues that could illuminate his personality before entering into this meeting. The whole conversation had been so shocking and unexpected that I was left only with fragments of impressions – the twinge of regret in his voice when he learned of mother's death, the spite when recalling how she'd severed contact with him. Reaching into my pocket, I pulled out the talisman stone, as though it could provide me with direction. I felt so lost without my parents here to guide me.

A sharp rap sounded against my window. I jolted upward to find a man standing beside my truck, only his torso visible. Frowning, I rolled down the window. The man reached out and gripped the window frame with hands the size of dinner plates, coarse black hairs dusting the knuckles of his sausage-like fingers. With a huff of exertion, he bent down and peered into the truck.

"Well, I'll be damned," he said. "You're Laurel, all grown up."

Electricity shot through my spine. This was it. There was no turning back now.

I pocketed the talisman stone, emerged from the car, and faced my uncle, stammering out an awkward greeting. We stood there for a moment, studying each other. Garrett wore a faded baseball cap over silver streaked hair. Stubble lined his pock-marked cheeks, not quite thick enough to obscure the knotted web of scar tissue marring his broad chin.

"Well, give your uncle a hug, won't you?"

Before I could respond, Garrett embraced me with his con-strictor-like arms, his foul breath warm on my neck. My heart lurched and panic flooded through me at the forced physical af-fection. I squirmed, desperate to get away. Even after releasing me, his vise-like hand lingered on my shoulder, pinning me in place.

"My place is just up the road. Get in and I'll direct you."

Though doubts about my decision crept into my mind, I forced myself to set them aside. As we drove, I snuck furtive glances at him, trying and failing to glimpse April within his blunt features. Then again, I didn't take after my dad, either.

When a passing freight train forced us to stop, Garrett broke the tense silence hanging between us. He cleared his throat and said, "How did she die? Joan, I mean."

"Car accident. She... fell asleep at the wheel."

"Shame."

I nodded, throat tight.

He didn't need to know about the drugs and alcohol in my mother's system.

He didn't need to know that I'd pushed her towards death.

And he didn't need to know that in my darkest moments, I wondered if she'd meant to kill herself.

The railroad tracks cleared, and we continued on in silence. After another mile, Garrett directed me onto a long gravel driveway lined with pines, where I parked beside a dented silver pickup truck.

"Well, this's it."

He heaved himself out of my truck. I followed behind him, gazing at his decrepit single-story home with apprehension. The smell of rot clung to my nostrils as I sidestepped past discarded garbage bags swarming with buzzing black flies, old furniture, and rusty yard tools littering his porch.

Garrett unlocked the front door, ushered me inside, and tossed his jacket on a chair. My eyes struggled to adjust to the subdued light straining through drawn curtains. The room stank of cigarette smoke.

"Bathroom's down the hall, if you need it," Garrett said. "I'll fetch us something to drink. Hope you're not a tea drinker. I've got coffee or water."

"Coffee would be great, thanks."

While Garrett prepared our drinks, I hurried into the bathroom and shut the door, breath hitching in my chest, pain throbbing through my pelvis. I splashed cold water on my face, trying to calm my system. This was my chance to get answers. Running away now meant losing that chance, perhaps forever. Despite the fear leaching through my veins, I needed to stay strong: for myself, and for April.

As I struggled to calm my thrumming nervous system, I surveyed my surroundings. The shower stall contained a bar of soap and a generic shampoo, the plastic curtain and bath mat speckled with black mold. Though I hadn't intended to snoop, I found myself inching open the medicine cabinet. It contained the usual suspects – toothbrush, toothpaste, floss, razor, deodorant – and some unusual ones – two medicine bottles for Prazosin and Paroxetine. Closer examination of the labels revealed they were used to treat symptoms associated with post-traumatic stress disorder. I wondered why he needed the medication. Though given his age, it was conceivable that he'd served in the Vietnam War.

A loud clanking noise, like dishware being jostled together, jolted me back to the present. With shaking hands, I quietly closed the medicine cabinet and took a deep breath before heading back. When I entered the living room, Garrett was balancing a tray laden with two chipped mugs, a carton of creamer, and a box of sugar. He frowned, staring down at the jumble of newspapers, magazines, and cigarette cartons layered atop the coffee table. I rushed over to help clear some space.

"Just leave it," he said.

"At least let me take the tray."

He shoved it into my outstretched hands, sending coffee splashing from the mugs, and threw his arm over the table. I placed the tray on the cleared surface, heart banging against my ribcage.

Garrett grabbed a mug of coffee and headed for a well-worn leather recliner held together by duct tape, which he'd positioned in front of an ancient television set. Dust billowed around him when he plopped into the seat. He swiveled the chair towards me and said, "Sit, sit."

I grabbed a mug and headed for the mildewed couch, which was coated in cigarette ash, crumbs, and what appeared to be animal hair. I sat down on the least offensive cushion and took a sip of coffee, more out of politeness than thirst, before placing it beside me on the floor. The taste barely registered on my tongue.

The couch cushion shifted. I whirled around and found two pale green eyes staring back at me. They belonged to a ginger cat with cream-colored paws and ragged fur. I smiled and reached out a hand towards her.

"Get off," Garrett growled.

Despite the warning, the cat continued to sit there, mewling plaintively. She strained her neck towards me, nose twitching, whiskers brushing soft against my fingers. I felt myself relax in her presence, as though she knew I needed comforting.

"For fuck's sake."

Garrett burst from his chair, grabbed the cat, and threw her aside like a piece of trash. She yowled and bolted into a corner. Horrified, I jumped to my feet, determined to comfort the cowering animal. When I approached her, she scurried away, tail between her legs.

"That's just Kitty. Leave her be," he said. "She's a stray. I don't much like animals, but she helps keep the mice and rats under control in the winter."

"You might've hurt her."

"She's fine. Sit down."

Too rattled and stunned to argue, I sank back onto the couch, alarm bells sounding within me. I wondered again if coming here had been a mistake.

"So. Joan never told you about me?" he asked.

I gave a slight shake of my head, orienting myself to the conversation. "No. Maybe she planned to at some point, I'm not sure. I never suspected she had a brother."

"Brothers. Me'n Brandon."

Mouth dry, I stared at him, incredulous. "Brothers? No. She would've... why didn't she tell me?"

"You really don't know anything?"

"No. Just tell me what the fuck is going on." I took a deep breath to compose myself and then added, "Please."

He sighed and removed his baseball cap, running a hand through his thinning hair.

"Joan and Howard aren't your parents."

I stared at Garrett, his words rattling around in my head, certain I'd heard him wrong. "What did you say?"

"I said Joan and Howard aren't your parents."

This time, there was no mistaking it. The blood drained from my face, sending the room spinning in a dizzying dervish. I clutched the arm of the couch to steady myself.

"You're wrong. Their names are on my birth certificate. They're my parents. They raised me."

"There're three Ryders. Me, your mom, and our older brother, Brandon. Brandon is your'n Maura's father. Joan is — was — your aunt."

"I don't believe you. You're lying. This doesn't make any sense."

"Joan adopted you and your sister. You must've been about two or three years old. It's Maura's fault. She told some teacher that Brandon — your dad — was hurting her. It got blown out of proportion. CPS and the police got involved. Brandon left town. Joan took you'n Maura in, and cut me out, even though I didn't have any part in it. And your mom — your birth mom — killed herself. That's the gist of it, anyway."

Each sentence sliced through me, cutting deeper and deeper until only a gaping hole remained where my heart once was. Tears pooled in my eyes.

I'd just lost my mother. Now I was losing another. And I couldn't bear it.

Garrett leaned forward, his hard black eyes devoid of any pity or compassion. "Maura ruined this family. She tore us apart. Even if Brandon hurt her, it wouldn't've been anything that wasn't done to him by our dad, you understand? Our dad'd drink too much, then holler, carry on, beat us, beat our mom.

Nothing we couldn't handle, though. It made us stronger. Made us smarter, too.

"But Maura was always sensitive. Weak. She made up some story about your dad hurting her. Tattled on him, probably over nothing. CPS liberals started a witch hunt, and that was it. Brandon had no choice but to leave."

My mind raced with a million disparate thoughts and feelings, all threatening to boil over. Despite how much it pained me, despite how much I wanted this to be a big misunderstanding, I knew deep down that what he said was true.

In this bright moment of clarity, everything clicked into place.

This was the reason for Maura's rage.

This was the reason why Joan refused to tell me the truth about our family.

Words and questions lodged in my throat, struggling to burst free. In the end, I choked out the most important one.

"What was she like? My birth mother?"

Garrett tossed his hands up, grinning, and the hardness in his expression dissolved. "Gorgeous girl. You're the spitting image of her, you know. You don't take after the Ryder side, your features are too fair. Yep, you definitely take after Irene."

My breath caught in my chest. Irene. My mother's name was Irene.

I wracked my mind, struggling to unearth some repressed memory of her lurking deep within me, waiting to be uncovered. For a fleeting moment, she glimmered before me: a pale figure in a blue dress, peering down at me with kind, sad eyes.

"She was a spitfire, that one," Garrett continued. "Got bored easily. Motherhood didn't suit her. Maura was a needy kid, and Irene didn't have the patience for mothering. I suspect she was jealous of you kids being the center of attention all the time. Brandon told me how she flirted with men for attention. Got smacked around because of that, but it never stopped her."

I flinched, the memory of my mother dissolving, marred by Garrett's cavalier mention of the abuse she'd suffered. Her identity was no longer her own, doomed to be forever filtered through another person's experiences and memories. How could I ever learn who she truly was?

Garrett's voice softened. "She cared about you kids, though. She was heartbroken when Maura made up those tales about abuse. Then, when everything fell apart, and she'd lost her entire family, she couldn't live with it. Hung herself from the tree in your backyard."

His words slammed into me like a sledgehammer. I closed my eyes, forcing the image he'd conjured from my mind. Tears streamed over my face as the heaviness of grief crashed over me once again.

Garrett cleared his throat and shifted in his seat, jarring me back to the present. My grief hardened into anger as I watched him sitting there, completely indifferent to my suffering, not making even the slightest effort to comfort me. As though the only reason he'd invited me here was to share his twisted version of the truth.

"What about Brandon? My father. What happened to him?"

"Like I said, he took off after Maura started spewing lies. Had no choice. A man's life, ruined, because of a girl telling tall tales. I haven't heard from him in decades."

My face twisted in disgust. How could he sit there and spew this nonsense? Women and girls don't lie about abuse. Only that wasn't strictly true. We lie about abuse by not speaking of it, choosing instead to bury our experiences, convince ourselves it hadn't happened, or that we misinterpreted what happened. Because if we told others about our experiences, if we accepted the horrific ways we'd been violated, there was always a risk that we still might not be believed. And the not believing would burrow into our scars and tear us in two.

Despite the stories Garrett weaved, I knew deep in my bones that whatever abuse our father had inflicted on Maura must have been nothing short of horrific.

11

When I left Garrett's house, he followed me to my truck and enveloped me in another unwanted hug.

"I know this was a lot to take in," he said.

A lump formed in my throat as I nodded. Overhead, the sky was streaked blood red, the sun inching towards the horizon.

"I need to go, before it gets too dark."

"Come back anytime. We can always talk more." Garrett's shoulders sagged, head drooping. "I don't get many visitors out here these days. It's nice to have someone to talk to. There's more I can tell you about the family. Me, Joan, our parents... your grandparents. Anything you want to know. No point in keeping secrets anymore."

April flashed through my mind, a reminder of the secret I still kept from him. A rush of guilt flooded through me at my silence.

"Oh, I nearly forgot." Garrett pulled a crumpled envelope from his jacket pocket and handed it to me. "I want you to have this. They're photos of your parents. Of your real family."

I accepted the envelope, mouth dry, and croaked out a thank you. We said our goodbyes. As I headed out, I snuck one last glance at him through the rearview window. His dark eyes flashed in the setting sun as he watched me depart.

Once I reached the main road, I pulled over beside an orchard, tree limbs heavy with apples. I stumbled out of my truck, legs shaking, and fell down, retching violently, over and over.

My stomach continued to heave long after it had emptied, each spasm forcing my knees deeper into the hard soil and exacerbating the ever-present cramp that plagued my every moment. Flies buzzed around me, frenzied, and my head swam from the stench of vomit and fermented, rotting apples. Tears spilled from my eyes, watering the earth. Soon, sobs wracked my body, chest tightening with each gasping breath.

I'd lost so much, so long ago.

After what seemed like an eternity, my body and breath quieted. I staggered to my truck and began driving home.

The sky had darkened to deep violet by the time I reached my cottage. The events of the day blurred together, dreamlike. I couldn't even remember the drive home. Once inside, I rinsed the sour taste from my mouth, then crumpled onto the couch, struggling to process my new reality.

Garrett's story painted a compelling picture of our family, one that provided answers to questions that had always bothered me. Though painful to accept, it seemed I had no choice.

Joan and Howard weren't my parents.

I pulled out the envelope Garrett had given me. When I removed the first photo, my own face stared back at me. I almost dropped the image out of shock before realizing who it was.

My biological mother. Irene.

My breath caught in my chest. I drew the photo closer, scrutinizing her features. We shared the same straw-colored hair, lanky limbs, and jutting collarbones. On me, these features were awkward, but on her, they were elegant. Endearing, even.

She wore a lightweight summer dress that clung to her curves, and her red lips were curled into a teasing smile. I could almost see her fluttering her dark lashes at the photographer. As I drank in the picture, I marveled over her grace and beauty, the comfort with which she existed in her own skin, so unlike myself.

I lived in my head, absorbed with new ideas or tasks or problems to solve. My body was an unwanted distraction, requiring food and clothes and regular bathing. I preferred worn jeans and hiking boots to dresses and makeup, and unlike other women, I didn't check my appearance in windows and mirrors multiple times a day, generally finding my appearance unchanged from one day to the next.

Where did I come from then?

Not from Irene, with her flirtatious smile and effortless beauty.

Not from Joan, with her soft round body and fear of snakes and spiders.

I pulled out the next photo. Irene grinned at me, her smile crinkling the corners of her blue eyes, as though laughing at a private joke. Her blonde hair was flipped over one shoulder and a few loose strands framed the heart-shaped face she shared with Maura.

And there he was, beside her.

Brandon.

My biological father.

I expected a chill to run through me, for the hair to stand up at the back of my neck, for his wrongness to seep into my bones.

Instead, I was filled with a curious sense of disappointment. He looked... normal, like the men I walk past in coffee shops and grocery stores every day. The type of evil that camouflages in with its surroundings, that your eyes skirt around, unseeing.

Brandon shared Garrett's muscular frame and Maura's wavy raven hair. He stared at Irene, but rather than sharing her joy, his jaw was clenched, tendons in his neck straining. They stood in front of a small ranchette, a 'Sold' sign staked into the yellowing lawn.

Flipping over the photo, I read the inscription, written in neat, delicate print, perhaps by my mother's hand.

Outside our first home! 8202 Maple Ave, Chicago.

I pored over the rest of the photos, absorbing the minute details of my parents' features, their body language, how they related to one another. It was as though I were reading runes, or the stars, trying to divine meaning from the way she smiled, or how he positioned himself in relation to her orbit.

Brandon was a sentinel, unchanging. Irene was mercurial, shifting from flirtatious to sullen as easily as a snake sheds its skin.

Any doubts about Garrett's story fell away as I studied the photos. It just felt right. This woman was my mother.

There were so many questions I wanted to ask her.

Had she known Brandon was abusing their daughter? Had she tried to intervene, only to fall prey to her husband's violence?

What had she been like? Had she loved me?

But I already knew some answers.

She abandoned me and Maura. She stood by while her husband abused their daughter, either out of blind ignorance or denial or helplessness. She ended her life rather than accept the consequences of losing her children.

Joan and Howard had been my true parents. I knew that deep in my bones. Howard and I might not have shared the same blood, but he'd treated me like his biological daughter. He'd shielded me from the angst between Maura and Joan, providing me with the comfort and safety that Joan couldn't. Our connection and love for one another was so strong that I carried it within me, years after his death. The talisman stone nestled in my pocket was a constant reminder of his steadfastness and guidance. I'd created a life for myself based on the lessons and experiences he'd shared with me.

Though I knew Howard was complicit in my family's lies, it was hard to hold him accountable for the deception. Joan was the architect of the secrecy. It was her family, her niece who had suffered at her brother's hands, and likely her choice to keep our history from me. Over time, Joan and I had deepened our relationship, finding our own form of closeness, to the point where the ties binding us together had been strong as steel, able to withstand anything. Now those bonds felt like gossamer threads, breaking one by one.

Joan's lies drove a wedge between me and my only sister, preventing us from forging a genuine relationship. As a result, I grew up with a stranger instead of a sister. Maura carried the burden of abuse and neglect and heartache alone when it should have been ours to share.

Now the lies had shriveled away, creating space for our relationship to bloom. Though my mind teemed with questions, I knew demanding answers from Maura might rip open her old wounds, leaving her bare and bleeding, just to satisfy my hunger. And that wasn't fair.

There'd been enough secrecy in this family. She deserved to know that she wasn't alone anymore. Picking up my phone, I sent her a message.

I met with Garrett. He told me everything. I'm sorry.

I spent the next day in bed, mind adrift on a tumultuous sea. In what was becoming a familiar pattern, I neglected research and chores, choosing instead to grapple with the complex waves of emotions pulsing through me.

Anger that Joan and Howard had built my childhood on a bedrock of lies.

Rage at my biological father for his abuse and cowardice.

Grief for the loss of my biological mother.

Sorrow for the horrors Maura had been forced to carry alone, for the chance at sisterhood we'd been denied, for the silence Maura still perpetuated, even after telling her I finally knew the truth.

When I awoke Monday morning, a sense of dread and helplessness coiled around my heart. I groaned and heaved myself into a seated position, swiveling my neck, trying to work out the kinks. My body was a lead weight, anchoring me to the bed.

Facing the week felt akin to swimming upstream, when all I wanted was to surrender, allowing the water to enfold me in an icy embrace. If I sunk now, I might lose the strength to rise again.

Instead, I focused on the tasks ahead of me. I needed to check in with Luis's lab assistants about their progress with my blood samples. Having some new data might give me something to do besides sifting through the lies my parents had fed me.

I dragged myself out of bed, showered, and dressed, then headed to the kitchen for a late breakfast of oatmeal and coffee. My phone buzzed atop the kitchen counter. I grabbed it, hoping Maura had finally replied to my message. My heart sank when I realized she hadn't. There was a series of text messages from April going back several days, asking me if I had any updates about our search for Garrett. Unable to muster the mental and emotional fortitude to respond, I finished my breakfast, threw my phone in my bag, and headed to campus.

When I approached the ecology lab, I heard Luis and Petra conversing in low tones through the open door. Their conversation skidded to an abrupt halt when I walked in. Petra glanced up from her desk and shot me a forced smile, eyes sunken and bloodshot. Luis stood next to her, wearing a rumpled plaid shirt, his face flushed. I forced a tight smile by way of greeting, unable to muster the energy to be drawn into their conversation.

"Do you know if your lab assistants have finished processing my samples yet?" I asked.

"Mmm, I'm not sure," Luis said. "But they're working this morning if you want to talk to them. They're in the lab down the hall."

"Thanks."

I strode over to my workspace, threw down my bag, and pulled out my laptop, more out of habit than necessity. An uneasy silence settled through the cramped space. Though my back was to Luis and Petra, I could feel their eyes boring into me. My skin prickled with unease.

Could they sense the despair and angst roiling within me? Was my desperation exuding from my pores like a pheromone, a primitive alarm bell ringing out to warn others to steer clear? My breath hitched, the sound in the silence as jarring as a gunshot. I didn't want to be here. Couldn't be here.

Before I started spiraling, I gritted my teeth and took a deep breath, trying to soothe myself. All I needed was my data. Then I could hole up somewhere quiet. Allow myself to get lost in the comfort of numbers and statistics; in the objective, emotionless reality of science.

When I turned around, I found Luis blocking my path. His sudden presence was jarring, and I stumbled away from him, my hand instinctively settling on my heart. He politely ignored my distress and instead asked, "Petra and I are going out for coffee soon. Do you want to join?"

I swallowed and forced myself to speak, latching on to a weak excuse. "I have too much to do, sorry."

His face fell. "Okay, no worries. But we need to catch up soon, yeah?"

"Sure, maybe later this week." The answer sounded false even to me, but I couldn't pretend that everything in my life was normal. Not while the wound in my chest was still fresh and bleeding. Avoiding interactions entirely seemed easier than allowing others to see the pain blooming within me.

I brushed past Luis and headed towards the other lab space on this floor. Giggles echoed down the hall, competing with the hum and whir of centrifuges. I entered the room and spotted Luis's assistants, Erica and Rob, curled up on the scuffed floor next to our storage fridge. Pipettes and dirty test tubes littered the lab bench, and the faint coppery scent of blood and disinfectant filled my nostrils.

Erica shrieked with laughter, nestling deeper into the crook of Rob's arm. They were watching something on Rob's phone, sharing the same set of headphones. His muscular shoulders were hunched forward, sending his mop of curly black hair over his pimpled face, smirking as he stared at the screen.

A flash of annoyance flitted through me. "You're getting paid to process samples, not watch YouTube videos."

Erica's head jolted upwards. She yanked out her headphone and scrambled away from Rob, round face blooming into the same furious shade of red as her frizzy hair. Rob's gaze flicked up at me before settling once again on his phone.

"We're on a break," he said.

I opened my mouth to retort when my eyes snagged on the charging cable running from Rob's phone to an outlet on the wall. The cord from the adjacent refrigerator sprawled across the floor. Panic coursed through me. I lunged for the phone charger, yanked it out, and tossed it aside.

Rob burst to his feet. "What the hell!"

I plugged in the fridge and stuck my hand inside to check the temperature. Cool, but not cold. Hands shaking, I rummaged through the glass vials of samples within.

All mine. All possibly damaged. A summer's worth of work that I couldn't afford to lose.

Slamming the door shut, I turned around, fists clenched at my side, all the anger and anxiety churning within me ready to spill over. "Please tell me you already processed my blood samples."

"We're almost done," Erica said. "Just a few more days. Promise."

"How many do you have left?"

"We've done, like, all of them, basically," Rob replied. He was now slouched against the wall, arms crossed over his chest, a single headphone still lodged in his ear.

I closed my eyes and pinched the bridge of my nose. "I cannot believe I have to explain this to you, but you do realize that unplugging a fridge full of samples so you can charge your cellphone is a bad idea, right?"

The blood drained from Erica's face, leaving her pale skin almost translucent. Her eyes darted to Rob, who was eyeing me with something close to disdain on his face.

"I'm so sorry, it was a stupid mistake," Erica said.

"I want these samples processed ASAP. I need to know if they're still viable."

She nodded vigorously, curls bouncing across her shoulders. Rob scowled and turned his back to me, still absorbed with his cell phone. I bolted towards him, grabbed his arm, and tugged the headphone out of his ear.

"Are you even listening to me?!"

Rob peered down at my hand with incredulity, which was still wrapped around his bicep, tight enough that my fingers ached from the exertion. I released him as if shocked, revealing pale streaks on his tanned skin from where my fingers had dug into his flesh.

"You can't tell me what to do. I don't work for you," Rob said, rubbing his arm. He reeled in his headphone cord, frowning as he examined it for damage. I resisted the urge to slap it out of his hand.

"You're right. You don't work for me. You work for Luis, and he won't be happy to learn that his lab assistant is a mindless, careless idiot who contaminated the lab samples that were his responsibility. Now do your job, or you'll risk losing your work-study."

I left Erica cowering at a lab bench and stalked back down the hall, dragging my legs. Fatigue clung to my body like a bulky winter coat and a dull ache bloomed behind my eyes. Without the data to distract me, all I wanted was to go home and crawl back into bed. Coming in today had been a mistake.

When I entered the lab to retrieve my belongings, Luis was standing by the door, pulling on his coat, Petra close behind him.

"Did you find Erica and Rob?" he asked.

"Yeah, just in time to rescue my blood samples," I said, then explained what happened.

"Fuck, that's unacceptable. I'll talk to them."

"Good."

"Petra and I are about to grab a coffee. Sure you can't join us?"

"Can't. I've got a headache. I'm going home."

I headed towards my desk and grabbed my belongings. Luis opened his mouth to protest, but Petra grabbed him by the arm and murmured something in his ear, her face tight. His eyes flashed, but he nodded, head turned towards her. I raised an eyebrow, curiosity tugging at me, but said nothing. Before they could pull me into their conversation, I brushed past them and left.

Once outside, I blinked at the onslaught of bright morning light and took a few steadying breaths. Cold air flooded my lungs, triggering another wave of pain through my skull.

My phone vibrated. I pulled it out. It was April. I sighed, knowing I couldn't avoid her forever.

"What's up?" I asked.

"Hey! Just checking in, since you haven't been answering my texts?" The words raced from her mouth, brimming with nervous energy.

"I haven't found Garrett, if that's what you're after."

"Oh. No, that's okay," she said, though her tone was laced with disappointment. "I get that it might take some time before you locate him. It's just... I've spent my whole life dreaming about him, you know? And now, finally, being so close to finding him, meeting him... I'm having trouble waiting." She laughed nervously.

A sense of unease gnawed within me as I recalled my encounter with Garrett. He'd dismissed Joan and Maura and Irene's experiences and defended my abusive father. Was he someone I wanted to bring into April's life?

"That's not the only reason I called. I've been thinking a lot about you lately. About how your parents kept Garrett a secret for all those years. It's just so... strange."

I tightened my grip, struggling against the surge of anger and frustration boiling within me. "Yep. But they're dead now, so I'll never get to ask them about it. And my sister might as well be dead, because she won't talk to me about it, either. So yeah, I'm not okay, but bringing it up isn't helping."

For a moment, April fell into a stunned silence. "You're right. It was stupid to even ask. I'm sorry."

The line went dead. I shoved the phone into my coat pocket and resumed walking towards the parking lot, hardening myself against the twinge of guilt curling in my gut. My entire world had imploded because of April. She was a constant, nagging reminder of my parents' lies. I still hadn't figured out how to tell Garrett about her. Still, part of me regretted my impulsivity.

My phone buzzed again. Relief coursed through me at the chance to make things right between us. I answered it without looking.

"April, I'm sorry—"

"I can't believe you didn't listen to me. How could you?!"

Maura's fury-filled voice leapt from the phone. I skidded to a halt, grasping the trunk of an oak tree to steady myself.

"Well, you didn't leave me much of a choice," I said, reeling. "You could've just told me."

"I wanted to, when we were younger, but Joan wouldn't allow it. She wouldn't let any of us."

"But why? How could she expect to keep it a secret forever?"

She sighed. "You were so young when it happened. Joan wanted to give you a fresh start. We argued about it constantly, but she wouldn't budge. It was exhausting. After a while, I just gave up."

Realization washed over me. I closed my eyes. "That's why you two always fought. She wanted to keep our parents a secret from me, and you didn't."

"Something like that."

My heart shattered. I slid against the tree trunk, legs crumpling, dead leaves crackling beneath me. A student strolling through the quad threw me a curious look.

For years, Maura had been struggling to maintain the charade that Joan had forced upon her without her consent. No wonder she'd broken off contact with me. I was a constant reminder of what she'd gone through, yet I'd emerged unscathed, living in blissful ignorance.

"Why didn't you tell me the truth, after Mom — after Joan died?"

She hesitated, as though weighing her words. "Because over the years, I realized Joan was right. There's no point in bringing up the past. Not after you'd built a life centered around Joan and Howard as your parents. Your real family. I know how close you were with them. I didn't want to take that away from you.

"I came to the funeral because I thought we could start fresh, with Joan and Howard gone. I knew you'd be struggling with Joan's loss, but I didn't anticipate how upset you'd be with me. My issues were always with them, not you. I wanted to start over, focusing on the present. But you're still stuck in the past."

"Can you blame me? These secrets ruined my childhood. I spent years wondering why you hated me, why you always pushed me away. I deserve to know why."

"How much did Garrett tell you?" she asked. Her voice was guarded. I flailed, trying to find the right words.

"He... he told me that our father was... abusing you, but that you made the whole thing up. Or most of it, anyway."

Her voice cut through the phone, sharp as glass. "So he's still spewing that bullshit."

"I didn't believe him. You wouldn't lie about something that serious." I shook my head, tears filling my eyes. "All these years, carrying that burden, being told not to speak of it... I'm so sorry, Maura. I knew Joan and Howard were only trying to protect me, but they only made things worse. For all of us."

We both fell silent, Maura's still unspoken story hanging between us, just out of reach, like the leaves swaying overhead. My mind brimmed with questions. I bit my lip until I tasted blood, determined to stop them from spilling out. I couldn't risk scaring her away, not when we were finally talking, after over a decade of silence.

"I suppose you want to know what happened."

My breath hitched, heart lurching against my ribcage. "Yes. Of course I do."

"Did you tell Garrett about that girl? Ann?"

"April. And no, I didn't. She knows he's her father, but doesn't know that I found him."

"Good. That's good." She took a deep breath. "If I tell you, you need to promise you won't contact Garrett again. Make sure April doesn't, either. He's a bad person, Laurel. He'll destroy her."

Her words sent a chill down my spine. My shoulder tingled with the phantom touch of Garrett's vise-like hand, holding me still. In my mind's eye, I saw him throwing his cat across the room, black eyes glinting with malice.

Perhaps Maura was right. Despite April's insistence to the contrary, her daydreams of the father she desired might be preferable to facing the disappointment of the one she had.

Maura was offering me something I'd waited my entire life for: the chance to rebuild our relationship on a foundation of truth, rather than lies.

All thoughts of April fled from my mind as I found myself intoxicated by that lure, helpless in Maura's grasp.

"Fine," I said. "I promise."

12

I spent the next few days avoiding my research. Though Erica and Rob finished processing my samples shortly after our encounter, I couldn't muster any interest in evaluating the data. The long hours I'd spent in the lab last week felt like a distant dream. So much had changed since then.

After returning home, I'd texted April to apologize for losing my temper, but she didn't respond. It was probably for the best. I was about to meet with Maura and the conflicting promises I'd made to each of them weighed heavy on my shoulders.

On Thursday, I pulled into the near-vacant parking lot at Silver Beach, along the shore of Lake Michigan. Maura chose the meeting location. Every summer growing up, Joan and Howard would rent the same cabin with its peeling paint, cobwebs, and mice scurrying through the walls. I never grew tired of running breathless and ecstatic down steep sand dunes, of splashing in the icy water, of building sandcastles and swinging from vines in the nearby forest. Howard and I spent hours together canoeing, birdwatching, and searching for salamanders lurking beneath rotting logs, the two of us happily lathered in mosquito repellant, sunscreen, and soil.

Maura had a decidedly less rosy view of those family trips. She'd spend her days at Silver Beach sulking, brow furrowed, fair skin burnt and peeling, while I bronzed in the sun, lips smeared and sticky with mint ice cream.

Now, decades later, I sat perched upon a splintering picnic table as I waited for her to appear. I ran a finger over the rotting table, black holes burrowing into once fresh pine, and studied the graffiti scrawled across the neighboring restroom's walls, wondering when this place had begun to decay.

The crunch of gravel caught my attention. Maura emerged from a trail in the woods with a man I didn't recognize, her hand clasped around his arm. Upon catching my gaze, he stared at me warily and rubbed a hand across his stubbled chin. Maura untangled herself from his grasp and raised a hand in greeting, her face troubled.

I hopped off the table and headed towards them. Maura tugged at the long loose braid that rested like a rope down her chest as she watched me approach, her expression guarded. She wore an oversized cardigan over a black dress that whipped around her thin legs with each gust of wind.

As I neared them, the man placed a protective hand on Maura's shoulder. She shot him a grateful smile, squeezed his hand, and murmured something in his ear. He kissed the crown of her head and took off down the trail, shoulders hunched, hands shoved into the pockets of his jeans.

"Who's your friend?" I asked.

Maura's cheeks flushed, and she struggled against the upward tug of her lips. I wracked my mind, trying to remember the last time I saw her genuinely smile, but came up short. This might be it.

"That's James. We're..." Her eyelids fluttered close. "We've been together a few years."

"That's great. I'm happy for you."

A lock of dark hair shrugged loose from Maura's braid. She brushed it aside and stared towards the shore, eyes glazed.

"Brings back memories, doesn't it? Being here again, after all these years?" I said.

She smiled wryly. "You'd always count down the days until our annual trip. When the day arrived, we'd wake to find you already buckled in the car, with a tote bag stuffed with books and crayons and whatever snacks you could scrounge up. You'd sit there for hours as the rest of us finished packing. When we'd turn into the parking lot..."

"I'd lose my shit."

Maura nodded. "You were lucky, growing up."

"We both were. Joan and Howard were good parents."

Maura scowled and stalked towards the beach, her delicate feet leaving small depressions in the sand. I scrambled to keep up with her, heart racing, desperate to prevent her from slipping away from me. Then she whirled around, eyes ablaze, and I skidded to a halt.

"Joan and Howard weren't our parents. Understood?"

I nodded, swallowing back the lump in my throat.

"Good," she said, her voice softening.

We drifted down the beach. Seagulls flocked around us, cawing at one another as they rooted for food in the coarse sand. The waves crashed against the shore in rhythmic pulses.

Maura stopped at an inlet and peered over the water, shielding her eyes from the midday sun breaking through the clouds. Wisps of hair fluttered over her flushed cheeks. Her mouth opened and closed a few times, as though considering where to begin. She took a deep breath and turned towards me.

"I need you to understand how difficult this is for me. When I left home, I was in a dark place. I never imagined I could experience the life I have now. I'm in a long-term relationship with a loving partner who sees and accepts me for who I am. I'm doing meaningful work, teaching art to vulnerable children and teenagers who need someone who understands. I have a beautiful home where I'm safe and loved."

As she spoke, Maura's eyes shone, her face filling with wonder, as though she didn't quite believe that the life she was describing belonged to her. For a moment, I didn't recognize her. I struggled to reconcile the strong, capable woman in front of me with the scared, angry child she'd once been. This was the version of my sister I'd spent my childhood yearning for.

"It's taken years of therapy and work for me to get to this point," she continued. "And even with all the goodness in my life, I still carry the damage from my childhood. Still struggle with it, every single day." Her face darkened, eyelids fluttering closed, and she took a deep breath.

"I know you want the truth about our family. I get that, Laurel, and know that you deserve it. But it comes with a cost. To both of us." She caught my eye and spoke her next words slowly and deliberately. "You need to understand that what you're asking is for me to relive my trauma, and to traumatize you in the process."

My mouth went dry. I swallowed, collecting my thoughts. Maura clasped her hands in front of her and gazed at me intensely, searching my face. I wondered if she wanted me to leave, relieving her from the burden of our shared inheritance. A small part of me wanted to give her that release. But this was my only chance to get answers. I know she wouldn't give me this opportunity again. If I walked away now, I'd spend the rest of my life regretting it.

"I know this is hard for you, but I need to know the truth. Please, Maura. You don't have to carry this on your own anymore."

For a fleeting moment, Maura's body tensed, like a deer under the watchful eyes of a predator, readying herself to escape. The moment passed as quickly as it occurred. She shook her head slightly and straightened her back, drawing her slight frame to its fullest extent. Despite her display of strength, dread settled deep in my gut. I wondered if I was truly prepared for what came next. Before I could second-guess my decision, Maura began to speak, and I had no choice but to listen as her story shifted the ground beneath me.

"Growing up, I learned at an obscenely young age that I needed to pay attention to Dad — our actual Dad — because things could get ugly and dangerous fast. So I learned to watch him. Hide. Make myself small, invisible. I tried not to get in trouble. It was better not to be noticed.

"That worked sometimes, but not always. Sometimes, hiding wasn't an option. That was the worst, the feeling of not having control. Of being trapped. Like whenever Dad would drive and start screaming about something, swerving over the road while other drivers honked and yelled at us. Sometimes, if we were lucky, Mom could convince him to pull over and she and I would walk home. Other times, we were trapped in a car with a madman.

"There were some calm moments too, after they'd had their drinks. They'd joke, flirt, laugh. But then the fighting would start again. I don't even remember what about." She stared, unseeing, at the bubbling foam, the rise and fall of surf inches from her feet. "All those horrifying hours spent cowering in my room, listening to them yelling and shoving and slapping, and I still don't understand why."

Memories flashed through my mind, parallel to her own, though a decade apart. Maura and Mom, arguing in hushed tones behind closed doors. Blow-ups in the car, or over dinner. And me, never knowing why, forever searching for that one crucial detail that would help it all make sense.

"I never understood why Mom wanted another kid," she said, casting me a sidelong glance. "I don't think she enjoyed being a mother. She'd play with me, and take care of me, yes, but it was in fits and bursts. Eventually, she'd get bored with me, or things would get too hard. She wasn't like other moms. She never seemed interested in me." Maura turned away, voice brittle. "It's so absurd, thinking back on it. I mean, for kids, their parents are their life. Their whole life."

She clammed up. It was as though someone had flipped a switch inside her. Her shoulders slumped, eyes clouded over, lower lip trembling. Silence descended upon us — for a minute, then two. I wondered if she'd lost her nerve. When she finally spoke again, her voice wavered, and she avoided my gaze.

"That's when it started happening. When she was pregnant, with you." Her words fell from her mouth slowly, like honey dripping from a spoon. My whole body tensed. "He started coming to my room at night. He told me that if I told Mom, he'd hurt her, and you, and it'd be my fault."

Chills ran down my spine. My nails bit into my palms as I stared at my sister, bile rising in my esophagus, pelvis throbbing in pain. Something inside me urged me to run, but I found myself frozen, unable to do anything but listen in growing horror.

Not this. Please, not this.

"I blamed myself. I thought I must've done something wrong, must be wrong, for this to happen to me," she said, pressing her eyelids shut. "I thought he'd stop after your birth, but he didn't. Instead, it made it easier for him.

"Mom had... changed. She used to be so vibrant and full of life, if a little self-absorbed. But she was preoccupied with you, and just so... sad. I was invisible to her. It's like she didn't realize she had another child.

"I've always wondered if she knew what was happening, and ignored it. Maybe she was afraid of him, or couldn't muster the strength to intervene. Maybe she didn't know at all. I don't know which is worse." She shook her head as though trying to dislodge a fly from her ear. "Guess it doesn't matter now."

Her gaze flicked towards me. I forced my face to go blank, not wanting her to see the turmoil and anguish roiling within me. A shadow crossed her face. She traced her foot along the nebulous boundary separating sea from sand, then eased herself into a crouched position, resting her chin on her knees.

I lowered myself to the ground beside her, heart thrumming against my ribcage, like the wings of a hummingbird. Time slowed down. The moment stretched on and on, the air between us vibrating with tension. Then Maura spoke again, and everything unraveled.

"I was in Mrs. Hernandez's seventh grade English class when it happened," she said. "It felt like someone was squeezing my insides. I was bleeding all over my chair, so I ran to the restroom. There were these big shiny clots falling out of me. I'd had my period before, but this was different. It hurt so bad, and there was so much blood. I was certain I was dying."

Maura recited the story as though she were running lines from a play. Though her voice was flat, an edge ran through it like an undercurrent, so sharp I thought she might shock me if I touched her.

"The nurse found me and called an ambulance. I spent the next few days being crowded by doctors and CPS agents and police officers, begging them to believe what he'd done to me. Because I couldn't hide it any longer." Her voice cracked. "I was only twelve."

Maura's face screwed up, and she wrapped her arms around herself as her body quaked with muffled sobs.

My shoulders and chest ached, breath shallow and uneven, hands tingling. I felt untethered from my body, drifting, observing from above, unable to speak, unable to accept the horror hanging between us.

After what seemed like eons, Maura settled into stillness, wiping her nose with the back of her hand. "Well, you heard the rest from Garrett. Dad ran off. Joan took us in. Mom..." Her words skidded to a halt, and she inhaled sharply, shuddering. "And Garrett alternated between denying the whole thing and accusing me and Joan of bringing it on ourselves."

"What happened to you wasn't your fault," I said, squeezing her shoulder. "None of it was your fault. You know that, right? You were just a kid."

She didn't respond, face blank, unblinking. I felt completely helpless, unsure of how to respond, only knowing I wanted to soothe her pain, somehow. Trying again, I said, "I wish Joan and Howard could've taken us in sooner. I wish... I wish our mother, our actual mother, would've done more to protect you."

Maura unfurled herself and pierced me with a dagger-like glare. I recoiled, removing my hand. "You're right. It shouldn't have happened. Because Joan could've prevented it."

I frowned, puzzled. "What do you mean?"

"I wasn't Dad's first victim. Joan was."

13

I stared at Maura in disbelief, certain I'd heard her wrong; but knowing I hadn't. My chest tightened, each breath a struggle, like drowning on dry ground. I dug my palms into the sand, willing the beach to swallow me whole and release me from this waking nightmare. When I finally mustered the strength to speak, my voice cracked.

"What do you mean, Joan was his first victim?"

She shot me an exasperated look. "What do you think? Our dad abused Joan when they were growing up. His own sister. And she buried it. By the time she finally told me, it was too late. He'd already done to me what he'd done to her. She could've protected me, Laurel, but she chose to protect him instead."

My mind conjured an image of Joan's body splayed across the steering wheel, shards of glass glittering around her, speckled red with blood. I thought of her crippling depression and anxiety, nursed with alcohol and numbed with medication. All because of the unbearable suffering that she'd buried away, unwilling to acknowledge or address. Instead, she allowed her wounds to fester until it destroyed her and those she loved.

Yet despite Joan's many flaws, the instinct to defend her was overwhelming. She was my true mother, and my best friend, and she wasn't here to share her own story.

"That's not fair. You can't blame Joan for what happened to you. She might've been afraid of him, or thought she wouldn't be believed, or was ashamed of her own abuse."

"She took us in because she felt guilty."

"She took us in because she loved us," I insisted. "Because she was a good person."

Maura scowled. "She wanted redemption. I wouldn't give it to her, so she focused her attention on you. That's why she forbade us from telling you the truth. She knew if you found out, she'd lose you, too."

"I can't listen to this anymore." I stood up and started down the shore, feet sinking and sliding in the soft sand. Maura made a soft noise of disgust and scrambled to keep pace with me.

"You can't run away from this, Laurel. You wanted the truth, even after I warned you about what it meant for both of us. Well, here it is." She gestured with her arm, as if displaying a dinner spread, lip curling into a grimace. The tranquility and calm strength she'd exuded earlier had dissolved, as had the despair and sadness of mere minutes ago, replaced instead with the familiar spite-filled version of the sister that had tormented my childhood.

"You've got some nerve, demanding that I relive all the fucked-up shit I went through for your benefit, then thinking you can walk away from it. Well, you can't. And neither can I. Maybe now you realize how good you had it, growing up in ignorance."

Desperate to get away, I stumbled into the surf, gasping as cold water lapped around my ankles. Maura grabbed my arm to steady me.

"Leave me alone," I said, shoving her.

Maura staggered backwards, mouth opening into a ring of surprise, arms wrapping around her belly. Vindicated, I turned around and trudged onwards, sand sticking to my wet feet.

"You're just like her," Maura called out.

I skidded to a stop. Even though I knew she was baiting me, that I should ignore her, I spun back around. Maura's fists were clenched by her side, a look of pure fury upon her face.

"What do you mean?" I asked.

"You're making this about you, just like Joan did. I came to her at the darkest point in my entire fucking life. At first, she tried comforting me, and I thought I could trust her. I so desperately wanted to trust someone. But then I realized she only wanted to ease her own guilt. She didn't care about me. If she did, she would've intervened."

Maura spat her words like venom, voice rising and crashing with the waves. I staggered along the beach like an injured deer as she stalked behind me.

"You act like Joan was this great mother to you, but she wasn't," Maura hissed. "She lied to you. Manipulated you. Turned you against me."

Tears pooled in my eyes. "She didn't turn me against you. There was no need. Whenever I tried to get close to you, you pushed me away. Then you abandoned us. You abandoned me. I needed you, Maura."

"Are you kidding me? I never meant to break off contact, but once I left, Joan wouldn't let me see you. She was worried I'd tell you the truth. Then you got older, grew closer to Joan and Howard. By that point, it seemed too late for us."

The words hit me like a punch in the gut, pushing the air from my lungs, leaving me breathless and stunned into silence.

After Maura moved out, Joan insisted it had been Maura's decision to break off contact with everyone, including me. She said Maura's emotional disturbances made it difficult for her to form meaningful relationships. I'd accepted the explanation without question, though now I saw the kernel of truth lurking within the lie. Maura's struggles with depression made sense in the context of this secret history.

If Maura was telling the truth, it meant Joan had intentionally isolated me from my sister. The realization made my stomach churn.

"I didn't know. I'm sorry, okay? It's not her fault. I should've... I dunno, challenged her more."

Maura's face twisted into a mask of disgust. "And yet you're still defending her. She manipulated you, used you as an emotional crutch for her own feelings of guilt and inadequacy. You could've gone to Yale, Laurel. But she convinced you to attend Hildegard, so you could care for her. Enable her."

"You don't know what you're talking about. You weren't there, didn't see how bad she was, after Dad — after Howard died. She needed me. It was my choice to stay, not hers."

Maura shook her head and scoffed. "I thank God every fucking day for that miscarriage, because it got me away from him. You should be thankful for it, too, because if it hadn't happened, you would've grown up in that house, and eventually Dad would've started visiting your bedroom at night, just like he did to me. And your precious, infallible Aunt Joan wouldn't have done a thing about it."

Something inside me wrenched apart. Tears streamed down my flushed cheeks and my body shook, chest tight as I gasped for air. I stumbled through the sand, hurrying towards the safety of my truck, leaving Maura behind.

For the first time in our lives, I was the one running away.

14

I staggered back to the beach's parking lot, my eyes blurred. A gust of wind rattled through the trees, whipping my hair across my cheeks. Maura's partner, James, sat atop a picnic table, hunched forward, hands clasped over his head. As I approached my truck, he scrambled down and barreled towards me, his face scrunched in concern.

"Where's Maura?"

"Still on the beach."

He ran his fingers through his hair, idling behind me as I searched for my keys. Then he cleared his throat and asked, "How'd it go?"

I threw him an incredulous look, not bothering to hide my agitation. Maura had upended everything I thought I knew about my childhood, my family. I'd barely had time to process her story, and certainly didn't want to rehash it with him.

James nodded in understanding, as though realizing the absurdity of his question, and smiled weakly. "It took a lot of courage for Maura to show up today. I hope you know that."

Not responding, I unlocked my truck and opened the door. Before I could sit down, James grabbed the door, holding it open, a hopeful expression on his face. I glared back, resentful that he was inserting himself into matters that didn't concern him.

"Maura's a remarkable person," he said. "It's incredible what she's overcome, the life she's built for herself. I feel fortunate she's chosen to share it with me. She still has her struggles, but she's worked hard to move beyond her childhood. I know what you learned today was difficult to hear, but with time and the right help, you can move beyond this, too."

"She hasn't moved beyond anything," I snapped, thinking of how she'd eviscerated Joan, who was barely one month in the ground.

James shook his head sadly. "She's probably triggered, that's all. It might not seem like it, but she cares about you."

"No one in this family ever cared about me. Not enough to entrust me with the truth. Especially not Maura."

"You have the truth now. Get a therapist, take some time to work through this on your own. Then you and Maura can start over, on equal footing, focused on the future."

The earnestness in his voice made me laugh in disbelief. I'd spent years of my childhood dreaming of Maura's attention and affection, only to be disappointed. There was no reason to believe this time would be any different. "I've waited my entire life for that. But now I want to get as far away from her as possible."

I yanked open the truck door, hopped inside, and started driving, tires crunching against sand and gravel. My eyes flicked to the rear-view mirror, seeing Maura emerge from the beach like an apparition. James hurried over and wrapped his arms around her, resting his broad chin atop her head. A lump formed in my throat. I tore my eyes away.

Clouds swelled low over the forest. A few scattered rain-drops drummed against the roof of the truck, then the sky gave way, unleashing a torrent of water that streamed down the windshield in sheets. A flash of lightning illuminated the horizon, followed by a clap of thunder.

Overwhelmed with helplessness, I coasted along the road, mind adrift upon a tumultuous sea. The depths of deceit seemed boundless. My family had fed me a steady diet of lies, to the degree that even my own childhood memories seemed false.

My thoughts drifted to Chris. I wondered if she knew about my parentage and Maura and Joan's abuse. I wondered if she'd been complicit in my parents' subterfuge. She'd been Joan's best friend, after all. Surely she knew something of the truth.

Regardless, Chris was the only person with whom I might disentangle and talk through all I'd learned. The only person who might understand what I was experiencing. I headed to-wards her place, a sickening feeling festering in my stomach, harmonizing with the dull ache in my pelvis.

Upon arriving outside Chris's bungalow, I sprinted from my truck to her porch, rain lashing against me. My clothes soaked through within seconds, clinging to my skin.

After ringing the doorbell, I waited a minute. Then two. Just as I was about to leave, the door swung open, and Chris blinked at me, eyes bleary. Though it was late afternoon, she still wore plaid pajamas, and her black hair was flattened against her ear.

"I'm not hungover, just jet-lagged," she said, stifling a yawn.

I opened my mouth, ready to yell and scream and accuse her of keeping Joan's secrets at my expense, but instead, I crumpled. Her eyes widened, and she dragged me inside by the elbow.

Out of habit, I kicked off my sandals. With each step, water dripped from my limbs and sand sloughed off my feet, like a trail of breadcrumbs leading to a life I could never reclaim.

Chris didn't seem to mind the mess I'd brought along and ushered me over to the couch. I sank down into the cushion, unable to stop my body from trembling. Tutting, she grabbed a blanket, coaxed me to lie down, and draped it over me. Warmth seeped into my bones.

I nestled my head onto Chris's lap as silent sobs wracked my body. She stroked my hair, the sensation transporting me back to my childhood.

"It's okay if you're missing her. I do, too," she murmured into the crown of my head.

"You don't understand. I miss my mom. My real mom."

Chris stiffened. I untangled myself from her embrace and searched her eyes, but she avoided my gaze, confirming my worst suspicions.

"You knew. You knew all along."

She sagged, face drawn, not bothering to deny it. Raw fury lashed through me.

"You lied to me. I'd expect this from Maura, not you."

Chris wrung her hands, gazing at me with pleading eyes. "I'm sorry, Laurel, but I had no choice—"

"I don't want to hear it. I don't care if Joan ordered you not to tell me. It still doesn't make this okay."

"She was my best friend. Helped me more times in my life than I can count. I couldn't betray her trust, Laurel."

"You should've told me the truth after she died. Especially since you know how difficult it's been, not having Maura in my life."

Chris frowned and gave a light shake of her head. "Maura never recovered from losing her biological parents. You were a constant reminder of what she'd lost. There's nothing I could've said or done to fix that."

Hysterical laughter bubbled up from within me. Losing our father was the best thing that ever happened to Maura, which meant Chris was as clueless as I'd been.

The story spilled from my mouth. About the abuse. Joan's silence. I attempted to erase the false narrative that Joan had fed us, yet I choked on the words, as if the story she'd indoctrinated me with was fighting back -— the story of Maura as the ungrateful child, Joan as the selfless mother. How I stumbled into the truth in an attempt to address the chronic pain tormenting my every moment.

By the time I finished, Chris's cheeks had drained of color and the lines crossing her forehead had deepened, as if she'd aged ten years in a few minutes.

"Fuck, Laurel. Joan told me your parents were unable to care for you anymore. I didn't ask why. It didn't feel appropriate." She groaned and buried her face in her hands. "What a fucking joke. Decades of friendship, and Joan never said a word. It's like she was a stranger."

"I guess she lied to both of us."

Chris's cat bounded up and plopped onto her lap, as though sensing her distress. "At least you still like me, Pepper," she said, stroking his glossy black fur. He purred, kneading her leg with his white mitten paws.

"I like you most of the time. Not so much today, though."

"Fair enough."

Pepper turned his attention towards me, butting his head against my shoulder. The tension residing in my back lessened as I rubbed his velvet cheek.

"This is my dad's fault. He's still out there, you know. They never caught him. He could be harming other children."

Chris sighed and shook her head. "You can't think like that, Laurel."

"That's the problem, isn't it? Everyone acts like he's dead. Nobody's ever made things right."

"Laurel. Laurel, just stop." She reached out and grabbed my shoulders, which had crept up towards my ears. Her dark eyes searched my own as if she could see my blood boiling beneath my skin. "Don't go down this path. Trust me, I know."

"No, you don't."

"Look, when I got pregnant at seventeen, my mom kicked me out. I spent a lot of time and energy trying to repair things with her until I realized she'd never treat me right, no matter what I did. So I gave up and moved on with my life."

"I'm not in the mood for one of your fucking life lessons right now, Chris," I said through gritted teeth.

"You're working to fix a problem that isn't your responsibility," she continued, ignoring my outburst. "Accept what you've learned, process it, and move on. Leave the rest in the past where it belongs."

My jaw tightened. I pushed up to standing, strode toward the door, and forced on my sandals. Chris scrambled after me.

"Laurel, listen to me. Please."

Whirling around, I stared her down, ignoring the flash of alarm in her eyes. "I'm sick of everyone telling me what to do, how to feel. You don't get to decide how I should cope. Let me deal with this fucked-up shit on my own, on my terms."

I bolted outside into the torrent of rain, leaving a shaken Chris behind.

That night, I raged.

I wanted to rip my father to shreds for the horror and suffering he'd unleashed upon my sister, and his sister. But I couldn't, so I tore myself apart instead.

The storm whipped through trees and battered against my windows as I stalked through my home, clawing at my hair, screaming until my throat was as raw as sandpaper. Whenever I prodded a facet of Maura's story, pain radiated through me, as though I were being consumed from the inside out.

As excruciating as it was to learn about my parentage from Garrett, it was nothing compared to the turmoil churning within me now. My stomach twisted as I thought of the horrible abuse Maura had suffered through as a child, with no one to protect or save her.

It was no wonder she'd wrenched herself free from our family's jaws. How could she love or trust any of us after the damage and neglect she'd endured?

I finally saw Maura for who she really was. Not the rage-filled teenager that lashed out at the slightest provocation, but the frightened child cowering within her, who viewed everyone as a threat.

My chest tightened as I reflected on what Maura told me about Joan. Ever since my visit with Garrett, I'd clung to the narrative that Joan's reason for keeping my parentage a secret was to protect me, birthed from the well of a mother's unconditional love. That I could accept. It made Joan's deception, though still painful, easier to bear. But if Maura was right, Joan lied to me out of guilt, not love. If Joan actually cared about us, she would have intervened during our childhood, revealing our father for the sick, twisted fuck he was.

Joan and Maura's lives were intertwined in ways I'd never imagined. Both of them were victims of the same man, forced to endure untold pain and suffering and horror, betrayed by someone who should've protected them.

Of all the Ryder women, somehow I alone had emerged unscathed. I knew I should feel relief — gratitude, even — but instead guilt slammed down on me, pressing the air from my lungs.

Maura was right. If she hadn't miscarried, I would've faced the same fate.

The storm outside settled into an uneasy murmur. Violet darkness coated the windows, save for brief flashes of jagged lightning that tore across the sky. My frantic pacing stalled, then halted, as exhaustion settled upon me.

I trudged upstairs and cocooned myself in the tangle of sheets and blankets atop my mattress, burrowing myself deeper into the warm bed. Running my hand along the soft contours of a fleece blanket, I tried to quiet the messy jumble of thoughts and feelings colliding inside my head. It was no use. Despite my fatigue, I knew sleep wouldn't come for me that night.

Instead, I leaned over, tugged open the drawer to my bedside table, and pulled out a few photos of Joan, smoothing away invisible creases and tracing the lines of her smile with a fingertip. I squeezed my eyes shut, trying to conjure her in my mind's eye.

All I saw was her coffin.

In retrospect, it seemed foolish that I'd blamed myself for Joan's death. Her depression and substance abuse weren't because of my impatience or neglect, or Howard's death, or Maura's estrangement, but symptoms of the unspeakable tortures inflicted upon her by her own brother.

Her death was his fault. He was the reason she got into that car, drunk and high. Not me.

My father lurked at the center of this tangled web, a swollen spider that devoured everyone who stumbled across his path. He'd destroyed both of my mothers. Maura and I could never move on or heal while he still roamed free. While he was free to hurt other children. Free to destroy more lives.

His disappearance hadn't brought closure. Instead, the wounds he'd inflicted had festered. Joan had succumbed to them. Unless our father paid for his crimes, Maura would, too.

15

Two days later, I turned onto Maura's street in Chicago. A pair of towering catalpa trees stood outside her brown brick townhouse, their massive pea pods scattered across the sidewalk, branches obscuring the darkening sky. After parking, I stood beneath their expansive canopies, wondering how Maura would react when she found me on her doorstep unannounced and uninvited.

Setting my jaw, I scaled the steps to Maura's townhouse and rang the bell. After a moment, the door creaked open and James peered out at me, frowning. I pressed my lips together into a tight smile.

"I thought you wanted to get as far away from Maura as possible," he said drily. "You're headed in the wrong direction."

"I need to speak with her. Is she home?"

"No. And she probably wouldn't want to see you, anyway. I mean, you could've just called, saved yourself the trip."

"She never answers my calls."

He ran a hand through his disheveled hair, exasperation flicking across his face. "Why are you here, Laurel?"

I bristled, thoughts running through my mind at his intrusiveness. I'm here because I want to find my father. Because

Maura might have suspicions about his whereabouts. Because she's my sister, and I deserve to see her. I admitted none of these things.

"I wanted to talk more about what... about our family. I still have questions."

He shut the door. I figured he was telling me to fuck off, but a moment later, he emerged with a worn leather jacket.

"Maura's not home right now. I was about to grab some dinner. You want to come?"

"Yeah," I said, relief flooding through me, "let's do that."

We walked towards the bustling nearby street, and James ushered me into a small Mexican restaurant tucked beneath the train tracks. I blinked as my eyes adjusted to the harsh fluorescent lights reflecting off polished tables. We sidestepped past the crowd of people milling around the checkout counter and slid into a small booth. A young waitress hurried over to our table, balancing a tray ladened with two menus, two cups of water, and chips and salsa.

After placing our orders, James grabbed a chip, scooped up a hefty portion of salsa, and shoved it into his mouth, crunching loudly. I wrinkled my nose and took a sip of water. The train rumbled overhead, momentarily drowning out the cacophony of the restaurant.

"Where's Maura?" I asked.

"She's teaching an evening art class at a community center. Mostly retired folks. They absolutely adore her. Same with the children and teens she works with, through art therapy, helping them through their own journeys towards healing. Plus she's really talented, too. Not like other so-called artists who teach classes but don't create anymore. Here, look at this."

He pulled out his phone, tapped the screen, and slid it across the table towards me. I picked it up and studied the image: A painting of a woman entwined in the trunk of a tree, its canopy ablaze with sunlight.

"Good, right?" James asked.

I nodded, momentarily at a loss for words. It was good — the play of light and color, the way the woman captured your attention, demanding to be seen, yet determined to keep her secrets. Maura had always been talented, but this was beyond anything she'd produced in sketchbooks or on easels growing up.

I handed back the phone to James. He stared at the image again, nodding in admiration, before pocketing the phone.

"When is Maura's class finished? I really need to talk to her."

"Look, she was pretty upset after your visit. She puts up a hard exterior, but she's actually quite sensitive. Caring, even. Especially now that... well."

I rolled my eyes. That didn't sound like Maura. But then I remembered her painting and the art classes, and realized he knew a version of her she'd never shared with me. The thought sliced through me like a knife.

"Meeting with you was pretty overwhelming, having to re-live everything again. Ever since you learned about Garrett, she's been having nightmares. It's getting worse. I woke up last night to the sound of her screaming. It was agonizing, watching her relive her past, unable to do anything but hold her and wait for it to end."

A lump formed in my throat. I hated to think that I was causing her more pain, even though I knew I wasn't the one responsible — our father was. He needed to be punished for what he did to her.

"I'm sorry she's hurting. That was never my intent. I only wanted to learn the truth."

"Then you should understand why it's a bad idea to speak with her right now."

"But I still have questions."

"Such as?"

I hesitated, considering how much to share with him. Evading the question would provoke suspicion, and he seemed to be Maura's gatekeeper. Better to be honest.

"I was curious if our dad's tried getting in touch with her, or if she knows where he is."

James scrutinized me, his brown eyes cold. "Maura hasn't seen or heard from him since he ran off. She wants nothing to do with him, for reasons that I assume would be obvious. Please don't bring this up with her. She'll spiral."

The server placed a burrito the size of a football in front of me. My mouth watered. I began shoveling food into my mouth, ignoring the stab of pain as heat seared my tongue. James drenched his burrito in hot sauce before slicing it open, and steam billowed out, clouding his glasses.

"Has anyone looked into his whereabouts since he disappeared?" I asked.

James shook his head and set his fork down, a pinched expression on his face. "Look, I know where you're going with this. Even if Brandon was alive and was found, pressing charges wouldn't change anything. It would only force Maura to face her abuser and relive everything he put her through. She's suffered enough."

"But he might be hurting other people. Children."

"It's not her responsibility. And it's not yours, either."

"It's the right thing to do."

"This is fresh for you. You're hurting, I get it. But this happened a long time ago. Maura's moved on, or is trying to, at least. But this kind of emotional damage lingers. Transforms. Even when you think you've beaten it, done the work, it sticks with you. Because sometimes you're carrying the trauma of your entire line."

"I'm not following."

James stabbed his burrito with his knife, sending hot sauce and salsa oozing across his plate like blood. He tapped his fork against his plate, face troubled, as though considering how much to share.

"Your grandfather — Joan's dad — used to beat on your grandmother, and on Brandon and Garrett, too. From what Maura's told me, it seems like Joan avoided the worst of it. Then Brandon went on to beat on your mom. And if you trace your family history back, well, I'm certain you'd find that your grandfather's father hurt him, too."

I shivered, burrowing deeper into my coat. The guts of my burrito lay splattered across my plate. The sight of it made my stomach churn.

"Abuse begets abuse," he continued. "Children pick up and repeat those behaviors, unless someone breaks the cycle. It only takes one generation. Seeing your father behind bars isn't a substitute for your own healing. Maura's already worked hard to move beyond her childhood. You can too."

"Seems like you've thought a lot about what's best for us." It was meant to be sarcastic, but James took it literally.

"I'm a social worker," he said, shrugging. "I work with kids who're dealing with trauma. Helping them process what's happened to them. I even have cases at Maura's childhood school."

"Maura's school? What's it called?"

"Philomena Middle School. They have excellent teachers." His eyes clouded over. "I sometimes wonder what her life would've been like if she had a normal childhood, a normal adolescence..."

James droned on, his words fading into the background. I wracked my mind, trying to remember Maura's story. She'd been in class when her miscarriage occurred. And her teacher's name. What did Maura say it was?

Hernandez, I realized. Mrs. Hernandez.

A plan began to form.

"Laurel."

The roar and bustle of the restaurant sprang back into sharp relief. My gaze snapped back to James, irritation flicking through me. I pictured him working with kids and teens, smug and self-assured in his faded jeans, Converse all-stars, and band t-shirts beneath ripped flannel, spilling out unwanted advice and psychobabble like an overflowing dumpster.

"So you think being a social worker means you know what's best for her. For us."

"Yeah, I do. Maura needs to work through her shit by herself. She's dealing with her own trauma and the trauma passed down the Ryder line for generations. It's a lot for one person to carry."

"I'm dealing with it, too."

"What you're dealing with is different than Maura," he said coldly. "She was abused, taken from her mother, placed with adoptive parents, who didn't have a clue how to help her. To make matters worse, they forbade her from talking about what she went through. Joan and Howard did that so you could have a normal childhood. Maura was harmed in the process. Collateral damage."

I glowered at him. How dare he speak so assuredly about my childhood, with only Maura's side of the story to inform his opinion? He didn't know how Maura wreaked havoc in our household, leaving me in constant fear of her angry outbursts, even while I remained desperate for her affection. If our father had been found and punished during our youth, Maura might have found peace. Closure. We might've had a chance at being sisters.

"I get that you're dealing with your own issues, Laurel. But you can't ask Maura to help you process this. It's too triggering for her. Get yourself a therapist. Take some time. Work through this on your own."

"I don't want a therapist. I want my sister."

"That's what I want, too."

"Then help me get through to her."

He shook his head, eyes full of pity. "I've meddled enough already. Who do you think convinced Maura to attend Joan's funeral? To tell you the truth after you learned about Garrett?"

My stomach clenched as realization flooded through me. Maura hadn't wanted to speak with me at all. It had been James all along.

"She'd been doing so well. I thought she could handle it," he said. "I was wrong. Meeting with you was too intense. She's having nightmares and crying spells again. I'm having to remind her to eat. Please, keep your distance from her, at least for now."

Hot, angry tears pricked the corners of my eyes.

James never intended for me to see Maura tonight.

After paying the bill, we walked back in silence. When we arrived outside their townhouse, he stopped and turned around, positioning himself between me and the door. Behind him, a phantom shape floated across the white curtain. My heart leapt in my chest.

"She doesn't want to see you, Laurel," he said gently. "I texted her from the restaurant."

My heart sank. "Tell her I'm sorry for what happened on the beach."

"I will. Take care of yourself. Remember what I said."

He opened the door. A splinter of warm light pierced from the archway through the dusk. Then the door closed and snuffed out the light, leaving me alone in the burgeoning darkness.

16

After leaving Maura and James's place, I camped out at a nearby forest preserve, lying atop an air mattress in the bed of my truck. I was used to roughing it, having spent the past few summers sleeping beneath the expansive western sky after days spent tracking mountain lions through the wilderness.

Camping in Chicago was different. The sky never darkened, the stars constantly straining to break through the city's sickly yellow glow, and I found myself unable to drift into sleep.

Though Maura refused to speak to me and James insisted she didn't know where our father was, I wasn't ready to admit defeat. Not yet. Maura had suffered from unspeakable horrors because of Joan's silence. I couldn't let my silence jeopardize the lives of other girls. Even if it meant going at it alone. Even if it meant pushing Maura further away, if that was possible.

My conversation with James hadn't been a complete waste of time, though. Thanks to him, I knew where to look next for answers.

The following afternoon, after another sleepless night, I arrived at Philomena Middle School, which Maura attended before Joan and Howard adopted us. The place where she'd had her miscarriage, where she'd sought help from a school nurse wise enough to recognize the signs of abuse and get help.

The school was located in a quiet neighborhood, tucked behind a wrought-iron fence with a playground and school garden. I idled beside my truck, watching parents milling around the sidewalk until the harsh, grating noise of a bell pulsed through the air.

Students burst through the school's open doors, rushing towards buses, parents, friends. My gaze settled on a young girl with raven hair huddled by the door. She hunched her shoulders and hugged a stack of books tighter into her chest as students weaved around her in a mad frenzy.

A lump formed in my throat. She reminded me of Maura. I wondered what middle school had been like for her: grappling with the misery of adolescence and the horror of her father's abuse. Of being betrayed by her parents and her own changing body.

The girl's eyes brightened as a man strode towards her, a smile spreading across his face. My chest tightened. The illusion shattered as I watched the girl bury herself in his embrace before setting off together, his arm draped over her shoulder.

After the flood of students slowed to a trickle, I strode into the school. The halls echoed with the sound of sneakers squeaking against the basketball court and the pummel of a ball being dribbled.

When I entered the front office, I found a young man staring at an ancient computer monitor.

"You can sign in here for your conference slot." He tapped his finger on a clipboard perched beside him.

"That's not why I'm here. I wanted to visit an old teacher. Mrs. Hernandez."

He looked up at me and smiled. "You're not the only one. Lots of people have been dropping by ever since she announced her retirement."

I nodded in agreement, relief coursing through me.

"You'll still have to sign in. And I'll need to see some photo ID."

After completing the form, I wandered down the hall, past lockers and bulletin boards crowded with audition notices and glittery posters for class elections, jolting me back into unwanted memories of my own adolescence. I felt a flush of gratitude that I wasn't thirteen anymore. Getting a PhD was hard, but middle school was worse.

The door to Mrs. Hernandez's classroom was ajar, so I nudged it open and poked my head in. A woman was wiping down a white board, panting with exertion. Her silver hair glinted in the stream of light pouring through the windows, and her patterned skirt brushed across the floor rhythmically as she worked. Book reports bobbed from wooden pins hanging from a clothesline that wrapped around the room.

"Mrs. Hernandez?"

The woman whirled around, a smile poised on her ruby-red lips, but when she spotted me, her smile faltered, and the color drained from her face. She raised a hand to her throat, clutching a silver pendant nestled beneath her pink blouse. I noticed later that it was a cross.

"Sorry if I startled you. I wondered if you had a few minutes to talk about an old student. Maura Ryder?"

She stumbled backward and landed in a student's chair. It skidded across the floor, emitting a grating noise that made me wince.

"Are you all right?"

When she didn't answer, I inched towards her, my brow furrowed. She shrunk away from me, eyes wide with terror. Her mouth opened, but no words came out. A flash of annoyance pulsed through me at her reticence.

"You're the sister," she said, her voice hoarse.

"That's right. My name is Laurel Lane. Maura Ryder is my sister."

She shook her head, a high-pitched giggle ripping from her throat. The sound sent chills down my spine.

"I thought you were your mother, here to haunt me," she murmured. "You're the spitting image of her, you know."

My shoulders tensed. "I don't remember her. My aunt raised me."

She didn't acknowledge my response. Instead, she wrung her hands and said, "I didn't know. I never suspected. You need to believe me. It's not my fault. I've lived with the guilt for so long, the knowledge that your sister was sitting in front of me and I saw nothing. Not until the day her blood pooled on that chair." She jabbed a finger at a desk near the front of the classroom. I flinched at the image she'd conjured.

"I'm not here to blame you."

"Then why are you here? Is your sister all right?"

"Yeah, she's fine. I just—"

"Oh, thank God," she said, clutching a hand to her chest. "I think about her every day, about how I failed her. Wondering what her life would've been like, had I helped her at the right time."

Her words, so similar to James's from the night before, sent goose pricks up my arms. She grew quiet, staring, unseeing, at the ground in front of her. I took a few tentative steps forward, recalibrating my approach to this conversation.

"What was she like?" I asked. "My sister."

Mrs. Hernandez's startled eyes met mine, opening wide in surprise.

"She's older than me, and left home at eighteen. We aren't close. I never really got to know her," I explained, sensing her confusion. "I've always wondered about her life, before we were adopted."

"Well, she was a quiet child. Sensitive. Not the most motivated student, or the most talented writer, but she had a creative spark. Her assignments always came back with doodles in the margins. I actually saved one of her drawings."

Mrs. Hernandez stood up and shuffled over to some filing cabinets in the corner of the room. She opened a drawer and began rifling through the contents, muttering under her breath. "Was it '98 or '99? Ah. Here it is."

With a flourish, she turned and handed me a sheet of paper. The front contained three typed questions, below which were hastily scrawled responses in Maura's familiar, looping handwriting. There was something on the back, too. I flipped it over, revealing a sketch of a rabbit, carefully rendered with the precise taxonomic detail I had tried and failed to replicate during feeble attempts to connect with my sister over boxes of crayons and colored pencils. Blades of grass were tucked in its mouth, its ears perked, nose scrunched, and eyes alert, as if monitoring its surroundings for an invisible predator.

It would have made Howard proud.

"It was early on in the school year," Mrs. Hernandez said, pulling my attention back to the present. "A beautiful fall day, too gorgeous to spend cooped up indoors. I marched the class outside, handed each student their assignment, and ordered them to find a quiet spot on the lawn. We were reading *Watership Down*. Imagine my surprise and delight when I flipped over Maura's worksheet later and found this. I asked her if I could make a photocopy, but she told me to keep it, so I stored it with other treasures from over the years: well-crafted essays from gifted students, thoughtful notes from students and alumni, things like that."

"Maura's an art teacher now," I said, handing her back the worksheet. "And an art therapist. Helping other children who were... who were hurt, like her."

"It brings me much comfort to hear that she's doing good in the world. She was always so kind-hearted. Despite everything that happened to her, I'm not surprised that she's still helping people."

Grief and sadness struck me, hard and fast, pummeling my gut. Grief for a version of my sister I never knew. Because of the lies she was forced to keep from me, I grew up with a version of Maura who treated me with indifference and downright scorn, rather than with the care and kindness she apparently extended to everyone else.

"There was another student in her class. Emily, I think her name was," Mrs. Hernandez continued, oblivious to my despair. "Emily was a late bloomer, much less developed than the other girls. After some of the boys noticed tissues sticking out of her top, she was bullied relentlessly. Everyone avoided her, afraid of being victimized by association. Maura didn't care, though. She was kind to Emily, always partnering with her for group assignments."

"Did she have other friends? Maura, I mean."

Mrs. Hernandez scrunched up her nose, nodding slowly. "A few girls, from the after-school art club that Maura attended. I don't remember their names, though."

"Do you... do you think they knew? Do you think Maura told them?"

The question hung between us like a dark cloud. Mrs. Hernandez paused before responding, her face darkening.

"I'm not sure, dear, but I suspect not. Shame is a powerful influence at that age. No one wants to be that student — the one whose parents are divorcing, or whose father beats up their mother. Maura, despite her quiet sensitivity and kindness, was no different, I imagine. But I told the authorities who she spent time with, in case it ended up being relevant."

"Told who? The police? CPS?"

"Well, yes."

A frisson of excitement coursed through me as I was reminded of the reason for my visit. "Do you remember who interviewed you, about Maura's case?"

She stiffened and crossed her arms across her chest. "Detective Harlowe was the main one. Pete Harlowe. I could never forget a name. It was more of an interrogation than an interview."

A name. It was more than I had allowed myself to hope for. Detective Harlowe might have suspicions about my father's whereabouts. Leads, even those long gone cold.

"He treated me like I did something wrong," she continued. "But I didn't know. I couldn't have known, not how the police wanted me to. I mean, I knew there was something off with your father, something wrong, but I couldn't call in the authorities based on a bad feeling." She paused for a moment, her eyes glazed over. "There've been other students since then. Two that I reported on. One was nothing. The other... wasn't. I might not've been able to save Maura, but I saved that other child. I saved him."

I nodded, grateful that something good had come from Maura's abuse. It was clear Mrs. Hernandez had grown to trust her instincts, vigilant for signs of trouble, determined to ensure her students were safe.

Mrs. Hernandez's attention snapped back to me, her eyes sharp and suddenly suspicious. "Why are you here, Laurel? There were other teachers that she was closer to than me."

My skin pricked as I weighed my response. She'd been honest with me, taken time to speak about an experience that still haunted her. It seemed only right that I return the favor.

"Because they never caught my father. I want to know why. You were there when... when it happened. I wanted to see if you were interviewed, if you remembered anyone working the case."

"Why not ask your sister? She'd certainly remember."

"I... don't want to drag her into this."

"Even if that's not your intent, your actions could open up old hurts. Undo what she's built. I understand that you and your family need closure, but closure might look different to her than to you. Keep that in mind."

I forced a tight smile, wondering why everyone felt the need to offer me unsolicited advice. Eager to pursue my new lead, I thanked her and began heading towards the door. The air shifted behind me, and her hand closed around my shoulder like a vise. She was stronger than she looked. I twisted around to face her, heart hammering in my chest. Her eyes were wide and wild, searching my own.

"Do you think she forgives me for not helping her?"

A complicated wave of emotions pulsed through me. Growing up, Maura had needed an adult on her side, someone looking out for her, whom she could trust. Mrs. Hernandez hadn't been that person. Maybe Maura blamed her for it, maybe not. Either way, it wasn't her fault.

The woman standing before me today was different from the woman Maura had known. She'd learned from her experience with Maura. She'd saved a child that might have otherwise suffered needlessly. No more women should be blamed or feel ashamed because of our father's actions.

"She doesn't blame you," I said gently. "It was our father's fault, not yours."

Mrs. Hernandez's eyes closed and her face slackened, tension draining from her body, replaced with an almost angelic disposition. When her eyes opened, they were bright, her shoulders relaxed, back straight.

"Thank you," she whispered.

Mrs. Hernandez's haunted face stayed with me long after our meeting. Though the miscarriage occurred decades before, it was clear that she was still consumed with guilt, forever tormented by the sight of Maura's blood.

I realized then that the black poison of my family had leached outwards, contaminating everyone it touched. How many others had my father infected since his disappearance?

A few days later, I located Detective Harlowe at the same police district that had handled Maura's case decades before and arranged a visit. When I arrived, an officer directed me to a cramped waiting area. Outside, the wind howled, rattling the windows, sending leaves and dirt swirling around my boots whenever the door swung open.

After a few minutes, the officer returned and escorted me to a desk covered in file folders, an old computer monitor, and a cracked mug. Detective Harlowe sat behind the desk, sunken blue eyes trained on the officer, scowling.

"I don't have time for cold cases when there're fresh ones needing attention."

"She's got a right to it. It's still her case," the officer replied.

Harlowe's scowl deepened, and he jabbed a chubby, pale finger at a metal chair. I sat down. After introducing myself, I told him about Maura's case and handed him the photo showing my parents outside their first home in Chicago.

"These are my parents. Brandon and Irene Ryder. Do you remember them?"

He leaned forward and squinted at the photo, nodding. "Yeah, I remember your mom. And the case, too. Nasty business. A long time ago, though. Figured you would've moved on by now. You were what, one, two years old?"

"It's been hard to move on, given that you never caught him."

Harlowe stiffened and wagged a finger at me. "You don't understand what it's like, working these cases. It's he said, she said. Your sister could've been experimenting with peers her age, if you catch my drift. There were questions, early on, as we were trying to figure out what happened."

"You can't be serious," I said, staring at him with incredulity. Maura had only been twelve. Victim blaming was bad enough, but this seemed even worse, given her young age. "She told you what happened. Why would she lie?"

"At first, she insisted it was just a heavy period. Even after doctors confirmed the miscarriage, she kept avoiding our questions. It wasn't until we brought in the social worker that she finally opened up and admitted that your dad hurt her. She said he threatened to hurt your mom if she told anyone. But none of that matters, anyway. Your dad's guilt was evident when he panicked and ran."

"Where do you think he went?"

"We don't know for sure, but his brother seemed like the obvious option."

I frowned. "Wait. You think Garrett helped him?"

"Well, yeah," he said, shrugging.

"But you were wrong. You must've been wrong. Otherwise, you would've caught him."

"Garrett lived out of state. We sent some local cops over to his place, but Brandon wasn't there. Since it was outside our jurisdiction, we couldn't follow up. It's how these things go sometimes. My money's still on the brother, though."

My chest tightened, an invisible weight slamming the air from my lungs. The room spun, sounds fading away. I thought of how Garrett had blamed Joan and Maura for what happened to Brandon. How he defended his brother, despite all of the evidence against him.

Garrett had lied to me. Like everyone else in our family. Now he'd placed me in the position where I was considering lying to April about her father, to protect her from his darkness and the darkness of this family.

I looked down at my hands and found that I'd pulled my talisman stone free, my thumb smoothing over the painted bird like a nervous tic. When I lifted my gaze, Detective Harlowe was eyeing the stone with interest. With effort, I forced my hand still and slipped the stone back into my pocket, glaring back at him.

"Even though you knew where he was, you did nothing," I said, struggling to keep my voice calm.

"Hey, that's not fair. We suspected but weren't able to confirm it."

"You could've done more. So much more. If he's harmed other children, that's on you."

Harlowe's face reddened with anger. "If you came here looking for someone to blame, blame your mother. She knew what kind of man your father was. When she called him from the hospital, she didn't just tell him that your sister miscarried. She

THE INHERITANCE | 155

asked if he was responsible. Then she completely broke down, became almost catatonic, ended up in a mental hospital. Totally useless to our investigation."

My mouth went dry, and for a moment, I couldn't breathe.

"Your mom knew what he'd been doing, and she couldn't live with the guilt. Why do you think CPS shipped you girls off to your aunt instead of letting you stay with your mom? She wasn't fit to be a mother."

Though I wanted to argue, the seeds of doubt had already taken root, their tendrils unfurling, joining the others buried deep in my mind.

If my mother had known the truth and chosen to remain silent, even when the evidence became too great to ignore, it meant both my parents had been monsters.

17

The Chicago house where I'd spent my first years of life stood deserted and empty. I pulled out the photo of my biological parents standing before this home, decades before, and compared it to the structure standing before me.

The once neatly trimmed bushes and lawn were now overgrown, and the windows were shuttered, giving the house a dark and imposing presence. Though the metal railings on the porch were once a cheery pink color, the paint had since cracked, revealing the rusted metal beneath, as though tinged with blood.

No one had cared for this place in a long time.

I'd come here after leaving the police station, hoping that the house might spark some newfound understanding of who my parents were. Meeting with Detective Harlowe had forced me to confront the painful possibility that my birth mother suspected that Maura was being abused and had done nothing. The thought had burrowed its way into my mind like a termite through wood. Sadness and anger coursed through me for all Maura had suffered through, but those feelings were also mingled with pity for my mother. She'd failed her children and never recovered from the loss.

Because I'd only spent the first years of my childhood inside its walls, the home evoked no memories. Instead, the stories that Maura had shared with me ran through my head, a never-ending loop of horror and misery that made me want to tear my hair out and scream until my throat was raw.

Being here was causing me more pain, but I couldn't wrench myself away. Like picking at a scab until it bled. After years of blissful ignorance, I deserved to suffer, to taste what Maura might have felt during her time here.

Though every fiber of my being was screaming at me to run, I forced myself into the backyard, my heart in my throat. A white fir tree towered over the unkempt lawn, its branches heavy with cones and needles. It was strong enough to support a child's makeshift swing, a rotting wooden plank hanging from two frayed ropes.

Strong enough to support the weight of my mother's lifeless body.

I caressed the gnarled trunk. Sap stuck to my fingers, sharp and pungent. I craned my neck and peered upward through the branches. A scar tarnished a branch high above me where the bark had been stripped away. Where another rope had once hung.

Wrenching my gaze away, I stumbled backwards, panic lodged in my chest. With tears streaming down my face, I fled through the gate. Away from my old home. Away from this place of darkness.

I wandered blindly down the sidewalk until it joined a path skirting along the curve of Lake Michigan. I climbed down the embankment and onto the blocks of concrete lining the shore.

The crashing waves spit a sheen of spray across me, soaking my clothes, but I was too numb to notice or care.

As I stared at the churning gray water, a feeling of helplessness descended upon me. I'd come here searching for my father, but the answers only peeled back more layers of deception. More unfortunate truths. Detective Harlowe's words rattled around my skull in a never-ending chorus, reshaping what I thought I knew about my family. My mind sifted through the stories I'd collected about my family members, attempting to separate truth from lies, but it was like trying to catch a fistful of sand adrift on the wind.

If Harlowe was right, Garrett had lied to me. He'd helped my father escape. Finding him meant breaking my promise to Maura and confronting Garrett about his role in my father's disappearance. It meant potentially jeopardizing April's chance of building a relationship with Garrett, no matter how ill-advised it might seem.

But I had no other choice. The thought of my father roaming free made my stomach churn. He'd caused enough damage. Both of my mothers were dead because of him. My sister was still consumed with anger and despair from the trauma he'd inflicted upon her decades ago. I couldn't live with myself if I stopped searching for him now. Not when the answers might be within my grasp. Not when I had the ability to make him pay.

Yet guilt slammed down on my shoulders as I thought of April and how I'd deceived her, through silence and avoidance, in a vain and misguided attempt to appease Maura's wishes.

I couldn't justify my behavior any longer. Our family had sustained its secrets through lies and deceit disguised as love for long enough. It was better to make room for the truth, allow it to spill out, rather than rely on the false security of secrets. April deserved to know her father, even if it meant facing crushing disappointment.

I'd tell April the truth, but there was something I needed to do first.

A few hours later, I arrived at Garrett's home, where I parked beside his truck. Indigo darkness had begun to creep over the horizon, coating the landscape in an unsettling stillness. A dim light glowed through the house's shuttered curtains.

As I shuffled towards the house, a small creature darted across my path. I flinched, heart fluttering in my chest, and knelt to look under Garrett's truck. A pair of glowing eyes, pupils black and wide as saucers, peered back at me.

"You scared me, little one," I murmured. The cat inched forward towards my outstretched fingers, nose twitching. My eyes widened as I noticed her matted fur, the way her loose skin hung from her bones. What had Garrett done to this poor creature?

"What the hell are you doing here?" Garrett asked.

I bolted up, loose gravel roiling beneath my feet, and the cat darted away. Garrett loomed on the porch, face illuminated by the amber glow of a cigarette dangling from his mouth. The sight of his imposing presence sent goosebumps marching up my arms.

"I wanted to talk. I called, but you didn't answer."

Garrett glowered at me, leaning against a rotting support beam. Climbing the stairs towards him, my nostrils filled with the foul stench of his body odor. I tried not to gag.

"I've been busy," he said. "This isn't a good time."

"I won't be long. Please. I came all this way."

He grunted, discarded his cigarette, and shuffled towards the door, body swaying. I trailed behind him.

Once inside, Garrett headed for the kitchen and pulled a beer from the fridge. He offered me one, but I refused. Shrugging, he collapsed into his recliner and groped on the table for a bottle opener. A football game played on the ancient television set in the corner, antennae stretching high towards the ceiling. I leaned against the kitchen table, its surface cluttered with dirty dishes, newspapers, empty beer bottles, cartons of cigarettes, and an open bottle of liquor.

"What do you want this time?" Garrett asked, his gaze fixed on the television.

Taking a deep breath, I recited the story I'd prepared on the drive over. "I talked to Maura. She told me what happened, why our father left. But I know it was her fault. She's always been so selfish, so attention-seeking."

Though the lies tasted like poison, I needed to catch his attention, win his trust. When I saw Garrett's eyes flicker, I knew my ploy had paid off.

"Well, I told you, didn't I? That girl's always been trouble."

"Because of her, I lost the chance to know you and my dad. It's not fair. Joan and Howard were good parents, but it's not the same. A daughter deserves to know her father, don't you think?"

"I don't know where he is, if that's what you're after. I told you that already."

"But you were such a good brother, defending him when no one else would. Surely he would've reached out to you for help? At least to let you know he's okay?"

Garrett didn't respond, eyes boring into the television. Though at first glance he seemed indifferent, the muscle in his jaw tightened, suggesting I'd struck a nerve.

"I'm not looking to cause trouble for either of you. I just want to talk to my dad, that's all," I pressed. "Don't I deserve that much?"

He swiveled in his chair and scowled at me. "How stupid do you think I am? You're just like all the rest of 'em, always pressuring me, wanting something." His words slurred together as he took another swig of beer, the golden liquid trickling down his chin. "I've been talking to this girl online, right? She's gorgeous. Russian. Young, tall, blonde, the works. She was gonna come over here, marry me, maybe give us some babies. But now she's asking for money, says she wants me to pay for the rest of her family to come here, too. She's taking advantage, you see? Playing games."

My face twisted in disgust at his crude characterization of the young woman and the insinuation about my own motives. "That's not what I'm doing. I just want to meet my father. Is that so hard to believe?"

Garrett struggled to standing and scowled, twisting his face into an unrecognizable mask. He waddled over to the table beside me and lit another cigarette. I recoiled as smoke poured from his gaping mouth, clogging the air in a toxic stench.

"You women are all the same," he said, inches from my face. "Always prying, always playing, always trying to get something out of someone. Your mom was like that, too. She was a whore. Brandon told me. He always caught her flirting with men at Maura's school, with neighbors. Sleeping around. I told him he needed to control her."

"Don't talk about her like that," I snapped, fists clenched at my side. I couldn't stand listening to another man weave stories about my mother, warping my perspective of the woman she'd been. Garrett sneered, seemingly amused by my reaction.

"There're no more family values anymore. Brandon didn't hurt your sister. Irene wanted out of the marriage, so she fed lies to Maura to tell her teachers. Backfired on her, though, when she lost the both of you. She got what she deserved, in the end."

I stared at him, incredulous, struck by how naïve it had been of me to expect him to cooperate, to expect him to show empathy for the unfortunate women who'd been captured by the orbit of the Ryder family.

Rage coursed through me, hot in my veins. The words spilled from my mouth before I could catch myself. "You've got some nerve talking about family values when you have a daughter you don't even know about."

Garrett stiffened, eyes narrowing. "The hell you talking about?"

"I'm talking about Simone Heller. You met her in a Chicago bar twenty-eight years ago. You slept with her. She got pregnant and had a daughter. April. That's how I learned about you. We matched as first cousins on a DNA test."

"Ah. I see what this is," Garrett said, wagging his finger at me. "It's a scam. Just like the Russian. This so-called daughter of mine and you are using some cock-and-bull story to make a grab for my money."

I clutched the hair at my temples, stifling a groan of frustration and anger. I'd expected denial from him, but not delusion. Telling Garrett about April in a moment of anger was a mistake, but I couldn't take it back. Instead, I doubled down, desperate to make him understand the situation.

"This isn't a scam. I'm not making this up. This is your daughter we're talking about. She wants to get to know you, that's all. We both want to know our fathers."

"I don't even know this Samantha woman."

"Simone. See for yourself."

Pulling out my phone, I showed him the photo of Simone that April had messaged me. In it, Simone held a drink in one hand, eyes slanted to the side, red lips curling into a begrudging smile, as if admitting she was enjoying herself, though she hadn't expected to.

Garrett squinted at the image, then snatched the phone out of my hand. His inky black eyebrows shot up and a giggle burst from his mouth.

"Oh, this's rich. I've never seen this woman in my life. And besides, I would never, ever fuck a—"

A roar burst from my lungs, drowning out the sound of his belligerence. His use of a racial slur to describe the mother of his child was my breaking point. Something inside me snapped. Everything went red as all of my pent-up pain, anger, and frustration boiled over. I lunged towards him, my nails scratching the back of his hand, grappling for the phone. Garrett lurched towards me, black eyes glittering with rage. I wrested the phone from his grasp and shoved him. Hard.

Garrett stumbled backwards, crying out. After steadying himself, he charged at me. His clammy hands groped at my chest, neck, arms. I could feel his putrid breath on my cheek, making my stomach churn. I yanked myself away, sending pain shooting through my side and pelvis. He lost his balance and crashed to the floor, upending the cluttered kitchen table. A sharp crack filled the air as plates collided with one another, shattering to pieces beneath our feet.

The sharp smell of alcohol filled the air as a liquor bottle spilled its contents over the carpet. Garrett tried to stand up but couldn't find his balance. Beside him, smoke billowed from his smoldering cigarette, dislodged from his mouth during the scuffle.

Panting, I backed away from his splayed body. His mouth was slack, breath stuttering. He clutched at his chest, wide wild eyes staring at me in terror.

I should've felt pity for this lonely, broken man, whose family had been torn asunder. Instead, I felt nothing but contempt and disgust. We might share the same blood, but he wasn't my kin. And he wasn't April's kin, either.

"You're pathetic. I don't know how you ended up with a daughter like April. I'm glad you aren't in her life. And I hope you never will be."

Garrett writhed on the floor, hands groping for me. I sidestepped over him and grabbed his laptop and charging cable.

"Consider this an intervention. No more online dating. I'm done with the men in this family treating women like shit."

I skirted around him, avoiding his hands scrabbling at my ankles. His mouth twisted into a grimace, and drool dribbled down his chin. He didn't deserve my help or compassion, not after how he'd treated the women in our family. I'd ignore his suffering the way he'd ignored Maura and Joan's. It was only fair.

The front door clattered shut behind me. I flopped into my truck and started down the driveway. A pair of eyes flashed in the darkness. I hit the brake, opened the door, and picked up the cat, nestling her trembling body in my arms.

Together, we drove away.

18

It was two days after my disastrous visit with Garrett and I was still reeling from the fallout. Being around my uncle had awakened parts of me lurking deep within, whose whispers were growing louder, goading me towards rage and violence.

Now I understood why Maura had warned me to stay away from him. I'd seen it through my own eyes; his rage, delusions, denial, misogyny, racism. I shuddered, recalling the press of his body against mine, his foul breath on my face, our shared blood thrumming in mutual agitation.

There was no possibility for reconciliation. Not after what that fight illuminated about him. Losing a potential relationship with Garrett mattered little to me. I'd spent my entire life without him, and absorbing the loss would be relatively painless.

But I couldn't say the same for April.

My stomach twisted as I recalled how Garrett had denied and degraded April's existence. How could they possibly build a relationship founded on such scorn?

I sat at my kitchen table, drinking a cup of coffee and staring at a bowl of cereal that tasted like cardboard, trying to figure out how to repair the damage between me and April. I needed to tell her the truth, but it felt impossible. The wound of learning everything I had was too fresh. How could I inflict that same pain on April, when she carried such high expectations for her father and their relationship? She'd be devastated to learn his true nature. Or worse, she could spiral into denial, refusing to believe me and demanding to meet and judge him for herself. Such a meeting might break her.

Groaning at the impossible situation, I shoved the cereal aside and buried my face in my hands. I felt movement around my legs, soft and subtle. I glanced down to see Garrett's cat, whom I'd renamed Ginger, peeking up at me with wide green eyes, the black pupils narrowing to slits in the morning light.

I scooped some kibble into a bowl. Ginger sniffed the air, pink nose and white whiskers twitching, and slinked out to investigate. The bowl rattled as Ginger devoured her breakfast with the frantic speed of a creature who had grown accustomed to hunger.

Once she finished, I crouched beside her and pet her in long, gentle strokes. It had taken awhile for Ginger to tolerate my touch and accept that I wouldn't hurt her. Red scratch marks still crisscrossed my hands from our first evening together, when I'd attempted, with little success, to groom her tangled coat. But now she was purring, albeit begrudgingly.

The scratches didn't bother me. Ginger had been acting on instinct, responding based on her history of neglect. My fingers tightened in her fur as I whispered a promise to protect her from harm, a futile attempt at redemption for failing to save my collared mountain lion's life. She, too, had been acting in her nature, and had died attempting to feed, care for, and protect her cubs.

Once, I thought those were actions instinctive to all mothers. Now I wasn't sure. Non-human animals were more complex than most people imagined, yet in some ways their behaviors were remarkably uncomplicated. They just acted, exactly how they should. Exactly how the indifferent world taught them to.

Ginger's bedraggled state was an improvement over my own. My hair hung limp around my face, the dull locks coated in oil and grime. I hadn't gone to the university or touched my research in well over a week.

On the kitchen table, my phone vibrated. I heaved myself up to standing and grabbed the phone. Luis was calling. I hesitated a moment before answering.

"Haven't seen you in a while," Luis said. "Where have you been hiding?"

"Chicago. Family stuff. I'm back now, though."

"Well, you should get over here. Richard's looking for you. He seems pissed."

My nostrils flared. I thought of the unread emails piling up in my inbox, the glitchy statistical code I still hadn't cracked, and the data from Luis's lab assistants sitting unanalyzed on my desk. The thought of facing Richard made me cringe, but the longer I avoided him, the worse things would get between us.

"You still there?" Luis asked.

"Yeah. I'll head over now. Thanks for the heads up."

"You bet. And stop by the lab once you're through with Richard. Petra and I could use your help with something."

I fell silent, mentally cataloguing the growing list of demands on my time and others' expectations of me. My chest tightened as I realized how overextended I'd become, both with my responsibilities and emotional bandwidth. I wanted to crawl back into bed and hide under the covers, escaping the pressures surrounding me.

"It's important, Laurel," Luis pressed. "Or we could come by later this week?"

"Sure." I couldn't muster the energy to argue, instead forcing myself to shove items into my bag. After saying our goodbyes, I headed out towards campus.

Upon arriving, I trudged through puddles towards Wallace Hall, splattering water across my jeans. Students hurried past me, umbrellas overhead, books and bags clutched tight against their bodies. When I approached the lab, I found Richard barreling towards me, a purple vein in his neck pulsating.

"There you are. We need to talk."

Richard grabbed my arm and yanked me into his office. Once inside, he released me, and my arm throbbed as my blood resumed flowing. He sank into his chair, hard eyes boring into me. My face flushed, shame blooming within me, wondering what I'd done to deserve this treatment.

"I received yet another unpleasant call about you the other day, Laurel."

"What are you talking about?"

"Steve Fletcher."

"Who?"

"For fuck's sake. Luis's lab assistant. His father called Dean Young and claimed you raised your voice and grabbed his son."

I closed my eyes as I realized what this was about. Steve's carelessness had almost destroyed an entire summer's worth of work, yet somehow I was the one in trouble.

"He unplugged a lab fridge and almost ruined my blood samples," I said. "When I confronted him, he threw a fit and stormed off."

"His father's an alumnus. Dean Young wants you to issue a personal apology."

After everything I'd been through the past few weeks, the pettiness of the situation felt absurd. Annoyance flicked through me. "In other words, he's a major donor, and she doesn't want to lose his annual donation."

The corner of Richard's mouth quirked upwards before he forced his expression back into a grimace. "Look. Steve sounds like a fucking idiot, but your behavior was still wildly inappropriate. You can't treat students that way."

I stared at him in disbelief, too stunned to respond. The hypocrisy was almost comical. Richard had literally grabbed me moments before. Where was my apology?

"In fact," Richard continued, "your behavior has been fucking appalling lately, and you're way behind with your work."

"I just buried my mother. I've been grieving."

"You can't keep using her death as an excuse for slacking off. And you shouldn't have asked Luis for his lab assistants. They weren't responsible for that work. You were."

"He knew I was struggling and offered them to me. I wouldn't have accepted the help if I knew what a big deal it would turn into."

"That's the thing, Laurel," he said, wagging a finger. "Everything turns into a big deal when you're involved. You've got a poor attitude. Always have. It was cute when you first started the program. I took your brazenness as a sign of intelligence. A spark inside you. But it's getting out of hand. I'm sick of cleaning up your messes."

Heat flared across my neck as fire bloomed within me, feeding on the rage I'd buried over years of being subjected to Richard's tantrums. I couldn't tolerate this treatment any longer.

"Well, I'm sick of you treating me and everyone else in this lab like shit."

The words spilled from my mouth, upending years of meekness and deference directed at my advisor. Richard stared at me, mouth ajar, his face darkening with anger at this unexpected response. With growing dread, I realized that I'd made things monumentally worse. I was spinning and spiraling towards a precipice, unable to slow, unable to grasp onto anything to stop myself from careening over the edge. Still, I forced myself to stand tall, hardening my features into a stony mask, clinging to the fleeting sensation of release that accompanied my words.

Richard's fingers coiled around the arms of Howard's old chair. "I'm trying to toughen you up so you're ready for your careers. I'd be doing you a disservice if I coddled you all the time. That's not how the world works. If you can't handle the pressure, then you're not cut out for academia, and you don't belong here."

I glowered at him, arms crossed over my chest.

He sighed. "Perhaps I'm partly to blame. I didn't think you were cut out for the program to begin with. The main reason I accepted you was because of who your father was. Maybe that was a mistake."

The words cut through me like a knife. My lungs emptied of breath. The corner of my heart reserved for Howard ached like an open wound. I struggled against the tears that threatened to spill over, knowing that he was manipulating me, trying to provoke a reaction. I refused to give him one. At least not the one he expected.

"Prove me wrong, Laurel," he urged. "Keep your head down, do the work. Prove that you belong here. Prove it to me. And prove it to your father."

My gaze slid away from Richard's smug smirk and settled on the sprawling view of campus visible through the rain-streaked window. I remembered coming to this office after high school and watching Howard lean out that window, cigarette in hand, ashtray perched on the sill. He'd wink at me, raising a finger to his lips, knowing full well the university didn't allow smoking inside the buildings. Our secret.

I realized then why Howard discouraged me from applying for this program. It wasn't because he thought I could attend a better school. The real reason had been staring at me this entire time, but I'd been too blinded by Richard's charisma to see it.

When I first started this program, I wanted nothing more than to impress Richard. It translated into years of putting up with and ignoring abuse, and sacrificing all aspects of my personal life not devoted to my studies or caring for Joan. It meant neglecting friendships and relationships, the only intimate contact restricted to fleeting drunken encounters with men and women whose names I'd forget by morning.

This program was destroying me from the inside out. I was sick of the posturing to get the best positions, the sniveling to secure the best grants, the bullying and taunts and condescension leveled at me by my so-called mentor. The expectations of the academy were so insidious that it was easy to get trapped beneath their weight without realizing you were being crushed to death.

Rather than supporting me, Richard seemed determined to quash my ambition, my morals, my values, to force me to fall in line with his way of thinking and doing things.

My research and this program used to be the cornerstone of my existence. Now it seemed so inconsequential compared to repairing my fractured family and ensuring my father couldn't harm anyone else.

The sharp moment of clarity sent relief flooding through me, like dipping into an icy stream on a sweltering day. I knew what I needed to do.

"If you don't want me here, that's fine. I quit."

19

I decided to take an official leave of absence from my studies, at least through the fall semester. The funds from my mother's estate, along with those from my father's, would be more than enough to support me financially over the next few months. Without my research to distract me, I could focus on locating my biological father, seeing him imprisoned, and destroying the power he held over our family.

Richard wouldn't let me go so easily, though. In the days following my decision, his emails flooded my inbox, each ping of a new notification akin to a mosquito buzzing in my ear. He seemed to view my leave as an empty threat, as if I were an errant teenager, running away from home for the attention.

Even after submitting the official paperwork with the university, Richard's emails only grew more frequent and urgent, asking me to reconsider. His initial emails were placating, but over time they became more manipulative, threatening to withhold his professional reference for future positions and revoke funding for my project. I soon stopped responding. The sense of relief and lightness that accompanied my decision was a more powerful motivator than Richard's criticisms and manipulations.

My attention had already shifted towards tracking down my father and reconciling with my sister and cousin, though I hadn't yet worked up the courage to speak with April. The thought of that conversation sent icy dread coursing through me. Instead, I'd been distracted with using Garrett's stolen laptop to discern my father's whereabouts.

There was only one problem. I didn't know the password.

Three days later, I was curled beneath a fleece blanket on my couch, Ginger nestled atop my lap, Garrett's laptop perched beside us. I glared at the machine, willing it to unlock and confirm my suspicion that Garrett had stayed in contact with my father for decades, but my efforts to guess the password had failed.

The muffled sound of a car door slamming shut, followed by a sharp rap on the door, grabbed my attention. Ginger scrambled off me, claws digging into my legs, and bolted out of sight.

I crept over to the living room window and peered outside, holding my breath. Luis and Petra stood on my porch, conversing in low tones. I exhaled and leaned my forehead against the door, mustering the energy for this unexpected visit. The door rattled as one of them pounded upon its ancient wood. Steeling myself, I wrapped my flannel shirt tight around me and let them inside.

"About time," Luis said. He surveyed the cottage with disdain, burrowing himself deeper into his gray wool coat. "Christ, Laurel, it's freezing in here."

"Trying to save on my utility bills." I approached the ancient thermostat and turned the heat up. The radiator rumbled to life, clanking and hissing. I usually preferred the wood-burning stove, but building a fire required more effort than I was willing to expend. There were more pressing matters that needed my attention.

"We come bearing gifts." Petra deposited a tray carrying three cups and a brown paper bag onto my coffee table, from which the smell of croissants and coffee wafted. My stomach rumbled, mouth filling with saliva. Petra shot me a tight smile that didn't reach her bloodshot eyes. My cheeks burned as I imagined how I must appear, unwashed and still clad in pajamas.

"I wasn't expecting you. Let me take a quick shower and change clothes. Just... make yourself comfortable."

I trudged back upstairs, washed my hair, and pulled on some leggings and an oversized sweater. When I entered the living room, I found Luis and Petra huddled together on my couch. Their murmurs came to an abrupt standstill when they caught sight of me.

After grabbing the remaining cup of coffee and croissant, I sank into the armchair opposite them and shoved the pastry into my mouth, its buttery flakes dissolving on my tongue, realizing too late that I was supposed to be avoiding dairy. I groaned in pleasure, and could feel my blood sugar beginning to stabilize after hours of neglect.

"We heard about your leave of absence," Petra said. "What happened?"

While I considered my response, I gulped down some lukewarm coffee. I wasn't comfortable telling them everything I'd learned about my family the past few weeks. Besides, it wasn't really my story to tell. Protecting Maura's privacy and dignity were more important than any emotional support I might need from my friends.

"I couldn't deal with Richard and my studies right now. There's too much going on with my family."

Petra's brow furrowed, concern marring her sharp features.

"I'm fine," I added. "You don't need to worry about me."

"For fuck's sake, Laurel. You're not fine. Look at this place." Luis gestured at the coffee table piled high with dirty dishes, unread mail, and empty wine bottles, the dirt-streaked floor, the moldering garbage bags stacked by the door.

My face flushed as I surveyed the once-tidy space, shocked at how quickly the cottage had fallen into disarray. I'd been too fixated on my family's deception and quest to find my father to notice. Petra elbowed Luis in the ribs and shot him a warning look. He shrugged away from her, scowling.

"It's okay to admit you're struggling," she said. "I mean, we all are. I get why you'd want to leave the program, especially after your mom's passing."

"I'm not coming back, if that's what you're getting at. At least not now."

"You shouldn't throw away your hard work and career because of Richard's inappropriate behavior," Luis said. "We know you've been having problems with him. We have been, too." He took a deep breath. "Which is why we're building a harassment and discrimination case against him."

I paused with my coffee cup halfway to my mouth and stared at Luis. He clasped his hands together in his lap, gazing at me intently.

"Wait, what?" I asked.

"It was Petra's idea," Luis said. "I mean, he treats us all like shit, but she's... she's had the worst of it. We just want it to stop. The university will have to listen to us if we all share our experiences."

He skirted his gaze towards Petra as if seeking confirmation. She shot him a reassuring smile before her gaze fluttered towards the floor.

I placed my cup on the table and sank back into my seat, considering how to respond. I'd grown so accustomed to placating Richard over the years that the abuse and manipulation had snuck in, so insidious that I hadn't noticed until recently. Yet I wondered how they expected to fix it.

"I wanted to tell you earlier," Luis added, breaking the silence. "Your first day back, when we had lunch together."

Realization settled over me as my memories flitted back towards that day on the quad, eating tacos and swapping stories. What would Luis have told me, if we hadn't been interrupted?

"I don't understand. You're almost done with your degrees. Why go through all this?" I asked.

Petra twisted the plain gold band on her ring finger, eyelids fluttering, and Luis squeezed her shoulder. She shot him a glance. He nodded as some unspoken agreement passed between them.

Petra took a deep breath. "Because I'm sick of hiding. I'm sick of pretending that what he did to me never happened."

The vitriol and pain in Petra's voice sent chills through me. My eyes snagged on her, noticing how she'd dug her nails into the couch like talons, eyes glinting like a predator about to make a kill. She'd transformed over the years, subtle and slow, building layer upon layer of keratin that had hardened around her like a protective shell. Then panic flooded through me as I remembered the argument I'd overheard between the dean and Richard weeks before.

They'd been talking about allegations. Petra's allegations. My mouth went dry.

"It started at a conference last year," she continued. "Richard got drunk, kept trying to... to touch me, kiss me. I rebuffed him. Reminded him I'm married, even if my husband still lives in Canada. The next day, Richard pretended like nothing happened. For a while, things returned to normal. I thought maybe it'd just been a one-off.

"A few months ago, I made the mistake of telling him I wanted to have children. He said I wouldn't need his recommendation for post-doc positions because I won't use my degree when I'm a stay-at-home mom. That's when he started making advances again, saying we should be together, that he can advance my career, if... if only..."

Petra went still and quiet, fists clenched atop her lap. My stomach twisted into a knot, tightening with each shallow breath. It felt like the ground had shifted beneath my feet, leaving me blind and staggering as I searched for solid footing.

Petra and Maura's stories weaved together in my mind, blurring around the edges, colliding into one brilliant, horrible reckoning about the men who had shaped our lives.

Suddenly, it was all too much.

"I can't do this right now." I lurched to my feet, legs quivering beneath me like toothpicks. "I just can't."

Petra and Luis scrambled up. Luis grabbed my shoulder to steady me. I shrugged it off.

"I know it's a lot to take in, and I know you're scared. But we need your help," Petra pleaded.

"You don't understand. There's no point. The university will side with Richard. They'll feign concern, lead a half-hearted investigation, and then dismiss your story. Nothing will change. I don't want to see you suffer through that, Petra. Not after what you've been through."

"So you think we should do nothing," Luis said, his eyes darkening. "Let him get away with it."

"No, of course not. It's... it's just..." I flailed, searching for the words to make them understand. Men like Richard behaved the way they did because they knew the system would protect them. I wanted to think that they'd believe Petra, that she would receive justice, but experience had taught me that systems created by men would always serve them first.

I wished Howard was still alive. He would've known how to navigate the inner workings of the university. He could've told us how to work within the system, or dismantle it from the outside. But he was dead, and we were just three students, powerless, fighting a system that would always protect itself.

Petra's face twisted in disgust at my silence. "This is the only way, Laurel. We can't give up our degrees and our careers over this. We came here as your friends, asking for your help. But if you won't help us, you're... You're no better than Richard."

I flinched at Petra's hurtful words, helplessness bubbling up inside me as I confronted yet another seemingly impossible situation. My eyes slid away from hers and snagged on a manila folder tucked beneath an empty wine bottle and a stack of unpaid bills on the coffee table. Something about the folder tugged at me, vying for my attention. Then realization struck, sudden and sharp.

The photo album wasn't the only item I'd found in my parents' chest. There'd also been a file folder with Richard's name on it, scrawled in Howard's handwriting.

I lunged for the folder, sending the empty bottle crashing to the floor. Luis yelped and scrambled away, Petra jerking away from him. "What the fuck, Laurel!"

Ignoring them, I released the binder clip holding the folder together and skimmed the first few pages, cursing at myself for not opening the folder sooner.

Howard had disliked Richard. He'd never spoken ill of him, but the signs were all there. An undercurrent of disdain that threaded through our conversations whenever I mentioned the possibility of attending Hildegard University and working with Richard. The gentle urging to apply to other programs.

It had never made sense to me. I was applying to graduate schools when Howard was diagnosed with lung cancer. It was clear Joan needed help after he was gone. Staying in Grenadier and attending Hildegard while caring for her was the logical choice, yet Howard had been completely opposed. Why?

The answer was in this folder.

Before his diagnosis, Howard had been helping another student build a harassment case against Richard. Six weeks later, he'd been dead, his lungs riddled with tumors. The case had died with him. The student had never received justice.

Heart hammering, I shoved the folder at Petra.

"What—"

"Just take it. Everything's there."

She combed through the sheets, eyes growing wide. Luis peered over her shoulder, his long, dark hair obscuring his face. Petra gazed up at me, mouth ajar.

With Howard's file, they could contact the woman Richard had harassed years ago, and urge her to come forward. It might be enough to sway the university. If it wasn't... well, I'd warned them about putting their faith in the system.

I only wish Howard had told me about Richard's true character when he had the chance. Though it was easy to assume it was another misguided attempt to protect me through lies, I realized his silence may have been to protect the student who had confided in him.

"Promise me one thing," I said. "This time, make sure Richard pays."

Before she could respond, the police arrived.

When I opened the door, I found two solemn police officers standing on my porch. I blinked at them, forcing my gaping mouth shut, mind fumbling to process their sudden appearance. My first thought was that Garrett had sent them to retrieve his stolen laptop and cat, and a nervous laugh burst from my chest, triggering concerned glances between the two officers.

Then I spotted Chris hovering at their periphery, wringing her hands, and my heart sank.

Not Maura. Not another suicide attempt. Please.

But it wasn't Maura. It was Garrett.

Luis and Petra left soon after the police arrived, but I barely registered their departure. I stood there, shocked, as the officers explained the situation to me with a calmness that bordered on infuriating.

First responders had found Garrett dead at his home a few nights ago, with flames lapping at his feet. Their working theory was that he'd been drinking, passed out with a lit cigarette, and set the house on fire. The neighbors saw the smoke and flames and called the fire department. They saved the house but were too late to save Garrett. The suspected cause of death was heart failure triggered by smoke inhalation.

"The police were outside your mom's place, looking for her," Chris told me later, after the police had left. "I was working on her estate when they showed up. Garrett listed her as his emergency contact, along with someone else named Walter Corbin that they couldn't reach. Maybe a friend or coworker? Anyway, I explained Joan had passed on, making you next of kin, and led them here."

"So I would've found out about Garrett eventually," I said, a lump growing in my throat. "All he needed to do was die."

Chris squeezed my shoulder and headed for the kitchen, leaving me in numbed, shocked silence.

Garrett was dead because of me.

I'd smelled the sharp scent of whiskey when the bottle crashed to the floor. I'd watched the golden ember of his cigarette smoldering on the carpet. I'd watched, indifferent, as he clutched his chest, unaware that it was the gesture of a dying man.

Or perhaps deep down I realized he was having a heart attack but did nothing. I pushed the thought aside, unwilling to probe it more deeply, unsettled by what it might mean.

Chris curled up beside me and pressed a mug of coffee into my hand. I nestled it against my belly, allowing the warmth to seep into me. It was easy to slip into the familiar pattern of allowing Chris to care for me. Though I still resented her role in my parents' deception, I was glad she was here.

"Did you tell April about her dad?" she asked.

"No. There was never a good time. And if I tell her now..."

"She'll be devastated."

I nodded, mouth dry. Then the guilt slammed into me, pressing the air from my lungs, its weight threatening to crush me to death. Panic tightened around my chest, replacing the numbness of the initial shock.

It was hard enough working up the courage to tell April about her father's true character. Now I had to tell her he'd died, that I was responsible. How would she ever forgive me?

The desire to tell Chris about my role in Garrett's death bubbled up within me, aching to burst free. I couldn't carry this guilt alone, not with the pain and grief of learning the truth about my family still so raw.

"Chris, there's something I need to... to..."

The words perched on the tip of my tongue, ready to spill out. It would be so easy to tell her, to replace guilt with relief. Instead, I choked. The shock and pain and guilt were too great. Not about losing Garrett, but what it meant for April and our burgeoning relationship.

"It's okay. I accept your apology," Chris said, patting my knee. "I'm sorry about how our last visit ended, too."

"No. It's not that. It's…"

It's that I'm the reason Garrett is dead.

I'm the reason April will never know her father.

And with Garrett gone, I may never learn what happened to my own.

"Laurel? Are you okay?"

Chris's voice jolted me back to the present. I shook my head, attempting to dislodge the dark thoughts crowding my mind.

"I'm fine. It's nothing."

She narrowed her eyes at me. "If you're still mad at me, fine. But don't sit there and lie to me. I know you're not okay."

The dam within me broke, unable to withstand the building pressure, both from Chris and from myself. "What do you want me to say? That I'm panicking because I need to tell April that I found her dad weeks ago but kept it to myself? That because of me she'll never know him?"

"I just want to help you, that's all."

I clutched the hair at my temples, nails digging into my scalp as I grappled with the storm of emotions within me, the racing thoughts threatening to drive me mad with anguish. Though I hated asking for help, to admit that I was struggling, I couldn't see a way forward on my own.

"You want to help me?" I asked. "Then tell me how to fix things."

"Start by telling April about her father."

"But how? He wasn't a good person, Chris."

She considered this, frowning. "There's no reason you need to tell her that. It would only bring her heartache, and she's got enough heartache coming her way."

"Lying to her, even by omission, would make me as bad as Joan. I can't do that. I won't."

"Joan wanted to protect you, that's all. Is that so wrong?"

I glowered at her. After seeing firsthand the destruction and turmoil Joan and Howard's deception had wrought within our family, I struggled to understand why she still thought they made the right decision.

"How can you continue to defend her? She lied to you, too."

"This isn't about me and Joan," Chris said, her jaw clenched. "This is about a vulnerable young woman who needs your help."

Her words thrummed within me, my heart aching, and I felt myself deflate. Deep down, I knew she was right. I should've told April about finding Garrett weeks ago. I needed to tell her the truth and help her through whatever came next. Even if it hurt.

After Chris left, I stood on my porch, staring at my phone. As my finger hovered over April's number, I finally understood why Joan and Howard had lied to me. I felt that urge now, borne of the fierce desire to protect someone from the pain of knowing a horrible truth about their past.

Joan never had children of her own. Though I could never ask her why, I suspected I already knew the answer, glimmering at the edge of my subconscious.

Perhaps she understood that the Ryder line had to end.

20

A week later, I craned my neck, trying to glimpse April through the crowds on the platform at the train station. The smell of fumes assaulted my nostrils and tickled my throat, spurring a coughing fit.

When she disembarked the train, I almost didn't recognize her. April's face was wan, unmarked by makeup, and a cluster of pimples sprouted angrily from her chin. She wore joggers and a sweatshirt, and the laces of her untied gym shoes dragged across the scuffed concrete. A small duffel bag was slung over her shoulder.

She scanned the platform, frowning, and I waved to catch her attention. When she spotted me, her forehead creased, and she trudged over, shoelaces slapping on the pavement.

"Thanks for coming." I flashed her what I hoped was a sympathetic smile and squeezed her arm. She muttered something inaudible under her breath and jostled free from my grasp, scowling.

A week had passed since I'd learned about Garrett's death.

The phone call to April had been excruciating. She'd fallen into a stunned silence when I told her about his death. I explained how Garrett revealed who my true parents were, how

Maura filled in the rest. That the shock of learning about our family's sordid history prevented me from reaching out to her sooner.

I didn't tell her I was there when Garrett died.

I didn't tell her that Maura urged me to keep him a secret from her.

I didn't tell her how Garrett reacted when I confronted him with the truth.

It didn't matter in the end, though. The outcome was the same. Her father had died a stranger.

Though my home was a short drive away, the minutes dragged on, tight with tension. April rested her forehead against the window of my truck, eyes shut. I opened my mouth to break the silence, but clammed up. What was there to say? I'd left her father to die, flames licking at his lifeless body.

But she couldn't know that. That much, at least, I intended to keep from her.

As I turned onto the gravel driveway leading to my cottage, I spotted Maura through the trees. She paced across my porch, hugging an oversized black cardigan around her midriff. A strand of dark hair swept across her face and she brushed it aside, appraising April as we headed towards her.

I pushed past them, leaving them to their awkward introductions, and unlocked the door. Together, we entered my cottage.

I hadn't expected Maura to show up. Then again, she'd always been unpredictable. Maybe I'd gotten through to her for once, made her understand how important it was to set aside our differences and support April. After all, she was our only cousin, though I could tell she was struggling to accept that Garrett had fathered a child.

Whatever the reason, I was glad to have Maura here. I think April was, too. With Garrett and Joan dead and Brandon gone, the three of us could begin fresh, no longer beholden to the narratives that our parents had set for us.

Now we sat around my kitchen table, Garrett's cremains in a nondescript box in front of us, while tears trickled down April's face.

"Do you think he would've wanted to meet me, if he hadn't...?" April gestured towards the cremains, stifling a sob.

"Yes, of course," I said, rubbing her back. "Once he recovered from the shock."

How easy it was to fall into the pattern of lying. Was this how it started for Joan? Spinning little white lies until you were caught in a web of your own making? When protecting those you loved, sometimes it was easier to sacrifice trust and truth for comfort and reassurance.

Maura gazed askance at me, raising a single arched eyebrow, her way of signaling that she'd caught me in the lie. My eyes darted away from hers, my cheeks flushing. Keeping this secret from April, or at least massaging the truth, was different from the secrets Joan and Howard kept from me. Unlike me, April hadn't grown up surrounded by the fallout of her father's actions, never knowing the real reason for the emotional chaos churning around her.

"What about my mom? Did he say anything about her?"

"He didn't remember her when I showed him the photo. I'm so sorry."

April laughed softly. "No wonder he had a heart attack. He learned he had a grown-ass daughter with a woman he didn't even remember sleeping with."

"The heart attack wasn't your fault. He lived alone, drank a lot, smoked a lot. Something was bound to happen, eventually."

Something like me.

"It's better for you this way," said Maura. "He would've disappointed you."

"Maura, please don't."

"It's better that she knows the truth, Laurel. Joan kept things from you to protect you, but it only made things worse. Secrecy isn't the answer. It only prolonged your suffering."

"Stop treating me like I'm not here," April said, brow furrowed, "and tell me what you're talking about."

"Please, Maura. Don't do this. Not now."

Though I meant to tell April about her father's flaws — with a generous sprinkling of fibs to make it go down easier — it needed to be done at the right moment. With tact. Something Maura neglected when her temper flared up.

Growing up, I learned to recognize the signs that meant Maura was on the verge of an outburst, a panic attack, a crying spell. The way her bottom lip would twist or tremble; the hardening of her jaw; her body coiling like a spring, every muscle tensed for a fight.

The signs were there now. Maura's calm exterior was calcifying, her delicate features twisting into a familiar mask of simmering rage. I collapsed into my seat, defeated, knowing I'd lost her. There was nothing I could do to intervene. I could only watch it happen and clean up the damage later.

Maura leaned forward. Staring April straight in the eyes, she said, "This will be hard to hear, but you need to hear it. Garrett was a piece of shit, just like our dad. Well, not quite as bad, but bad enough. He beat on Joan pretty regularly. And it didn't stop when they got older. I remember watching Garrett grab Joan's hair, drag her down the porch steps, and throw her against a car because she hadn't brought enough beer for whatever dumb fucking holiday we were celebrating. I was maybe, oh, eight years old?"

I closed my eyes, wishing I could disappear, struggling to accept how quickly things were unraveling, like a spool of thread tumbling down a hill.

"No, you're wrong. My mom said he was gentle, affectionate, kind—"

"But he didn't stick around. Your mom didn't even tell you his name. She might've lied to protect you."

"It was a one-night stand. She didn't get his number. She didn't even know she was pregnant with me until months later."

"Maura, stop it. This isn't helping," I said.

Her face darkened. Ignoring me, she turned towards April. "You wanted to know your father? Now you do. Accept it, process it, move on. Blood doesn't matter."

April's fists clenched atop the table, training her piercing glare on Maura. "But it does matter. It matters to me. I feel like a stranger in my family. My stepfather couldn't care less about me. My half-sister basically hates me. And you know why? It's because I'm different from them. Because I'm not from them.

"I'm walking this tightrope, caught between these two sides of myself. Too white, and too Black, both at the same time. My half-sister Rochelle acts jealous because I have lighter skin, which is completely fucked up, while my neighbor calls the cops on my Black friends and family whenever they come to my building after dark."

Tears streamed down April's face, as though a dam inside her burst. "I was a kid when I learned what it meant to be Black in this country. After begging and begging my mom for ballet lessons, she gave in. But when she took me to the first class, the dance teacher said hip-hop lessons were on a different day, then questioned whether we could even afford the fee. We should've gone to a different studio, but my mom's proud, and wanted to rub the bigotry in that woman's face. So I took the ballet lessons, and worked my ass off to prove I belonged there." She clenched her jaw. "It's impossible to figure out who I wanna be, who I am, when the world keeps making those decisions for me. Do you know how exhausting that is?"

I shook my head, face burning.

"There's an entire part of me that's written on the surface of my skin that I don't have access to," April continued, voice thick with tears. "It's completely cut off, just... static. I thought finding my dad, my other family, would change things. But it was stupid to ever think that. You'll never know what it's like to live in my skin, and I'll never know what it's like to live in yours." She drew in a ragged breath, choking down a sob. "This whole thing was a mistake. I should've listened to my mom and let it go when I had the chance."

Before I could react, she bolted from her seat and rushed outside. The backdoor clattered shut behind her, leaving me to reflect on the collateral damage my search for the truth had left in its wake.

21

Maura and I sat at the kitchen table in silence, contemplating April's words, her rage, her despair. Despite our shared blood, the lives we'd navigated, the families that raised us, and the color of our skin had molded us into disparate individuals. Led us down different paths. I thought our shared inheritance was strong enough to bridge those differences, but now I wondered if we were simply strangers, forced together by genetics and circumstance.

My gaze flicked to Maura's, who had been uncharacteristically silent since April's wholly justified outburst. As though sensing my gaze, she shivered and pulled her cardigan tight over her belly, glancing through the window at the deepening twilight into which April had disappeared. I'd invited them to spend the night so we could deepen our bond, but we were drifting farther apart, like brash ice floating on a lake in the dead of winter.

That's what the Ryder family does to its children, I thought. Cracks grow and widen until they fissure and break.

"You could've been gentler with April," I said. "She just lost her dad after searching her entire life for him. It's a lot to deal with."

Scowling, Maura turned to me. "She wanted the truth, so I gave it to her. It's not my fault she wasn't ready to hear it. But she should've been. I mean, what was she expecting?"

"Why did you even come? Do you even care about her? About us?"

"Our family's had enough secrecy. April needs to understand who her dad was. The sooner she accepts that, the sooner she can move on. The sooner we can all move on." She took a deep breath. "Secrets are their own form of trauma. Even if they stay hidden, there's always leakage, and the damage can be just as devastating. You should know that by now."

I made a disgusted noise and headed towards the stove to make dinner. I needed to do something with my hands before I ended up strangling Maura.

Whether or not she meant to, Maura's radical honesty was pushing April away, just like she'd pushed me away during our childhood. With Garrett gone, the three of us could finally get to know one another, instead of filtering our interactions through our relationships with our fathers.

Maura didn't understand that. Her actions were slowly dismantling what was left of the Ryder family and severing the tenuous bonds holding us together. She was falling back into the old patterns of our childhood, lashing out whenever someone tried to get close. I was regressing, too — could feel the familiar sting of Maura's rejection, the helplessness that shrouded our interactions, the sensation that I was playing a dangerous game blindfolded and without the rulebook, knowing one wrong move could detonate Maura.

"Laurel."

I sighed and faced her. "What now?"

"Cell service is spotty. I need your internet password so I can connect my phone and send James a message."

"I don't know it. Just use my laptop. It's in the living room," I said, sharing the password.

Maura nodded and left.

I started preparing dinner, chopping tomatoes for a salad while the pasta cooked atop the stove. As I worked, my eyes drifted to the window, where burgeoning darkness coated the abandoned farm and forest, obscuring April's presence. I wondered if I could fix things between us, help April move through her grief. If she even wanted my help.

Maura stormed into the kitchen and grabbed my arm. The knife slipped and sliced my finger. Pain bloomed across my fingertip. I yelped and cradled my injured hand as blood pulsed from the cut, dripping onto the cutting board and the scuffed tile floor. The knife landed on the counter with a thud.

"Why the fuck do you have Garrett's laptop?" Maura yelled, waving the computer over her head.

My eyes widened. I spun away, struggling to think of a response while my finger screamed at me. I couldn't tell her the truth. James had already warned me against pursuing our father. Mentioning my plan would send Maura spiraling, and she was already on the verge of a breakdown.

"Answer me, Laurel. Why do you have his laptop? How did you even get it?"

I turned to face her, wrapping a dish towel around my injured finger, which throbbed in protest. "I picked it up when I got his cremains so it wouldn't get stolen."

"No. Don't lie to me. You're trying to track down Brandon." She stood tall, fists clenched by her side, but the display of strength wasn't enough to disguise the flash of fear in her eyes.

I pressed my lips shut as my mind roved to come up with a response, juggling all the promises I'd made and broken. Maura shook her head, lip curling into a grimace.

"This is unbelievable. I told you to drop this. James told you to drop this. Why are you dragging me back into all this shit?"

My shoulders sagged in defeat. I felt bone-weary, and sick of the deceit. "So you admit it. You knew Garrett helped Brandon disappear. That's why you told me to stay away from him."

"I didn't want you talking to Garrett because he's a misogynistic drunk."

"Maybe so, but he might've known what happened to our father. And everyone ignored it."

"You can't blame me for that. I was a kid when Brandon disappeared. I was busy being poked and prodded by doctors, answering a thousand painful questions about what he did to me, forced to relive those horrible moments over and over." Her face crumpled. "Please don't make me go through this again. You promised me you'd let this go."

"I'm sorry, but I can't," I said, giving a slight shake of my head. "Not while there's a chance he could hurt other children. Garrett helped him get away, I'm sure of it. I can find him. Then we can make sure he spends the rest of his life in prison."

The floorboards creaked. We whirled around and found April standing in the doorway, her face pale. My heart sank as I realized she'd been standing there, listening to us this whole time.

"You're the reason Laurel didn't tell me about my dad," she said, eyes locked on Maura's. "You didn't want us talking to him."

"He was dangerous. I was only trying to protect you."

April turned to me. "Were you going to tell me about him, if he hadn't died?"

"Of course. I was waiting for the right time."

She raised an eyebrow, gazing at me askance, as though unsure whether to believe me. "Did you even tell him he had a daughter? Or was that a lie, too?"

"I wouldn't lie to you about that."

April's face twisted with anguish and grief, shoulders slumping. Beside her, Maura stood still as stone, avoiding eye contact with us.

"There's pasta on the stove," I said finally. "We'll all feel better with some food in us."

I replaced the bloody dishtowel with a bandage and salvaged what I could of the meal. Maura placed the laptop on the table, eyeing it warily. We ate together in silence, save for the clink of metal forks on plates. The pasta was overcooked; the salad wilted, yet color flushed across Maura's porcelain face as she ate. April and I worked through a bottle of red wine, though Maura refused.

Once Maura's plate was clean, she turned to me and said quietly, "You need to stop trying to find Brandon. I get that you're still reeling from what you've learned, but this isn't healthy. For either of us. Your obsession with him is harming me. I haven't felt this way since our meeting at Silver Beach."

I set down my fork and took a sip of wine before responding. "I just want to make things right."

"It's too late for that. You need to process this and move on. We'll never be able to have a relationship if you're stuck in the past." Maura turned towards April, whose face was stony. "That goes for you, too. It might be hard for you to accept, but you're better off with Garrett dead. He's not someone you'd want in your life. Though I suppose if he was alive, Laurel would go on another crusade to hold him accountable for all the fucked-up shit he did to our family. Our avenging angel."

My face burned. It felt as though my guilt was dripping off me, like a foul stench I'd never be rid of. Maura's words wormed their way into me, dredging up feelings I'd been struggling to suppress. Because I realized she might be right. Didn't part of me crave vengeance, even more than justice? Wasn't part of me secretly relieved that Garrett was dead, a fitting punishment for his role covering up our father's crimes?

Did I truly regret his death?

Before allowing myself to probe those thoughts further, I leapt up and whisked away the dirty plates, the dishes clattering in my shaking hands. After setting them aside, I gripped the edges of the counter, the cold surface biting my palms, and willed my shuddering breath to calm. Willed those dark thoughts to dissipate. I turned my mind instead to Maura.

Maura's singular focus on her own pain had blinded her to my suffering. She wanted me to come to terms with our shared past in a way that fit her needs—alone, out of sight, with minimal disruption to her. She didn't understand how her behavior during our childhood made things worse for me. Thanks to

Joan and Howard's misguided attempts to protect me, and the police's failure to apprehend our father, I grew up in an unstable household, watching, helpless, as Maura destroyed herself and pushed everyone who loved her away.

How many other families might our father have ripped apart in the intervening years? How many more families might he destroy in the future? I wanted to ensure others didn't suffer needlessly, too. That was how I could move on. Why couldn't she understand that?

Upon returning to the table, I found April glaring at Maura, her fingers clenched so tight around her wine glass I worried it would snap in two. If she didn't hurl it at Maura first.

"Can either of you think of someone besides yourselves for once, for fuck's sake?" April said. "My dad just died. Maybe that was inevitable. But I could've known him, even for a short while, if you hadn't kept him a secret from me. You stole that chance from me, and I'll never get it back. I'll never learn for myself who he was."

The snide look slid off Maura's face.

"You think you know what's best for me, but you don't," April continued, voice trembling. "I thought you wanted to help me cope with his death. That you'd apologize for keeping him from me. But you're too busy bickering about your own shit to consider what I'm going through."

April shoved her chair out from the table and cradled the box of Garrett's cremains in her arms. "I'm gonna take what's left of my dad and scatter his ashes in the wooded glen. It's peaceful. A place he might've liked. But thanks to you, I'll never know."

The back door clattered shut behind April, her father's ashes cradled in her arms. Maura rose from the table, flustered. "This was a mistake. I should go."

"No. Stay," I said. "It's too late to drive back home."

Maura peered uncertainly through the kitchen window, where darkness had settled upon the landscape, thick and oppressive, unmarred by city lights. A pang of worry coursed through me as I thought of April alone, scattering her father's ashes by the light of the crescent moon hanging low on the horizon.

I wanted to help April, support her during this difficult time, but the tug of Maura's whirlpool was too strong. Despite knowing I risked drowning, I didn't know how to free myself. Maura held her gaze for a moment, calculating. Then, resigned, she nodded. I exhaled in relief.

"Throwing Brandon in prison won't make up for all the ways he damaged me," she said. "So I'm asking again. Please let this go. For me."

I opened my mouth to argue but stopped when I caught sight of her. The anger Maura wore like a shield had dissolved, replaced instead with vulnerability. Her doe eyes were wide and glassy. She tugged at her cardigan, lip trembling, then encircled her arms around her body protectively, like vines curling around a tree trunk. For a fleeting moment, I caught a glimpse of the scared little girl she once was. That perhaps she'd always been.

"If I find Brandon, I'll find a way to hold him accountable without involving you," I said. "That's all I can promise. He's my father, too. Let me deal with the hell he put us through in my own way."

Maura's face hardened. She lunged for Garrett's laptop and threw it against the wall. A crack jolted through the air. Bits of plastic, glass, and metal shot out like shrapnel. I threw my arms up to protect myself.

Once I recovered from the shock, I fell to my knees and fumbled with the mutilated laptop. A crack marred the screen, splintering from a center point like a spider's web. When I tried turning it on, nothing happened.

Maura's boot stamped down on the keyboard. I yelped and withdrew my hand before her foot smashed down again and again, pulverizing the laptop.

Hot, angry tears streamed down my face and panic rose, overwhelming, in my throat. I clasped my hands over my ears, rocking back and forth on the floor, my pelvis seizing.

Silence descended, save for the sound of my ragged breathing. Maura stepped away, panting, grim triumph on her face. The laptop was demolished beyond repair. I staggered to standing, rage coursing through my blood. "You had no right."

Maura jabbed a finger at my chest, glaring up at me. "I had every right. I'm protecting myself. Brandon's been out of my life for decades now. I won't let you bring him back into it."

I clutched my hair so I wouldn't grab Maura by hers and let out a strangled cry of frustration.

"This is over, Laurel, understand? I don't want to hear anything else from you about finding Brandon. You have no idea how triggering, how damaging, this is for me. I've worked my ass off to build a safe, happy life with some semblance of normalcy. I won't let you take that from me."

"I can't even look at you right now," I muttered. "Maybe you should leave."

For a split second, Maura looked startled, almost remorseful, before her face hardened again. "You think it's easy for me to look at you, Laurel? You're wearing the face of our dead mother. You're lucky you don't remember her. Because if you did, you couldn't look at yourself in the mirror without being reminded of how she failed us."

The words cut through me, lodging under my skin like splinters. A surge of rage welled up within me. Every grievance and heartache I'd ever experienced because of Maura roiled through my mind, like magma churning beneath a volcano. The pressure was too great. I exploded.

"You aren't the only one who's been damaged by our father. I know he didn't hurt me the way he hurt you, but I suffered from the fallout. My entire childhood was dictated by your emotional instability. I didn't have any close friends growing up because I was scared you'd have a screaming match with Joan if I invited classmates over. I tried to be the perfect child, because I knew Joan and Howard had their hands full with you.

"I sacrificed so much to care for Joan and Howard after you left home. Putting their needs before my own. Now I'm stuck in my hometown, parentless, on leave from a graduate program that I only chose because Joan needed me close after Howard died. A graduate program I'm beginning to regret signing up for.

"No one told me why you were so angry and sad, so I spent my childhood thinking that it was my fault you hated me," I continued, tears streaming down my face. "Thinking you didn't love me. Wondering what I did to make you abandon me. Why you chose to break off contact with your only sister, when I needed you."

"I sent you letters," Maura shot back. "You never responded. You chose Joan and Howard over me. How do you think that affected me?"

Her words caused me pause, my raw anger replaced with confusion. "What are you talking about? What letters?"

Maura laughed quietly, her shoulders slumping as she shook her head. "Of course. You never got my letters. Even after Joan promised."

"Promised what? Maura, you aren't making any sense."

"After I left home, I wrote to you. Birthday cards, postcards from trips, letters. Joan promised me she'd pass them on to you. I figured she'd read them first, make sure they fit her narrative, but I never thought she'd keep them from you. When you didn't write back, I assumed it was because you didn't care. God, how could I have been so stupid?"

I stumbled backwards as if pushed, a visceral reaction to Joan's betrayal. Because I'd never received any letters from Maura. If I had, I would have cherished them, kept them safe, read and reread them until the words were etched in my mind and I could recite them by heart. Joan had purposely kept them from me, destroying those letters as surely as she destroyed any chance for our sisterhood.

Despite the freshness of this wound and what it meant, I recognized this latest revelation as an unwelcome distraction. Maura was a master manipulator, just like Joan. I couldn't let her redirect this conversation when so much was at stake. Dwelling on what could have been was a luxury I couldn't afford. I straightened, mustering my strength, unwilling to back down now.

"None of that matters anymore, Maura. I get that Joan and Howard made it impossible for us to have a relationship. You've had time to recover. This is fresh to me. Raw. So if you're asking me to put your needs first, I won't. I can't. Not again. It's time for me to start making my own choices."

I fell silent, lungs aching, as though I'd finished running a marathon. Maura stood still, studying me with a quiet intensity. When she spoke, her voice was calm and deliberate.

"I'm sorry you had a difficult childhood, but it wasn't my fault. I hope you can understand that. Joan and Howard insisted on staying quiet and pretending nothing happened, even when you deserved to know. But it did happen," she said, her voice breaking, "and their denial meant that we spent our childhoods without the help and love we both needed. I didn't have the skills or coping mechanisms in place to process what happened to me, and we both suffered as a result.

"But you know the truth now. You have the chance to heal. We have the chance to start over, focused on the future, not the past. We could be sisters again. I get that you need to start prioritizing yourself after putting Joan and Howard first for so long. But Pursuing Brandon won't change anything. It's only going to cause us both more pain."

I shook my head helplessly, desperate for her to understand. "I can't pretend he doesn't exist. I won't. Not when there's even the slightest chance he's hurting other children. You might be willing to ignore that possibility, but I'm not."

Maura's face paled. She swayed on her feet and leaned against the table to steady herself. Her chest began to heave, breath labored and shallow. Alarmed, I moved towards her, but she raised a hand to stop me. She turned away and gripped the back of a chair, shoulders hunched. After a few agonizing minutes, her breath steadied. She took a sip of water with trembling hands before facing me again. The color was high in her cheeks, her eyes trained on mine. When she spoke, her voice quavered, even as she carefully enunciated each word.

"After Joan died, I hoped we could start over. I wanted you in my life. I still want you in my life. That's why I came to her funeral. But we can't have a relationship if you insist on focusing on the past and refuse to respect my boundaries." She took a deep breath. "I need you to hear me. If you don't let this go, I'll never forgive you. I'll cut off contact, this time for good. You'll be dead to me."

My breath hitched, as though she'd punched me in the gut. I tightened my hands into fists, jagged nails biting into flesh. My cut finger throbbed in protest, and fresh blood seeped through the bandage, forming a ragged red circle.

It was an impossible choice. How could I choose my sister, whose love I wanted more than anything, if it meant abandoning children who might be harmed by our father's continued existence?

My sister, more than anyone, knew exactly how to break my heart.

"I'm not sure I can do that, Maura," I said quietly. "This is too important to let go. But I want you in my life, too. That's all I've ever wanted. There has to be room for both."

Maura's shoulders sagged and she squeezed her eyes shut. She stood there, unmoving, for several seconds. When her eyelids fluttered open, her eyes were hard, jaw set.

"If that's your choice, then I need to leave," she said. "But I hope you change your mind. For both our sakes."

Maura gathered her belongings and walked out the door, leaving me among the ruinous remains of my family.

22

I woke the next morning to the sound of creaking floorboards emanating from the living room downstairs. Ginger, nestled in the crook of my bent leg, stirred and stretched her limbs before stalking towards the stairs, signaling it was time for her breakfast. I pushed myself up to sitting, clutching at my aching head.

After showering and dressing, I wrapped my blanket around myself and headed downstairs to feed Ginger. My wool socks kicked up dust, the small flecks illuminated by the bright morning light. I'd tried cleaning up before April and Maura arrived but found myself less and less motivated to complete chores, which had in recent weeks felt mundane and insignificant in light of my family's dark history.

Yesterday evening, after scattering her father's ashes, April had returned to the house, eyes swollen and puffy. She didn't seem surprised to find Maura gone. When I asked her if she still planned on staying, April had nodded and settled on the couch, with her overnight bag and belongings neatly laid out on the coffee table.

Now the fleece blanket was folded, the lumpy pillow propped up against the couch cushions, and April was nowhere in sight. My heart started pummeling against my ribcage at her unexpected absence. Still reeling from Maura's abrupt departure last night, I wasn't sure I could handle it if April had decided to leave, too.

A shadow flitted across the curtain. My breath hitched. I wrenched open the door and exhaled with relief when I spotted April curled up on a wicker bench, gazing at the grove of trees adjacent to the cottage. Perhaps the location where she'd scattered Garrett's ashes last night. She turned to peer up at me, blinking, and burrowed her hands deeper into her coat pockets. The tension she'd worn in the creases of her forehead and the set of her shoulders last night had melted away. I sat down beside her, my heart rate slowing.

"I didn't want to wake you, so I came out here," she said, stifling a yawn.

"Thanks. I was worried you'd left, too."

"Yeah. Speaking of, what happened to Maura? Why'd she take off last night? Was it because of me? Talking about our dads was clearly hard for her."

My face flushed, memories of the fight with Maura last night flooding my mind. In some ways, it'd been inevitable, with decades of pent-up heartache and anger finally erupting. Maura and I were like two magnets, repelled by the force of each other's presence. This time, I worried the damage might be irreparable.

April didn't need to know the details of our fight. I didn't want to drag her into our mess. This was between Maura and me.

"Maura leaving had nothing to do with you," I said. "Her default setting is to run away when things get hard. It always has been."

"I get why she warned us to stay away from my dad. Especially given all the fucked-up shit that happened to her. I know she was only trying to protect me. But it still sucks, the not knowing him."

An image flashed in my mind, of Garrett scoffing at the photo of April's mother, a racial epithet on the tip of his tongue. Heat flashed across my neck at the memory, made even worse by April's honesty and vulnerability about her experiences as a Black woman the night previously.

Was there anything redeemable in her father?

Was there anything redeemable in me after leaving him to die?

A heaviness settled on my shoulders, pushing deep into my gut, but I steeled myself against it, instead focusing on how I could support April.

"When Joan died, I wrote her a letter. It helped, with the grief. You could do the same for Garrett."

"I don't know, Laurel. Maybe I will, one day. But right now, part of me wants to forget this ever happened and just go home."

We settled into a tense silence, punctuated by birdsong and the creaking of tree limbs. I gnawed on my thumbnail, consumed with guilt, wondering what our relationship would look like, now that April had seen the ugliness of our family.

Nothing held us together any longer. We'd found and lost Garrett. April could retreat to the safety and comfort of her old life, come clean to her mother about what she'd learned, and forget she'd ever met me. I only wished I could've brought her some closure before she vanished into my past.

"Don't feel obligated to stay in touch," I said, unable to coax the bitterness from my voice. "You've seen what our family is like. If you think it's better to cut off contact, I'd understand."

April faced me, jaw tight. "Is that what you want, Laurel? To drop me and go on this wild crusade against your father?"

I stiffened under her scrutinizing gaze, unwilling to respond.

"That's the real reason Maura left, isn't it? She's right, you know. Your obsession with him is unhealthy. It's not good for either of you."

"I don't expect you to understand."

She shot me an exasperated look. "Of course I understand. I was obsessed with finding my dad, too, but things didn't turn out as planned. They won't for you, either."

I shook my head, refusing to believe her words. Our situations were completely different. We were both searching for our fathers, but I held no unrealistic expectations for his character, nor did I desire a meaningful relationship with him. I knew exactly who my father was. He'd already disappointed and failed me in ways that were unforgivable. I didn't seek redemption or reconciliation. I sought justice. Yet in those fleeting moments when I was overwhelmed by anger and despair, I wondered if justice was sufficient.

April picked at a loose thread hanging from her jacket, gaze trained on the ground. She cleared her throat before speaking, her voice as slow and measured.

"I didn't sleep well last night. Kept thinking about what Maura said about Garrett. It made me think that my mom might've known more about my dad than she let on. Maybe Maura's right. She might've lied about him to protect me."

"What're you saying? You think it was more than a one-night stand?"

April's eyes fluttered close, tears beading on her dark lashes. She took a shuddering breath. "No. What I'm saying is that... maybe what happened between them wasn't consensual."

Her words forced the air from my lungs, reverberating through my head like a bird caught in a cage. Beside me, April crumpled. I wrapped my arms around her instinctively, desperate to offer her protection and comfort, though I knew it was too late. It had been too late the minute I told her the name of her father. She collapsed into my embrace, body trembling as sobs wracked through her.

"You don't know that," I said, even as shock and pain radiating through me. "Our fathers hid their true nature to get what they wanted. To hide in plain sight. It's only later that the ugliness came out."

Despite my words of comfort, despite wanting to believe she was wrong, the doubts had already taken root, spreading rotten tendrils through my mind.

Garrett had only been interested in what women could offer him. I'd seen him react with rage and disapproval when women expressed their own needs; insisted on controlling their own narratives. I couldn't imagine him giving much thought to consent. The thought made me shudder.

April shrugged out of my arms, sniffling, and wiped her nose on her sleeve. The sight of her red-rimmed eyes filled me with despair. Our family had broken her.

"Are you going to ask your mom about this?" I asked tentatively.

"No." She shook her head, face filled with grief. "I can't do that to her. It wasn't until yesterday, hearing Maura talk about her history, that I realized how painful it must be for my mom whenever I bring up my dad. Especially if it wasn't consensual. I've learned who my dad was. That's enough. I can't ask her whether I'm the product of... of rape." She choked on the last word.

My chest ached for April. The guilt I'd carried on my shoulders since learning about my role in Garrett's death lessened, allowing those darker thoughts from yesterday evening to percolate, once again, to the surface. Perhaps leaving her father to die had been exactly what he deserved. Maybe I could forgive myself.

"I was so caught up in my own pain last night that I ignored Maura's," April said, turning to face me, her eyes pleading. "It didn't even register. But I get it now. Especially when thinking about my mom. I get why Maura was so angry and upset. All this talk about our dads is forcing her to relive her abusive childhood. I can't imagine how scary and distressing it must be for her to consider facing your dad again. You need to stop searching for him. It's time for all of us to move on."

"I never meant for her to know. I can handle it without involving her."

"That's not the point. She showed up yesterday, Laurel. She showed up for both of us. She said things I needed to hear, even though it hurt. It's time we showed up for her."

My jaw clenched. Maura hadn't shown up for me. She'd shown up to make sure April knew the truth about her father. Ripping the bandage off in some misguided attempt to help April grieve and move on. Had April already forgotten how vicious and manipulative Maura had been last night?

I'd needed Maura to show up for me during our childhood, but she was so consumed by her own pain that my needs fell to the wayside. I spent my childhood desperate for her affection; watching, helpless, as her mental health deteriorated, culminating in the horrible day when I found her in her bedroom, wrists slit, blood pooling on the carpet, never knowing the reason why.

No one had helped her cope with her trauma. And no one had helped me cope with mine.

Maura understood the source of her trauma. She'd spent years working to address it. But mine was fresh, an open wound still spilling blood. Maura wanted me to follow her path of healing by addressing the symptoms, rather than the root cause. I wanted to heal by ripping out the poisoned roots of our past. Ensuring our father was held accountable for his actions. Ensuring he couldn't harm anyone else.

Why couldn't April and Maura understand that?

When we arrived at the train station an hour later, I paid for April's train ticket and accompanied her to the platform. Her silence hung over us like a dark cloud. With each breath, the distance between us expanded, a gulf I knew we could never truly repair, yet another gaping wound inflicted by the men in our family. A lump formed in my throat. I swallowed, shoving down the disappointment and panic simmering within me.

Once she boarded that train, I feared I'd never see her again.

The station bells clanged and lights flashed, jarring us both, and the train lurched onto the platform. I clasped April's shoulder and pulled her close, our foreheads nearly touching. She closed her eyes, tears gathering in the corners of her lashes.

"You're still my family, April. I'm here whenever you need me."

She didn't respond. She untangled herself from our embrace and boarded the train, never once looking back.

After the train winked out over the horizon, I wandered back to my truck and rested my spinning head on the wheel, feeling wholly alone and abandoned.

I never should have invited Maura to join us. Rather than helping us heal, she'd chosen to tear open old wounds and create fresh ones. Without her present, I could've eased April into the truth about her father, like easing into a warm bath. Instead, Maura had thrown her headfirst into a frigid lake lined with sharp, jagged boulders.

Rather than bringing us closer together, this weekend had ripped us apart, sent us tumbling into discrete orbits. The gravity of blood wasn't enough to hold us together. Our lives were too different.

Maura thought we could escape our shared blood by severing the bonds between us. But much more than blood bound us together. We were also bound by shared trauma, by the violence and abuse perpetrated by our fathers, and our father's fathers before them, embedded within our bodies and blood. Our inheritance.

The violence within our family also affected more than just us. I thought of Mrs. Hernandez's haunted eyes. Of my birth mother hanging from a tree. Of the other children my father might harm. Might have already harmed.

I couldn't stop searching for my father now, not even with Maura's threat of estrangement hanging over me. Her version of closure and healing was cutting off everyone who reminded her of her past, which was as effective as amputating a limb to stop the spread of blood cancer. How could she expect us to have a relationship focused on the future without acknowledging our shared history?

I'd find closure by facing our monster and destroying it.

Even if it meant losing Maura in the process.

23

I was certain, now more than ever, that Garrett had helped my father evade the police. I'd hoped to find evidence of Brandon's whereabouts on Garrett's laptop, but Maura had smashed it to pieces. What's more, Garrett was dead, and the police were useless, leaving me in the exact position I'd started.

The only remaining option was to revisit Garrett's place and see if he'd left behind any evidence linking him to his brother. Hopefully, the fire hadn't rendered his house into a pile of ash and rubble.

An hour later, I arrived outside what remained of Garrett's house. The exterior, at least, appeared untouched by the fire, though the porch was so littered with junk it was a miracle it hadn't ignited. I only hoped the fire department extinguished the fire before it destroyed any important documents — bank statements, phone bills, address book, even letters — that might suggest ongoing communications between Garrett and my father.

I parked and approached the house cautiously, worried about its structural integrity. Shredded yellow caution tape hung limply from the doorjamb. The front door stood ajar, the lock broken and doorknob mangled, jagged splinters of wood hanging from the frame.

Something about it tugged at me, a sense of unease I couldn't quite place. I shrugged it aside, telling myself the fire department must have kicked the door open in their hurry to reach Garrett, and that the recent storms had ripped down the caution tape.

I slipped inside and was immediately assaulted by smoky, stale air that wound its way into my lungs. A hacking cough burst from my chest, my throat burning. After catching my breath, I blinked, my eyes adjusting to the darkness. Faint light strained through the drawn curtains, illuminating the silky ash that blanketed every surface, erasing all color, like a black-and-white movie.

My footprints joined others crisscrossing through the ash, converging around a scorch mark that trailed from the carpet up the wallpaper. I stiffened, thrown back to that terrible moment when Garrett writhed on the floor, clutching at his chest, scrabbling at my ankles, peering at me with pleading eyes.

The evidence of my presence that night was everywhere. Shards of glass from the broken liquor bottle glittered in a narrow beam of sunlight; the legs of the overturned coffee table were charred, sticking out like oversized matchsticks, and Garrett's recliner was now a blackened husk.

Lungs tightening, I wrenched my gaze from the scene of destruction, a nagging reminder of my guilt that threatened to suffocate me. I forced the memories from my mind and focused on the reason I was here. Part of me wanted to leave, but I knew I couldn't. There was too much at stake.

My gaze settled on the massive work desk and filing cabinet shoved in the living room corner, but shock coursed through me as I realized that someone had pulled the drawers from their sockets and upended them on the scorched carpet, as though to rifle through their contents. The disarray went beyond Garrett's general disorderliness and any damage that the firefighters or police could have inflicted.

Dread coiled in my gut. I thought of the splintered door, the broken lock, the nagging feeling of wrongness permeating through the claustrophobic space.

I realized I hadn't locked the door after leaving here the night Garrett died. Garrett had been in no shape to lock it himself, which meant the paramedics and firefighters must have locked it afterwards to prevent looting. Yet the door had clearly been forced open.

Someone had broken in after the fire.

The realization sent a jolt through my body. I stumbled backwards, my heart rattling out a silent alarm, my ears filling with the sound of my ragged breathing. I felt light-headed from sipping the rancid air.

Though I knew the burglar was likely long gone, I crept deeper into the bowels of the house and scoured the remaining rooms in search of intruders. Once confirming I was alone, the tightness in my chest eased somewhat, and I focused my attention on salvaging what I could.

I started my search in his bedroom, which had been unscathed by the fire. As I stepped inside, my boot nudged against something buried beneath a discarded jacket. I rummaged through the jacket pockets and found a cell phone. A wave of nervous anticipation surged through me. Garrett might have used the phone to contact my father. It was an old flip-phone model, and the battery was dead. Impatient to peruse its contents, I grabbed the charging cable snaking across the floor and plugged in the phone.

While the cell phone charged, I turned towards the dresser and began rummaging through wrinkled clothes, in search of an address book, journal, anything that might contain my father's contact information.

My hand brushed against cold metal. I stiffened. A moment passed. Taking a deep breath, I wrapped my fingers around the object and pulled it out into the muted light.

I stared at the gun.

The phone chimed, the sound deafeningly loud in the enclosed space, so startling that I nearly dropped the weapon. Hands shaking, I placed the gun aside and picked up the phone, reviewing the notifications for missed calls and messages.

They were all from one person. Walter Corbin.

The name sounded vaguely familiar. I wracked my brain, trying to place it, before remembering that Garrett had listed him as an emergency contact, but the police had trouble reaching him.

Walter had been calling and texting Garrett nonstop since his death.

Where are you?

Why haven't you answered?

Has something happened?

Before I could ponder the messages' significance, a rap sounded at the door.

My body tensed, waves of panic crashing over me. Another knock sounded, louder this time, more urgent. I lunged for the gun, gripping it in my sweat-slicked palm, and tiptoed down the hall, wincing as floorboards creaked beneath my feet, wondering if it was the police or the burglar, come to finish the job.

When I reached the front door, I opened it a crack and peered out. The man standing on the porch wore a broad-brimmed hat and jeans smeared with dirt, with a pair of gardening gloves hanging from his back pocket. He scratched the graying stubble lining his cheeks and shot me a tight smile that didn't reach his eyes.

"What do you want?" I asked, not bothering to hide my annoyance at his unexpected intrusion.

"I'm Emmett, I live next door. I saw your truck, wanted to make sure everything's all right."

"Everything's fine."

"Well, I'd liked to believe that, but I'm not accustomed to seeing trespassers in my neighborhood."

"I'm not a trespasser. I'm Garrett's niece."

"That's strange, seeing as he never mentioned you."

My fingers tightened around the door. Of course Garrett hadn't mentioned me. Instead of supporting the women in our family, he chose to help my father evade justice. Because of that choice, Garrett had died a lonely old man, without any friends or family, his only relationships relegated to online chat rooms.

"We weren't close," I replied.

"Hmph. And here I was, thinking you were that mail-order bride Garrett was always bragging about."

I glared at him, my face stony, jaw clenched. Emmett's off-color joke was bad enough, but it was made worse by April's earlier admission that she suspected Garrett's encounter with her mother hadn't been consensual.

Eager to be rid of this busybody, I shoved the gun into the waistband of my jeans and started slamming the door. Emmett shoved his foot in the gap. Anger coursed through me. I didn't need another misogynistic asshole getting in my way.

"Now just wait a minute," he said. "The fire really shook me up. I'm the one who called 911, you know. They said it wasn't arson, but who knows? First someone claiming to be his brother shows up, then you. What am I supposed to think?"

The world fell away, save for the blood pulsing through me, and the soft thudding of my heart as I contemplated what this meant. "Wait. Garrett's brother was here? What did he want?"

"Said he hadn't heard from Garrett, wanted to check on him. I guess no one told him he'd passed on."

"Tell me everything that happened." My throat went tight. Out of fear or hopeful anticipation, I wasn't sure. "Everything about him."

His gaze flicked to the damaged door, eyes widening. "Look, I don't want any trouble. I don't even know if you're telling me the truth about who you are."

"Here's what's going to happen, Emmett. You're going to answer my questions, or I'm going to call the police and tell them you're trespassing and forced your way into my uncle's house."

His face reddened, the muscles of his jaw twitching, sending ripples through the needle-like stubble on his chin. I pulled out my phone and waved it in his face, quickly losing patience while also desperate to hear his story. "I can call the police now, if you like."

His shoulders sagged, and he removed his foot from the door.

"Okay then. Let's start over," I said. "When did this man show up?"

"A couple of days ago."

"What was his name? What did he look like?"

"Mm, Walker, maybe?"

"Walter," I said, dazed, thinking of the notifications on Garrett's phone.

"Yeah, that's it. Walter. He must've been a few years older than Garrett. Said he needed to check on him. That's when I got suspicious. I mean, surely he would've known he was dead?"

"Did he say anything else?" I pressed.

"No, nothing. He left right after I came by. I should've called the police, though. Something about him didn't sit right with me. Did... did he break in?"

"Yeah," I said, eyes flicking to the ransacked living room. Emmett cursed under his breath, but my thoughts were elsewhere.

What had he been searching for?

"Did you get his contact information?" I asked.

"No. He left in a hurry."

I groaned in exasperation. Nothing about my family was easy. Emmett was a busybody, but not an especially good one. "What about his car? Do you remember anything about it?"

"Oh, it was a real beater. Honda Civic, I think. Must've been silver at one point. Gray now. Ohio plates." He hesitated for a moment, then asked, "Who was he? Who was that man?"

I paused, gripping the door frame, shoulders heavy as the truth crashed over me.

"My father."

24

When I arrived home after leaving Garrett's place, the sky had curdled to slate gray and icy droplets battered against the cottage. The gold and scarlet leaves adorning the trees this morning were now hanging limp and tattered from their branches.

I found Ginger cowering beneath the porch, cream-colored paws stained brown with mud. I coaxed her back inside and attempted to wipe away the mud and water droplets snagged in her coat, with little success. Guilt flushed through me at the sight of her distress. It was my responsibility to protect her and keep her safe.

The shards of Garrett's laptop still littered the kitchen floor, along with drops of blood from my sliced finger. My jaw tightened. I lunged for a dish towel and began scrubbing feverishly at the scarlet stains until my palms were red and raw and my wounded finger screamed in protest. Then I swept up the remains of the laptop, scouring the ground to ensure even the tiniest fragments were disposed of, desperate to eliminate any reminders of my fight with Maura. Once the kitchen returned to a semblance of normalcy, I collapsed against a cabinet and cradled my head in my hands as the events of the past few days crashed over me.

So much had changed since the prior evening. At the time, I thought Maura didn't want me finding our father because she couldn't face him again. Now I wondered if she'd destroyed Garrett's laptop because she feared the truths I might unearth within its depths.

I understood why she was afraid. It was easier to believe our father's life ended when he'd disappeared, than to face the possibility that Garrett had been protecting him this entire time.

Her fears were justified. Because of my persistence, I finally had proof that Garrett had maintained a relationship with our father after his disappearance, and likely helped him disappear to begin with.

Garrett had kept his brother's location a secret for decades, but rather than pressure the police to question Garrett, Maura and Joan had severed their relationship with him, destroying any chance of seeing their abuser thrown in prison.

Instead, my father created a new life for himself as Walter Corbin, free from consequence, while his daughter, sister, and wife dealt with the fallout of his actions. For him, the intervening decades might have represented a chance to begin anew. For Joan, Maura, and me, the intervening decades were filled with pain, anguish, and untold suffering that had lingered and festered long after he disappeared.

In the absence of justice, we'd been forced into an uneasy limbo, without any chance of closure. Maura had been so badly damaged by his actions that she refused to discuss his continued existence, much less pursue his overdue punishment.

Stopping my search now wasn't an option. The challenge was finding a way to hold him accountable while protecting my sister from further pain, if that was even possible.

If I didn't stop him, the cycle of abuse would repeat. Others would get hurt. Might have already been hurt. It was on me to ensure he couldn't harm anyone else.

I was the only one capable of doing what needed to be done.

Over the next few days, I scoured the messages and call logs on Garrett's phone to learn more about my father and formulate a plan. He'd spoken with Garrett regularly, and Garrett provided him with financial support, sending money without question whenever he requested it.

I also learned that my father had turned to religion in his later years. He often sent Garrett invitations to join services and events at his church. Garrett, like me, had no interest in religion, and my father, like many Christians, appeared to have no interest in respecting Garrett's secularism. Because of my father's incessant nagging, I learned where he'd been hiding, and a plan took shape.

The following Sunday, I parked outside the Church of Hope and Faith in the rural town of Three Oaks, Ohio. According to the text messages, my father attended church services here regularly. What's more, my father had been foolish enough to be captured on camera. I'd found photos of church events featuring him posted on the church's website and social media accounts.

It seemed my father had slipped into his new life so thoroughly that he'd forgotten he was a fugitive. I was here to remind him of that fact.

I leaned forward against the steering wheel and scanned the herds of people swarming the church, trying to glimpse my father. My eyes kept snagging on a group of children flitting back and forth across the church lawn like starlings at dusk, laughing and carefree. The sight made my stomach churn. I imagined my father watching those children from the shadows of the church like a fairytale monster.

The bell tower tolled, the sound rattling around my skull. The children abandoned their game and joined their parents queuing at the church doors. I forced myself to unclench my jaw and scrutinized the remaining parishioners trickling inside. None of them were my father.

My heart sank as I realized I would need to attend the service. Given how much I resembled my biological mother, I was concerned that he'd recognize me and bolt before we had a chance to speak, so I tucked my hair beneath a knit hat and wrapped a scarf around my neck before heading towards the church.

When I entered the narthex, a squat man with watery eyes cast me a disgruntled look before handing me a program. He gestured at me to remove my hat, but I ignored him, instead pulling it tighter over my ears, and hurried into the nave.

The air vibrated with the sound of organ music; the notes blending together into a cacophony that made my head ache. I skirted around the rear of the church and sank into an empty pew beside a stained-glass window through which bright sunlight streamed.

I studied the congregation, straining to spot my father within the crowded church, but it was useless. The church was packed, and everyone had their backs to me, a sea of people with graying hair. I stifled a groan, frustrated with the situation and worried that my father might have gone underground after Garrett's death. Being in the church rather than the safety of my truck made me feel dangerously exposed.

A woman, man, and their teenaged son hurried into the church, their bickering audible even over the roar of the organ, and filed into the pew beside me. The man in the pew ahead of us swiveled around and cast a disapproving glance at them, and the woman muttered, "Sorry, sorry," under her breath.

The teenager plopped down beside me, slouching, his oversized collared shirt not quite tucked into his wrinkled pants. I scooted away, not wanting to draw attention to myself, but his mother lodged herself into the space between us. She wore a boxy dress with a harsh floral print, her graying hair cut short in a quintessential suburban mom style that made her look older than I suspected she actually was.

"I'm sorry about him," she whispered, gesturing towards the boy. "My son would rather be at home playing video games. He's too old for Sunday school, so he's stuck here with us. We're trying, but it's a hard age. I'm Ellen, by the way."

I smiled politely but didn't respond, instead burrowing deeper into my seat. During the service, I couldn't keep still. I ran my thumb over and over my talisman stone with such feverish energy that my skin burned from the friction. My eyes roved across the pews, searching for my father, my mind racing through questions and possibilities.

What if he already saw me and left?

What if he wasn't here?

If he was, was I strong enough to face him?

By the time the service concluded, my eyelids were heavy, fatigue and boredom clouding my vision. The triumphant chords from the organ echoed against the vaulted ceilings, mingling with murmurs and laughter, jarring me back to the present. I blinked, unraveled my limbs, and gripped the pew in front of me, studying each person who drifted past me, their shining faces relaxed and renewed.

Ellen scooted closer until her shoulder brushed against mine, orienting herself away from her son and husband, who were arguing about lunch options. "Did you enjoy the service?"

"It was fine."

"Will you be staying for the reception? There's juice, coffee, tea. Cake if we're lucky. You can meet the rest of the congregation and Pastor Michael?"

"Sure," I said distractedly. Anything to get her to leave me alone.

Ellen tittered, then departed with her family. The church was almost empty, with no sign of my father. Panicking, I jumped to my feet in time to spot Ellen disappear down a corridor leading to an adjacent building. I hurried behind her, my boots squeaking against the tile floor, and entered a large hall, reminiscent of a school cafeteria.

The burnt, bitter smell of cheap coffee in industrial-sized pots wafted through the air. A young boy darted past me, his lips stained red with juice, and grabbed a plastic plate topped with a slice of sheet cake.

I hovered beside a rack of folding chairs, surveying my surroundings. A sinking feeling grew inside me as the minutes ticked by with no sign of him. Soon doubt began to fester within me.

Perhaps coming here had been a mistake. A dead end. My father could have left town after learning of Garrett's death, concerned someone would piece together Garrett's role in his disappearance, as I had. He'd probably ransacked Garrett's place to remove evidence of his location and pocket some cash, but had been interrupted by Emmett before he could discover the cellphone now tucked in my pocket.

Someone tapped my shoulder. My heart lurched. I whirled around and collided with Ellen. The piece of cake she held outstretched towards me smashed against my chest. It slid down my jacket, leaving behind a trail of sticky pink frosting, and hit the floor with a sickening plop.

Ellen's hand leapt to her mouth. "Oh! I'm so sorry. Walter, someone get Walter," she shouted. "He's our janitor, dear."

I scowled at having become the center of attention. Reaching into my pocket, I grabbed a tissue and blotted at the stain. It wasn't until Ellen ran off, wringing her hands, that I registered what she'd said. By then, it was too late. My head bolted upwards. The napkin fell from my hand.

Because there he was, staring at me.

Walter Corbin.

Brandon Ryder.

My father.

25

I gaped, staring at him.

My father's once raven locks had morphed into wiry, gray ringlets and his skin hung loose from his bones, but he still possessed the thick eyebrows and dark eyes he shared with Garrett. He wore faded jeans and a flannel work shirt that hung loosely from his skeletal frame.

Despite Ellen's yammering, my father's attention was on me. I saw his jaw go tight with tension. He thrust the mop he was holding at Ellen and stormed towards the exit, pushing people aside as he went.

Time slowed down.

I found myself paralyzed, feet rooted into the ground, panic threatening to overwhelm me. Blood rushed into my ears. I struggled to breathe, clawing at the scarf that circled my neck like a noose, hands sticky with frosting.

Willing myself to move, I staggered towards the exit and got outside in time to see a dull gray Honda Civic barrel past me, tires squealing as it swerved out of the parking lot. The possibility of losing him spurred me to action. I sprinted towards my truck, jumped inside, and slammed on the gas. He was stopped at an intersection up the road. I exhaled, heart pounding, and pulled behind him, leaving two cars between us.

The minutes stretched on as I drove down the country highway, eyes locked on his car, praying he wouldn't spot me. I placed the talisman stone on the dashboard like a compass, noticing with alarm that the painted bird had begun to fade, the stone's once glossy, smooth surface now dull.

When my father veered onto a gravel road, I slowed down and parked on the shoulder. I pulled up aerial imagery of the area on my phone, which showed that the gravel road extended about two miles into the woods, interspersed with a few scattered structures. Rather than drive in and risk being spotted, I'd have to walk instead.

A twinge of unease curled deep in my gut. I palmed the talisman stone, thinking through my options. This wasn't the plan. I'd intended to speak with him at the church, in public. But it was too late for that. If my father had any sense, he'd be packing and preparing to leave town. This was my last chance.

I crept through the forest, sunlight filtering through the canopy, illuminating the bare branches that scraped against my arms and the dead leaves that littered the earth. Two crows perched atop a snag riddled with broken branches, their beady eyes following me as I passed below them.

Navigating through the woods was familiar. Comforting, even. Soon my anxiety began to ease, replaced with sharp focus and a clear mind that came from years spent in the wilderness.

Eventually, the forest spit me out into a meadow, barren save for a mobile home perched in the center. It was the color of brown mustard, with rust staining the metal siding like a weeping wound.

My father's car was parked beside it.

I came to a halt and leaned against an oak to steady myself. Its trunk was charred and blackened, the scar rough beneath my fingers. My other hand crept into my jacket pocket and gripped the cool metal resting like an anchor at my side. I could also feel the warmth of the talisman stone as it brushed against my fingers. Taking a deep breath, I moved towards the house, leaves and pine needles crunching beneath my boots, the sound deafening in the still, dead air.

Every bone in my body screamed at me to run. To forget my father ever existed. To bury away the memories of my family's anguish and pain, slip back into the comforting lies on which I'd been raised. But my thoughts kept drifting back to those laughing children in the churchyard, to the horrific abuse my mothers and sister had experienced at my father's hands.

If I gave up, I'd never forgive myself. My willful inaction would make me just as responsible for any further abuse he perpetrated. I had to end this. Now.

I scaled the steps and pounded on the door. The world went still for an agonizing moment. Then the door swung open, revealing my father's snarling face.

"Do you know who I am?" I hated the way my voice wavered, how timidity swelled inside me, threatening to replace my fortitude.

"Of course I do. You think I wouldn't recognize my own daughter?"

"We need to talk."

"Like hell we do. I have nothing to say to you. Now fuck off and leave me alone."

He slammed the door shut, and a deadbolt clicked into place. Forcing myself to stay strong, I rattled the doorknob and pounded my fists against the door.

"I came alone. No police. Just you and me," I shouted. "I only want to talk. If you don't let me in, I'm going to tell everyone at your church exactly who you are. Exactly what you are."

I held my breath. Though silence greeted me, I could sense him lurking behind the door, like a malignant spirit. The door creaked open again. His eyes flickered, calculating, before he strode into the house. I followed behind him.

"How did you find me?" he asked.

"Garrett's phone. I found it at his place."

He scowled, his knuckles white as he gripped a kitchen chair.

"You'd been there, too," I pressed. "What were you looking for? Money?"

"What do you want, Laurel?"

The question took me aback. My mind surged with a cacophony of thoughts and feelings and memories, all fighting to be heard and acknowledged.

I remembered the pain in Maura's eyes as she recounted the story of her abuse.

I remembered the desperation in my mother's voice the night before she died, borne out of her own unresolved past.

I remembered the shock and horror I'd experienced upon learning the truth about my father. Since then, the pain and grief and anger had only wormed deeper and deeper inside of me, growing stronger and more potent each day, until I feared I'd never be free from their iron grip.

"I want justice. For Maura and Joan. For Irene."

Even as I said the words, I knew it was a lie. The darkness lurking within me was no longer a whisper. It rushed through me like a scream, overpowering in its intensity.

I was here for myself.

I wanted to see him suffer.

It was the only way I could move on. Anything other than his complete annihilation would destroy me.

His face darkened. In one swift motion, he threw aside the chair and charged towards me. My heart leapt to my throat. I skidded backwards, boots squealing against the laminate floor. He towered over me, his face beet red, the tendons in his neck straining under loose skin. I stood my ground, even as fear coursed through me.

"I'm the victim here. Not them," he hissed, jabbing a finger in my chest. "Maura and Joan ruined my life. I'd still have my family, if it wasn't for the lies they spread."

"After all this time, I thought you'd show some remorse. You fucked up a lot of people's lives. Including mine."

"You want to see fucked up? This is fucked up." He thrust a finger at a jagged scar just visible beneath the oily hair at his temple. "My dad threw me down the stairs. It wasn't even the first time. But on this special occasion, I cracked my head open like an egg.

"You think I was a bad father? Oh, you have no idea. You girls had it good. I supported you. But what did I get? A cheating wife and a lying daughter. I lost everything, forced to start over in this shithole, with nothing. I've suffered enough, dammit."

He kicked the garbage bin, spilling cans and bottles and rotten food across the floor. I backed away and bumped up against a shelf, the contents rattling. My heart pounded as my deranged father stalked through the confined space like a lion in a cage.

"You don't know what suffering is," I said. "And your exile isn't punishment."

He barked out a laugh. The sound made my skin crawl. Fear of him coursed through my blood, oppressive and paralyzing.

Was this what it'd been like for Joan and Maura? Living with him for years?

"It's your fault too," he said. "Irene wasn't the same after she had you. She laid around all day. Didn't bother to manage the house or be a wife to me. That's when Maura and I got close. She was the spitting image of Joan, you know. And Irene didn't even notice. Or if she noticed, she didn't care."

"Fuck you." It came out little more than a whisper. I could feel myself fading, weakening, reverting back to the scared little girl I once was.

"Your mother was a drunk and a whore. When she got pregnant again, I told her to get an abortion. She wasn't capable of caring for another kid. Hell, she couldn't care for the one she already had. But she insisted. And here you are. Her ghost."

Tears pricked my eyes, even as the blood boiled beneath my skin. "I've heard enough. It's time to turn yourself in."

"You can't be serious."

"I am, though."

"But I've changed. Moved on. Found belonging in a community of believers. God is the only one who can judge me now."

The hypocrisy made me shake my head in disbelief. He was even more delusional than Garrett. The realization helped dissolve some of my earlier fears. "You think they'll want you around, cleaning up their spills, attending church, being around children, after learning what you are? They'll run you out of town. It'll be hard, starting over somewhere else at your age. Garrett can't bail you out anymore. You won't survive."

He flinched, eyes flickering with uncertainty, the malice draining from his mercurial face. I inched towards him, regaining my courage in bits and pieces, emboldened by the flash of fear in his eyes.

"Turn yourself in. Live out the rest of your days in prison, where you belong. You'll have shelter, three meals a day, medical attention. Not too bad, all things considered. More than you deserve."

"I've worked too damn hard for what I have here. There's no way in hell I'll let you take that from me."

"Suit yourself. You want me to leave? That's fine. I'll go back to the church and tell them your real identity. Brandon Ryder, the fugitive. The pedophile. The rapist."

A strangled yell sprung from his chest. Before I could react, he rammed into me. My back crashed into the wall, knocking the wind from my lungs. His hands gripped my shoulders, hot and putrid breath stinging my cheeks. I clawed at him, desperate to free myself, panic bubbling up within me.

He threw me aside like a rag doll. My head snapped against the floor. Pain radiated through my skull, and stars sparked in my field of vision.

Something heavy landed on me, pinning me to the ground. I blinked, struggling to regain my vision. My father, eyes wide and crazed, straddled me.

His hands wrapped around my throat.

26

My lungs screamed for air as my father's hands tightened around my throat. I clawed at him, my vision blurring. Above me, his eyes bulged from their sockets like grotesque blue marbles.

Panic, red and raw, coursed through me, until it was all-encompassing. I fumbled in my pocket for Garrett's gun. It wasn't there. It must have been dislodged from my pocket during the struggle. I lashed my arm over the floor, groping for the gun, for anything.

Darkness danced at the edges of my vision. My fingers grazed a bottle. I arched my body towards it and curled my fingers around its neck.

I smashed it against his skull.

The impact reverberated up my arm like an electric shock. The bottle crashed to the floor and shattered, shards of glass shooting out like shrapnel. He howled and released my neck.

I hacked and spluttered, lungs gulping down air, rib cage expanding and contracting like an accordion. My trembling fingers probed the soreness blooming around my throat, and I cried out in pain.

Above me, my father clutched his head, which was streaked scarlet. His blood splattered onto my chest. Gasping for breath, I flopped over and crawled towards the door, muscles aching in protest. Slivers of glass dug into my palms while tears and snot streamed down my face.

A strangled cry ripped from his throat. He grabbed my legs and pulled me towards him. My chin collided with the floor, and stars once again sparked across my vision. Something deep inside me wrenched and tore apart, sending shockwaves of pain through my pelvis, a gasp of pain fleeing from my lips. My head was a throbbing, aching mess of pain and confusion.

Jostling one leg free, I kicked him again and again. Each impact sent spasms of excruciating pain through me, sharp and overwhelming. I pushed the hurt deep down, knowing that death would greet me if I didn't.

He grunted and released me. I scrambled away and hoisted myself up to standing. The room spun. Nausea set in, bile rising in my throat. I hobbled towards the door, legs wobbling beneath me as my core screamed in protest, using the wall for support.

Then I saw it. Garrett's gun. The smooth metal barrel glinted in a lone ray of sunlight. Without a moment's hesitation, I lunged for it and cradled the weapon to my chest. I turned towards my father, studying him with curious dispassion. He lay on his side, panting, blood trickling from the gash on his head.

I could leave. Call the police. Let them handle it.

But Maura and Joan shimmered in my mind's eye, reminding me of the system that failed them. Reminding me we couldn't rely on others to bring him to justice. It was my responsibility to make sure he paid for his crimes.

Though he appeared almost feeble, I knew how dangerous he was. How dangerous he'd always been. In that moment, I realized that ending the trauma of our bloodline meant paying with blood.

I steadied the gun at my father and pulled the trigger.

The shot was deafening. My ears rang, eclipsing all other sounds. A red rose bloomed on his lower chest. He stared at it, mouth gaping open, like a fish caught on a hook. Disgust and horror and shame pulsed through me. A gargled cry burst from his lips, shooting out a spray of blood and spittle.

"Please just die," I moaned. "Please, let this end."

But he wouldn't obey. He tried to push himself up to standing, but his hands slipped in his own blood.

I didn't want to watch him suffer. I just wanted him gone.

Hands shaking, I raised the gun again. My father's eyes widened in terror, hands outstretched towards me.

"No, please—"

I squeezed my eyes shut and pulled the trigger again. And again. Putting him down, once and for all.

Eventually, the ringing in my ears subsided, replaced by a deathly silence. My eyelids fluttered open. When I viewed the scene before me, I dropped the gun and crumpled to the ground, cradling my throbbing core.

My father was a twisted mess of limbs, his knees wrenched at unnatural angles. He glared at me accusingly, with glassy, unseeing eyes. His face was pale, like the belly of a dead fish. Blood pooled around him, saturating his clothes, coating his skull.

The magnitude of what I'd done crashed into me. Invisible ropes encircled my chest, pulling tighter and tighter until I couldn't breathe. Despite gulping down lungful after lungful of oxygen, breath shallow and labored, my lungs still screamed for air. My hands tingled, then turned numb, as though they were no longer part of my body. I clutched my aching head, wanting the pain to stop and for oblivion to set in. Tears spilled from my eyes.

I'm not sure how long I sat there, catatonic. Once my breath slowed, I reached my trembling hands into my pocket and pulled out my phone. My hands were shaking so hard I almost dropped it.

I needed to call the police. They'd understand. It was self-defense. I murmured the phrase, evaluating how it tasted on my lips, trying to convince myself it was true. Reminding myself it was true. At least, the only truth I could stomach, even as tendrils of uncertainty crept through my mind, casting doubt on my intentions. I was certain, however, that I was revolted and sickened by the violence I'd perpetrated and was desperate to distance myself from my actions.

I stared at the screen, but couldn't remember my passcode, uncertain if the memory loss was due to shock or a concussion. Or both. But it provided me with the chance to reevaluate my situation.

My father had attacked me first, yes, but I'd shot an elderly, unarmed man. My own father. How much sympathy would I garner from the police?

Hysterical laughter bubbled up from my lungs as I reflected on how horribly wrong everything had gone. Deep down,

I knew my father would never turn himself in. It had been foolish to even try. This outcome had always been inevitable. Why else would I have brought a gun I'd stolen from another dead family member? To defend myself, or to enact vengeance? These questions warred within me, exhausting and overwhelming. I set them aside, forcing myself to deal with the situation objectively.

Going to the police wasn't an option. Neither was disposing of the body. Too much could go wrong. Instead, I decided to transform the scene, make it look like a robbery, and eliminate as much evidence of my presence as possible.

But I'd have to act quickly.

I placed my phone and gun in my coat pocket, then pulled on my gloves and a pair of my father's shoes. With any luck, the police would see a man's footprints tracking through the house.

Then I ransacked the place. I overturned shelves, upended drawers, threw the contents of the medicine cabinet across the bathroom floor. I shoved his wallet and cell phone into my pocket, along with some cash squirreled away in his dresser drawer.

Upon opening the drawer to his bedside table, I froze.

Maura stared back at me.

Hands trembling, I pulled out a stack of photos. Though faded, they were in otherwise good condition, treated with care. On top were photos of Maura, on the cusp of adolescent, doe-eyed and innocent.

Beneath them were more photos, this time of other children. Playing on the church lawn. Eating cake in the church reception hall. Swinging from monkey bars at the playground.

Something inside me broke. My heart was being ripped in two. I'd wanted to be wrong, to find my father timid, remorseful, changed. Was this the extent of his sickness, or had he harmed these children, too?

Fierce rage boiled within me, raw and righteous. This could have been prevented.

If only Detective Harlowe had done his job.

If only Garrett hadn't shielded his brother from accountability.

If only Maura and Joan had pushed harder, instead of viewing my father's disappearance as an end to his sickness, focusing only on their healing.

Any guilt burgeoning within me faded, replaced with hardened resolve. My father had worn a mask for decades. The world needed to know the truth.

After carefully placing the photos of Maura in my pocket, I walked back to the kitchen. Vomit clawed up my esophagus as his pale face swam into view. I forced it down.

I fanned the remaining photos across his lifeless body. I removed my gloves, dipped my finger into his blood, and scrawled a word across the floor.

PEDOPHILE.

Then I left him there to rot.

27

Dark clouds swelled overhead as I drove down the lonesome stretch of highway, away from the scene of carnage I'd left at my father's place. Lightning flashed in my rearview window, followed by the low rumble of thunder. I gripped the steering wheel tight, palms clammy and sticky with blood. My eyelids kept dragging shut, but I forced them open, channeling my waning focus on the road. Every minuscule bump sent waves of pain coursing through my head, my spine, my pelvis.

I made it twenty miles before the nausea, weakness, and disorientation became too much. I pulled onto the shoulder.

Before leaving my father's place, I'd tossed the gun and his wallet, cell phone, and shoes into a garbage bag and thrown it in the back of my truck. Now, I shoved the bag deep inside a plastic storage container containing the radio tracking collars once used in my research. Then I grabbed a duffel bag full of emergency gear and stumbled into a nearby cornfield, each step sending pain through my aching pelvis.

The brittle, yellow stalks lashed against my body as I submerged myself into the field. The world contracted until all that remained was the dead vegetation pressing against me, the dirt beneath my feet, and the swollen sky above.

I collapsed to the ground, curled into a ball, and closed my eyes, raindrops pattering around me. My thoughts drifted to the death left in my wake.

What had I done? How had it gone so wrong?

Questions and uncertainties rattled through my mind, leaving me unsettled and nauseous. I tried pushing them aside, to no avail. The shock and suddenness of it all was too great.

I wondered when my father's body would be discovered. Someone from the church would eventually notice he was missing and check on him. The police would follow soon after. They would question members of the congregation.

Would the woman from the church remember me? Connect my random appearance to Walter's death?

The thought was like pushing over a domino. Soon, my mind generated a list of evidence I might have left behind. Fibers. Hair. Blood. Fingerprints, both mine and my father's.

Would the police realize that Walter Corbin was Brandon Ryder?

Would they trace him to me and Maura?

I groaned. I didn't regret killing the bastard, but I regretted the possibility that I might get caught.

My eyes snagged on the dried blood embedded beneath my ragged nails and speckled across my jeans. In a fit of revulsion, I tore off the clothes and threw them aside. Goosebumps pricked my bare flesh as the chill, wet air blasted against me. I grabbed fresh clothes from my duffel bag and pulled them on, wincing as I became acquainted with the various aches and pains radiating through my body. None were worse than the agony screaming through my lower pelvis, as though something inside me had been torn asunder.

Once dressed, I used a water bottle to wash my hands, scrubbing away blood and dirt until my palms stung. Though the rain was soaking through my fresh clothes, I refused to wear my jacket, which was coated with a congealing mixture of blood and cake frosting. Instead, I shoved the soiled clothes into the duffel bag and gingerly wrapped the scarf around my neck.

Before heading back to my truck, I collapsed to the ground and rested for a moment beneath the bloated gray sky. I longed for the simplicity of the life I'd led before learning my father's name. A time when I was free to wander through mountains and canyons, studying the secretive lives of animals, immersing myself in the intricacy of the natural world.

There was something soothing in the act of observing an animal behaving in its nature. A predator, stalking prey. A mother, caring for her cubs. Human society was corrupt and confusing by comparison. People behaved in ways too bizarre and horrible to contemplate, out of sync with the ancient rhythms of our animal nature.

Murderers and rapists were sometimes called animals, a term meant to denigrate. But it was human, not animal, nature I feared most.

Numbness began creeping through my limbs, dragging me down, blurring my awareness of my surroundings. I shivered, teeth chattering violently in my skull. If I stayed here much longer, I might lie down and never get back up. With herculean effort, every bone and muscle protesting, I struggled to my feet. I grabbed my belongings and headed through the field, craving home.

When I emerged onto the road, I found a police car idling behind my truck.

I skidded to a halt, sick with dread. The policeman glanced at me. His face was still soft with baby fat, despite the patchy mustache sprouting below his nose. I prayed he wouldn't notice my legs quivering, and reached instinctively for the talisman stone for comfort before realizing it was in my bloodied jacket.

"You can't park along this shoulder, miss. Nor can you trespass in that field."

"I'm so sorry, but I just got my period. There was blood all over my pants. I stopped to put in a tampon and change clothes."

The policeman's face turned green, and his lanky limbs wobbled like a scarecrow caught in a windstorm. He cleared his throat, struggling to compose himself. "Well, just, uh, move your vehicle."

Relief flooded through me. "Thanks for understanding."

I turned around and was about to open the tailgate when I remembered the incriminating evidence hidden inside. Heart hammering, I dropped my hand from the latch and shuffled haphazardly over to the driver's side door instead.

"Don't you want to place your bag in the back of your truck?"

My whole body stiffened. Turning around, I found the policeman frowning at me, his hand resting atop the door of his patrol car. I flashed him a weak smile.

"No, that's okay. I should keep the bag up front, in case I need some Advil for the cramps." I prayed he couldn't hear the tremor in my voice. "But I'm leaving, promise."

His brow furrowed, and he stepped towards me. The blood drained from my head. I stumbled backwards, panic bubbling within me.

A low rumble pierced the air, followed by a motorcyclist. She zoomed around the blind curve in the road, leaves and dust billowing in her wake.

The officer's jaw went slack, eyes gleaming. He hurried to his vehicle and careened onto the road after her, sirens blaring, leaving me and my bloody bag of clothes forgotten.

When I arrived home a few hours later, I grabbed the bags from the truck and trudged towards my cottage. Each step felt labored, as though wading through mud. Demons crowded my mind with images of my father's corpse. All I wanted was to clean the blood and sweat from my body and slip into sleep.

But I couldn't. Not yet.

Once inside, I shoved my father's wallet and shoes into the wood-burning stove, doused it with lighter fluid, and flicked a match atop the makeshift funeral pyre. My knees pressed into the hard floor as I watched the flames dance. The coldness in my bones began to thaw.

A shadow flickered at the edge of my vision. Ginger butted her head into my hip, purring, her body soft and warm against mine.

"You scared me half to death, little one."

I followed her into the kitchen and refreshed her food and water bowls. She'd been eating a lot. Gaining weight, too. Her once coarse fur was now glossy and soft, green eyes vibrant. Hard to believe this was the same frightened, malnourished cat I'd watched Garrett throw across a room a few weeks ago.

The acrid stench of burning rubber and plastic accosted my nostrils. I gagged and raced back into the living room. Black smoke billowed from the wood stove. The fire alarm wailed. Ginger bolted beneath the couch.

"Fuck."

I grabbed a fire extinguisher and doused the flames, revealing a charred, blackened lump. I yanked open the windows, then grabbed a chair and teetered atop it, straining to reach the alarm.

Once the wailing stopped, I staggered to the floor. Tears streamed from my eyes. My body trembled. Though I wanted to blame the smoke, I knew my distress was much more.

Ginger emerged from her hiding place, curled atop my lap, and began kneading her paws against me. The gesture only made me cry harder. My head throbbed and pulsed, mind sluggish. It was hard to think. Hard to do anything but sit there, paralyzed, anchored to the ground by Ginger's comforting weight.

There was still more to do. Clean the stove. Dispose of the remaining evidence. Wash my bloodied clothes. Get rid of the gun.

They could wait until tomorrow.

I dislodged Ginger from my lap. Once upstairs, I stripped off my clothes and turned on the shower. Seeing myself in the bathroom mirror was jarring. Bruises bloomed in a black ring around my neck. My eyes were red and bloodshot, the delicate skin beneath them dappled with the fine red spots of burst capillaries. My chin was scraped and bruised. A lump adorned the crown of my head. My belly was distended and swollen, throbbing with each movement.

My hands weren't much better. Despite my earlier attempts to clean them, my nails were still caked with dried blood, while cuts and scrapes crisscrossed my palms, and black soot coated my fingers.

I staggered into the shower. My legs and core shook, muscles straining to hold me upright. I sunk onto the bathtub floor, allowing the scalding water to pound against my back, washing away the sweat and blood and grime.

My eyelids fluttered close. I wanted obliteration. Instead, I saw my father's twisted, broken body.

I never suspected I was capable of such violence. But perhaps violence had always lurked within me, a birthright, waiting for the right moment to awaken. As though I carried the ghosts of my father, my uncle, my grandfather within me, stirring, restless, until bursting forth, like maggots from a bloated corpse.

I saw the jagged scar on my father's head from his own father's abuse.

I saw Joan's body, splayed across the steering wheel of her mangled car, her body saturated with drugs and alcohol used to numb the memories of her brothers' torture.

I saw Irene's body, hanging from a tree, her only means of escape after losing her daughters.

I saw teenaged Maura sprawled on her bedroom floor, wrists sliced open, the blood pooling around her like angel's wings.

This was our family's legacy.

Violence was embedded within the fabric of my being. Stitched into my blood and sinew. Shared with the Ryders that came before me. Passed from one generation to the next, like a grotesque family heirloom. The cancer of violence was as heritable as my blonde hair or Maura's brown eyes.

For years, my family had shielded me from our violent heritage. But learning the truth had cracked me open, allowing the darkest parts of myself to pour out.

I'd left my uncle to die in a tinderbox.

I'd hunted down and killed my father.

I'd committed those horrendous acts because of who I am. Where I'd come from.

A tree blossomed in my mind's eye: the roots nourished by blood; the branches gnarled and withering; the heartwood poisoned. How could anything good bloom from that tree? How could its seeds do anything except rot?

I opened my eyes. Water streamed over my face, tinged pink with blood. A sense of utter clarity and calm descended upon me.

Ending my father's life wasn't enough.

The cycle of violence and abuse needed to stop.

Our bloodline itself needed to end.

28

That night, I dreamed my father was chasing me through a dark forest. His clothes were drenched in blood. Rotting skin hung in pale strips from his skeletal arms. He loomed over Maura, poised to devour her body, sprawled at the base of an ancient pine. Blood poured from a gash in her belly. Her glassy eyes stared at me accusingly.

When I awoke, I was drenched in sweat, clutching my hammering heart as the nightmare faded. I instinctively reached to my bedside table for my talisman stone. It wasn't there. Panic coursed through me. I tore apart the cottage and my truck searching for it, but to no avail. After years traveling with me, the talisman stone was gone.

That was the last night I'd been able to sleep.

In the following weeks, my bed transformed into a battleground. I'd lay awake each night, eyes squeezed shut, praying my mind would stop its ceaseless chatter, the constant parade of gruesome images.

Empty bottles of red wine accumulated beside my bed. The alcohol helped a little. It numbed the pain, allowed me short bursts of sleep, though always punctuated by nightmares.

The day after I killed my father, I tossed the charred remains of the evidence in a public trash bin and buried Garrett's gun deep in the woods. I thought I'd feel better with the evidence gone. But my mind found other ways to torment me. I obsessed over all the evidence I may have left behind. The alibi I lacked. The breadcrumbs pointing me straight towards him.

When a rap sounded on my door a few weeks later, I was certain the police were here to arrest me. A curious mix of relief and dread flooded through me at the prospect. Maybe now I could finally sleep. Before surrendering to my fate, I closed my eyes, savoring the warmth of Ginger nestled beside me.

It wasn't the police. It was Chris.

I peered at her through a gap in the blinds. She paced back and forth across the porch, rubbing her gloved hands together.

"I know you're in there, Laurel!"

Though overwhelmed by the prospect of allowing the outside world to infiltrate mine, I forced myself to unbolt the lock, knowing Chris wouldn't leave. She barreled through the door. The grim determination on her face dissolved when she caught sight of me.

"Oh, honey, what's happened to you?"

I tried to speak but couldn't. Words lodged in my throat. Chris wrapped her arm around my waist. I collapsed against her. Despite her slight frame, she supported me with ease and led me to the couch.

My pelvis still ached from the damage the encounter with my father had inflicted upon it. I knew I needed a hospital, knew there was something deeply wrong inside me, but feared the questions that might follow. Questions that would lead to suspicion, unwanted attention, an investigation. I suffered in silence instead, praying the pain would dissipate, that my body would heal with time and rest.

"For fuck's sake, I can feel your ribs. When did you last eat?"

"I don't remember." My voice was hoarse. I ran my tongue over my lips, discovering they were dry and cracked. My eyelids drooped, fatigue enveloping me like a warm blanket.

"Laurel. Look at me."

She grabbed my shoulders. I forced myself to meet her gaze. Her forehead was creased, her dark eyes filled with worry.

"What's going on? I've been texting and calling, but no response. Did something happen? Something with April?"

I frowned, confused by the question. Though I hadn't heard from April or Maura since our makeshift wake three weeks ago, my thoughts often drifted to them, imagining what our relationships might be like, in the absence of our family's dark history. Despite my best efforts to bring us together, their silence confirmed my fear that our fucked-up family had withered on the vine before it had a chance to bloom. I'd hoped holding my father accountable would create the room necessary for us to grow. Now I understood that killing our demons wasn't enough. The trauma and violence resided within each of us. Our shared inheritance.

"The last time I saw you, you were planning to tell April about her dad, remember?" Chris prodded. "What happened?"

"Yeah. I told her about him. She's strong. Resilient. She'll be okay."

Though I desperately wanted to believe my words, doubts festered within me.

"Why aren't you at the university?"

"Leave of absence. Just until the end of the semester."

But I knew I wouldn't return to Hildegard. Not after what I'd done. Not after learning Richard's true nature. My future, once a bright map of possibilities, was now barren. Still, I longed for my past life immersed in the wild, with the scent of sagebrush on the wind, a flicker of movement in the canyon, a long tail disappearing into the trees. Something I knew I'd probably never return to.

"Something's going on with you." She narrowed her eyes at me. "I can't help you unless you talk to me."

"Just tired. Haven't been sleeping well."

She scrutinized me, one eyebrow raised. My eyes slid from hers, settling on the floor, which was covered in cat hair, litter, and dust. I wracked my mind, trying to remember when I'd last swept.

Part of me wanted Chris to leave me alone. Another part of me wanted her to stay. To lift me out of this mire I'd sunken into. But I risked dragging her down, too.

"You're in pain," she said finally. "I can tell. Did you ever get a diagnosis?"

"I'm fine."

She scrutinized me, then reached out and prodded my gut. Waves of pain crashed through me. I doubled over, gasping, unable to ignore the damage any longer. Chris recoiled, alarm etched in her face. "You're not fine," she said. "We need to get you to a doctor."

I didn't answer. Not that I could, anyway. The pulsing agony within my pelvis was too excruciating, overwhelming my senses.

"I'm going to call the health center, see if they can see you tonight. But first, you need to eat something."

Unable to muster a response, I allowed Chris to guide me into the kitchen. She rummaged through the fridge and cabinets, grumbling about the options, which were slim, even by my low standards. I wrapped my arms around myself protectively, tugging at the strings of my pajama pants, swaying on my feet like a waif. After a few minutes, she handed me a peanut butter and jelly sandwich and told me to sit down. As though I were a child again.

"Make sure you eat that. I'm going to start a fire. It's freezing in here. Then, doctor." She disappeared into the living room.

I picked up the sandwich and took a bite, grimacing as the stale bread sucked the moisture from my tongue. But my body was famished, and I scarfed down the rest of the sandwich with a newfound sense of urgency. I'd been remembering to feed and care for Ginger, just not myself.

Strength slowly returned to my body, the stabbing pain in my pelvis settling to a dull ache once again. I made myself another sandwich, and ate that one, too. Then I started eating peanut butter straight from the jar. I washed it down with a few glasses of water. My face flushed and my muscles thrummed with energy. I felt better than I had in weeks.

Maybe I could convince Chris I didn't need a doctor. It's not like the last one took me seriously. I had no reason to believe this time would be different. The house had fallen silent. Chris hadn't returned to check on me, to ask why I hadn't eaten or showered or slept in weeks, why I'd ignored the chronic pain, my silent companion.

I crept into the living room and found her sitting on the couch, unmoving. She stared at a piece of melted plastic perched atop her knee. A fire roared in the wood stove.

My heart sank. I wasn't sure how I'd missed it. Then again, I hadn't been in my right mind lately. It was inevitable that someone would find out. How could they not, when I could barely function?

When Chris met my gaze, her face twisted in anguish. She jumped to her feet and shoved the piece of plastic and her phone at me. I took them both, avoiding eye contact, wishing I could disappear.

"This is him, right? What did you do? Tell me, Laurel!"

I squeezed my eyes shut, as if ignoring this would make it go away. Chris grabbed my shoulders and shook me, calling my name over and over, forcing me to open my eyes and face the items clutched in my hands.

My father stared at me from his forged driver's license. Though the corners had melted, his assumed name was still visible.

Walter Corbin.

The license must have lodged itself somewhere within the wood stove when I burned his wallet. My mouth went dry. I turned my attention to the news article Chris had pulled up on her phone.

Victim in murder case suspected of being a sexual predator

THREE OAKS, OH — Last Sunday, a Seventy-year-old man was found dead of gunshot wounds to the chest at his home in Three Oaks. Members of the congregation of the Church of Hope and Faith grew concerned when the man, Walter Corbin, failed to appear at the church for Sunday service. In addition to being a member of the Church's congregation, he also served as their janitor and assisted with church functions, including occasionally teaching Sunday school.

The police reported to Corbin's mobile home for a wellness check, where they discovered the gruesome scene. At first, police suggested this crime was linked to a string of burglaries in nearby Prince County, the perpetrator still at large.

However, additional evidence unearthed at the crime scene suggests that Corbin's murder may have been more personal in nature. Police have questioned several families that attend the church after finding photos at the crime scene showing their children at church functions, raising the alarming possibility that Corbin may have been a sexual predator.

Today, that possibility became even more likely as a twenty-three-year-old woman came forward to allege that Corbin had repeatedly molested her when she attended the church with her family during a brief period eleven years ago. The woman claims Corbin threatened to have her family deported if she told anyone about the abuse. Our sources tell us that other alleged victims plan to come forward.

The detective in charge urged the public to remain patient as they sort through the evidence and investigate all possible leads.

The words blurred together. My stomach churned. I thought of that poor girl, frightened and alone, with no one to turn to after my father had abused her, threatened her, silenced her. She'd forever carry that trauma. It would shape who she was. Her sense of self. Her relationships.

I'd been too late to save her. Years too late.

My fingers tightened around the phone. This shouldn't have happened. Maura should have prevented this. She could have pushed the police harder. Hired a private detective. Gone at it alone, as I had.

Instead, she'd pretended our father's disappearance was akin to death. She never once acknowledged that her silence was its own form of abuse, enabling him to prey on other vulnerable young girls.

She'd begged me to stop searching for him. I thought it was because she couldn't face him again. Now I wondered if she'd feared this very outcome, terrified of confronting evidence that her silence cost other girls their childhoods. Their lives.

I thought finding our father would bring us closure. I thought it would bring us closer together. It seemed so foolish now.

"Laurel, look at me. Please."

My attention snapped back to Chris. She peered up at me, face ashen, her lower lip trembling. While I'd stood there, petrified, she'd been crying my name, shaking my shoulders.

"What did you do? Just tell me. Please. Whatever it is, we'll get through it. I can help you. Let me help you."

"I did what needed to be done. What no one else was willing to do. And I don't regret killing the bastard."

Chris's face crumpled. For a moment, she was silent. Then she started pacing, rambling about self-defense and lawyers and psychiatric help. The words spilled from her mouth even as her breath grew shallow and labored.

I grabbed her arm and forced her to face me. She was hyper-ventilating, sweat glistening on her forehead, eyes wide with panic. I squeezed her hand.

"It's okay. You don't need to fix this for me."

"But I promised Joan that I would protect you."

"I don't need protecting anymore."

"I failed you. I failed Joan. How could I let this happen?"

"It's not your fault. This is who I am. It was always going to end like this."

Chris sobbed and pulled me into an embrace. We held each other tight, supporting each other in our shared grief. Our cheeks pressed together, tears mingling.

"I need to call the police," she murmured.

I untangled myself from her arms and nodded. "You can do that. But there's something I need to do first."

29

Chris didn't stop me from leaving. I wondered if she secretly wanted me to get away, but I knew her conscience would eventually win out. It was only a matter of time before she called the police. She always did the right thing. Even when it hurt.

My looming arrest hung over my head, a scythe ready to fall. Before that happened, I needed to see Maura. I didn't want her to learn what happened from a police officer or a sensational news story. It needed to come from me – not only the news of his death and my role in it, but about his life, too. The one he'd assumed after disappearing.

She needed to know that I'd been right about our father. She needed to know that he'd hurt other children. She needed to understand that my actions were inevitable. His death was the only way we could find peace, and the only justice his victims deserved.

A few hours later, I arrived outside Maura and James's townhouse. The giant catalpas had shed their heart-shaped leaves, blanketing the sidewalk in a sea of gold. Three crows feasted on seeds spilling from the moldering mouth of a Halloween jack-o'-lantern perched on their neighbors' porch.

I took a deep breath and knocked on their door. The curtains shifted. Maura stared out at me like a ghost. After a moment, she opened the door, her cheeks flushed a rosy red and a crease burrowed across her forehead. She'd filled out a bit, her belly and hips curved and soft beneath a pair of black leggings and an oversized sweater. She clutched a wooden spoon in front of her like a weapon. I charged inside before she could stop me.

It was my first time inside Maura's place. A wave of longing struck me as I imagined the home we might have shared as sisters, absent from our family's darkness. My body brushed against the plants lining her windowsill, their dark green tendrils spilling out of pots, life bursting at the seams. An open sketchbook sat atop her coffee table beside a set of charcoal pencils and oil pastels.

My breath caught when I spotted the illustration inside. April stared up at me, depicted in precise detail and vibrant colors — her golden skin, scarlet lips, high cheekbones reflecting the light. Hope shone through her eyes, a smile playing at her lips.

There was another image, too. Though partly hidden behind the sketchbook, I knew what the illustration would show, even before pulling it out into the light. Unlike April's, my portrait had been rendered in black charcoal. In it, my jaw was clenched, shoulders tense, and there was a fierceness in my eyes that radiated devotion. Or madness.

Maura slammed the sketchbook shut, nearly catching my fingertips between its pages. She straightened her back and assessed me with calculating eyes, as though daring me to mention the portraits, then sidled over to the kitchen. I threw my jacket aside and followed her.

She removed the lid from a steaming pot and stirred it, hands trembling. Then she rested the spoon on a cutting board beside a chef's knife. My mouth watered at the fragrant smell of her cooking, reminding me of how my grief had starved my body.

"James will be home soon." It sounded like a warning.

"I found him. I found our father."

Maura's already pale face drained of color, leaving her so translucent I could see the spiderwebs of blue blood vessels beneath her eyes. Her shoulders tensed. She drew in a few shaking breaths, clutching the granite countertop.

"Garrett helped him disappear. He changed his name, moved to Ohio, even started attending church. It's where he met his next victims."

Maura's eyes widened with shock. She backed away from me, her chest heaving, breath coming in and out in ragged bursts.

"You could've prevented it," I said. "Instead, you did nothing, and other girls suffered."

"It wasn't my responsibility. The police should've done more, Joan should've done more—"

"It became your responsibility when it was clear no one else gave a fuck."

I'd expected her to respond with rage. Instead, her eyes instead welled with tears. I wondered why she hadn't asked what happened to him.

But then I realized that, somehow, she already knew.

"You didn't have to do it," she said, voice thick with grief. "He wasn't worth throwing away your life. Why didn't you listen to me and let it go?!"

"I did it for you. For us. So we could move on."

Maura shook her head, face haggard, as though she'd aged ten years. "That's what you've never understood. I've already moved on. As best I can."

"But without me."

"I just wanted a normal life, or at least the semblance of one. Doing so meant letting go of the past. It's the only way I could function."

"Even if it meant letting go of me? Even if it meant knowing he might be hurting other girls?"

Her face twisted, its delicate features obscured by the rage that always lurked beneath the surface. She charged towards me, jaw clenched. I stumbled backwards, butting up against the counter. Instead of accosting me, she headed for the fridge and pulled something from beneath a magnet.

"This is the reason I wanted you to stop searching for him." She shoved the item into my hand, eyes glittering with rage. "I was trying to protect myself from him so I could protect my family."

I stared at the image, struggling to make sense of what I was seeing. Of what it meant. My vision blurred, the surroundings fading into stillness. All my efforts had amounted to nothing.

Maura was pregnant.

30

"You're pregnant."

Maura nodded. She inched towards me and gently removed the ultrasound from my limp hand. Her loose hair cascaded over her shoulders as she held the image to her heart.

"How far along are you?"

"Fifteen weeks."

Relief flooded through me. "There's still time. It'd have to be soon, though. I'll go with you."

"I'm not getting an abortion, if that's what you're suggesting. I'm keeping him. James and I want this child."

Him. A boy.

"But we were supposed to be the last Ryders. You, me, April."

"What are you talking about?"

"You can't keep it. You just can't." I began pacing around the kitchen, clutching the hair at my temples. "That thing growing inside you has a piece of Brandon in it. Of Garrett in it."

"Brandon tried to steal my body from me a long time ago. I've spent my entire life trying to regain that control. After what... what he did to me, I didn't think I could even have a baby. I won't let you or anyone else dictate the choices I make about my body. Not again."

"But we can end things. Stop this cycle of pain and suffering."

"This baby will grow up in a loving home. Surrounded by people who care about him. That's how we move on. This represents hope, Laurel."

I stopped pacing and gripped the counter to steady myself. My heart thrummed and skipped. How could she not understand that she wasn't growing a child inside her, but a cancerous tumor, one that carried all the violence and trauma of our line?

"I'm having this child. I wanted you to be part of his life, but it seems impossible now, after what you've done."

Tears streamed down my face. "I'm sorry. I'm so sorry."

I inched towards her, my fingers drifting along the smooth granite countertop. Maura's face softened, and she stretched her arms out towards me.

"It's okay. I know what you're going through. You're hurting. You're consumed with hopelessness. You think it's impossible to move beyond your grief and anguish. But you can. I did, and so can you. You'll get through this. Chris and I will get you the help you need."

She embraced me then, arms wrapping like branches around my body. I closed my eyes, ignoring the stab of pain in my pelvis, burying my face against the crown of her head. Her dark, lustrous hair clung to my wet cheeks.

I couldn't remember the last time she'd hugged me. Once, this was all I ever wanted. But things had changed. I'd changed.

Though I still craved Maura's love like an insatiable hunger, our relationship had always been doomed to be one of separation and heartache.

Joan and Howard gave me a loving home and a safe childhood, but it wasn't enough to stop the darkness within me from bursting forth. It wasn't enough to prevent Maura from falling into a well of depression, self-harm, destruction.

The same would happen to their child. He was a Ryder. It was inevitable.

Maura's firm, round bump pressed against my stomach. I imagined the life within her womb growing stronger, feeding off her vitality, preparing to rip free of her body.

My fingertips brushed against coarse wood, then cold metal. I wrapped my fingers around the hilt, savoring this last moment with her.

Then I plunged the knife into her womb.

Maura gasped and sagged against me, still nestled in my embrace. Her hand writhed against mine, which still gripped the knife. The blade was buried in her belly up to the hilt. Warm, sticky blood coated our hands, pattered onto the floor.

I wanted to keep holding her, but my arms strained beneath her weight. She dragged us both to the ground. I cradled her head in my lap as her hands scrabbled against the wound. Her wide brown eyes roved, seeking out mine, clutching my hand. Tears poured from my eyes and fell onto Maura's smooth, white cheeks, like rain streaming down marble. I tasted salt on my lips.

Atop the stove, the lid on the cooking pot rattled. Boiling hot broth bubbled over, cascading down the oven, splattering around us. Maura drew in a shuddering breath, moaning with pain. Her mouth was tinged with scarlet. Though her lips moved, no words came out. Blood spurted from her belly in sickening pulses. Her eyelids fluttered, eyes rolling back to reveal the whites. I clenched my hands over my ears, smearing blood on my cheeks, unable to bear hearing her distress, unable to gaze upon her writhing body.

I realized that I'd killed her. Even if she wasn't dead yet. Even if it hadn't been my intent. I'd only wanted to kill the thing growing inside her. To destroy the last remnant of our family's lineage. To stop the spread of violence, of abuse, of trauma.

My trembling hands reached again for the knife. I loosened her fingers from the hilt and wrenched the knife from her body. She screamed, a keening, agonizing howl that lodged within my skull. Blood poured from her like a red wave, spreading across the kitchen floor.

"I'm sorry," I whispered. "So sorry. This is the only way."

I slashed my own wrists. Sheets of blood poured down my forearms. The room spun. I collapsed beside my sister, grasping her limp hand with my trembling one. Lights flashed through the curtains, piercing my eyes like shrapnel.

Maura grew still and quiet. Soon I did the same.

And the world slid into blackness.

31

In the darkness, I dreamed of Maura. She floated beside me, tendrils of hair circling her pale face in a halo. Blood billowed from her mouth, staining the water scarlet. She clawed and grasped at my legs, dragging me deeper and deeper into the murky blackness of the sea.

Even though I struggled to awaken, the darkness fought back. I battled against the riptide of exhaustion threatening to pull me down into fitful slumber, where Maura roamed like a vengeful spirit.

I didn't want her haunting me. I had enough ghosts.

When my eyelids fluttered open, I was greeted by an onslaught of harsh fluorescent light and the acrid scent of antiseptic. I blinked, straining to bring my surroundings into focus, trying to remember why it felt as though someone had ripped my heart out.

As my eyes adjusted to the glare, I realized white sheets pinned me to a hospital bed in a suffocating grip. I lifted my head. A wave of dizziness and nausea flooded through me. I groaned and collapsed against the pillow, struggling to choke down the bile rising in my throat.

I heard the low hum of medical equipment, the steady beep of my vital signs on the monitor beside me. Once the vertigo passed, my eyes slid across my body and rested upon the bandages wrapped around my wrists and forearms. Dried blood stained the crisp white gauze. A needle trailed from my left arm to a clear bag of liquid hanging from a metal stand.

My right wrist was handcuffed to the bed.

I jolted upwards, panic ripping through me. I struggled against the restraints, limbs thrashing, heart pummeling against my rib cage.

A door creaked open. Cold, callused hands pressed on my shoulders, holding me still. My eyes roved. Chris stood above me. Her face was drawn and haggard, hair mussed, and black rings circled her red-rimmed eyes.

"Just breathe, Laurel. It's gonna be okay."

I wanted to respond, but found my lips parched, voice elusive. The inside of my mouth tasted of poison and rot. I locked eyes with Chris and shook my head. Things would never be okay again.

Low murmurs floated through the air. Detective Harlowe strode into the room. He arrested me for the murders of Brandon and Maura Ryder.

My heart shattered when he said Maura's name. I thrashed and yelled and screamed and cried, trying to make them understand I hadn't meant to kill her, but my words came out garbled. Chris stumbled away, tears streaming down her face, shivering despite the warm glow of the overhead lights.

My heart rate spiked. The monitor beeped out a furious rhythm. Harlowe raced to the door and shouted something unintelligible. Nurses rushed in. I struggled away from their prying hands, sobbing. I couldn't let them pump me full of the poison that made the world foggy. Made the nightmares come.

But in the end, they restrained me. Cold leached through my veins, pulsing in time with my beating heart. The room blurred. My eyelids fluttered closed.

I'm not sure how long I stayed at the hospital, drifting in and out of consciousness, veins pumped full of drugs. Fleeting moments of wakefulness were punctuated by crushing guilt that pushed the air from my lungs, suffocating me.

Chris told the doctors about my symptoms, insisted that I needed help, unwilling to accept anything less than a barrage of tests. Despite the horrors inflicted by my hands, she was still willing to stand by me. Her persistence paid off. After weeks of slowly escalating pain culminating in the agony I'd experienced after killing my father, I received a diagnosis.

My ovaries were covered in cysts. Twisted, swollen masses, my body gone haywire. When my father attacked me, the cysts ruptured, spilling their malicious contents into my abdominal cavity, where the poison had festered. The gynecologist remarked her surprise that I hadn't gone to the emergency room, doubled over in excruciating pain. I told her that I couldn't face another indifferent doctor who dismissed my pain, insisted my problems were emotional, not physical.

They operated on me. Scooped out my contaminated, rotten ovaries, leaving me hollow and barren. No chance of children.

It was a relief.

After I'd recovered from my surgery, the police transferred me to the Deer Creek Correctional Center for Women. I spent my first few days there confined to a cell the size of a closet where harsh light rained down on me twenty-four hours a day. My bed was a thin rubber mat streaked with white scratches from the roving fingernails of a previous occupant.

Eventually, they moved me into the general population, and I was allowed to see visitors. Chris visited several times, though I'm not sure why. Perhaps she still viewed me as her kin. But every once and awhile I'd catch her staring at me as though I were a rabid animal that might snap its jaws around her neck. In those moments, I knew I was a stranger to her.

During her first visit, Chris explained what happened the night of Maura's death. She suspected I might visit Maura, so she called her, explained what I'd done, and begged her to be careful. When Maura opened her curtains and saw me standing outside, she texted Chris, and Chris called the police.

By that point, the police in Three Oaks had already identified me as a suspect in my father's murder. They had been inundated by a steady stream of young women affiliated with the Church of Hope and Faith, who accused Walter Corbin of childhood sexual abuse. After running his fingerprints, they realized Corbin was actually Brandon Ryder and pulled Detective Harlowe into the case.

The police told him about the strange young woman who'd attended the church's Sunday service the morning of Brandon's death. The same woman who'd been spotted parked illegally on the shoulder of a highway. The same woman who'd visited Detective Harlowe, asking questions about her father's whereabouts, clutching the talisman stone that was later found at the scene of the crime.

It turns out Harlowe wasn't as incompetent as I'd once believed.

By the time the police and paramedics arrived at Maura's home, it was too late to save her. Some days I felt relief, others despair, that they'd rescued me before I succumbed to death. It seems I have a knack for destroying those around me without destroying myself.

I pled guilty to both murders. It seemed easier that way. I wanted to move on, even if it meant spending the next three decades in prison. Later, some of my father's victims wrote me letters, thanking me for what I'd done.

I never responded. I just wanted to be left alone.

Over time, Chris's visits became fewer and farther between. I couldn't blame her. She'd been trapped in our family's orbit for too long. She needed to move on. I was comforted by the knowledge that Ginger was safe in her care.

Luis and Petra visited once. After contacting the former student Howard had been helping before his death, they learned Richard had harassed other students over the years. Together, they built a coalition and pressured the university until the system buckled. Richard left in disgrace. Luis and Petra transferred to new advisors and graduated this past spring. Against all odds, they received justice.

James never contacted me, though Chris said they stayed in touch. Consumed by grief, he moved to another state and tried to start over, but the deaths of his partner and unborn child loomed over him, a permanent stain on his soul.

I wondered if he hated me.

I wondered if he thought my imprisonment was justice enough.

I wondered if he wished me dead.

The worst part was April's silence. We hadn't spoken since she departed Grenadier on that train. I wrote to her several times, trying to explain myself. I didn't want her forgiveness, nor did I deserve it. Instead, I wanted her to understand that the Ryder line needed to end with her.

She never wrote back.

Until two weeks ago.

32

When April wrote and asked to be added to my list of approved visitors, I didn't know what to think. I'd taken her silence as evidence that she'd renounced the Ryder side of her heritage. Renounced me. Like Maura, she seemed to think that severing her connection with our family was enough to escape the trauma inherited through our bloodline.

It wasn't enough. She carried our family's darkness within her, just as I did. It was only a matter of time until it awakened.

Now, two years after I'd last seen my cousin, I sat at a table in the prison's visitation room, waiting with nervous anticipation for her to arrive. I closed my eyes and took a few deep breaths, trying to calm the rising tide of anxiety within me.

It was hard to find moments of stillness in prison, and today was no exception. The room filled with the sound of laughter, raised voices, sobs; the whir of the vending machine dispensing snacks; and the crinkle of chip bags, together creating a cacophony that sent my nerves aflame.

The chair across from me squeaked as someone dragged it across the floor. My breath caught. I opened my eyes and found April staring back at me, jaw clenched, eyes glinting, body as taut as a piano string. Her hair was longer now, styled in an intricate braid that draped over her emerald green sweater. The color made my eyes ache after being submerged in an endless sea of orange, beige, and navy for the past two years.

My cheeks flushed as she scrutinized me. I traced a fingertip self-consciously over the knotted scar tissue crossing the bridge of my nose, received in a scuffle a few months after lock-up. My once-blonde hair was streaked with premature silver, and the skin beneath my eyes was bruised purple from years of sleepless nights.

April's eyes slid to my bare forearms, which rested upon the table. The other prisoners were used to seeing the twin scars. The ones that mirrored Maura's.

I didn't care about the cruel, judgmental words that the other women whispered behind my back or shouted in my face about the jagged, silver lines. Taunting my failure to end my life. Goading me to finish the job. The words slid off me, like water over a window. It was necessary, in order to survive. But here with April, I felt uncharacteristically self-conscious, and found myself tugging the sleeves of my sweater over my wrists.

We stared at each other for a few moments, both orienting to the others' presence. Conscious of our limited time together, I broke the silence first.

"You never responded to my letters."

"I had nothing to say to you. Not after what you did."

"I never meant for her to die."

"But you were fine killing your sister's unborn child. Your nephew."

Though I'd expected her anger, her words still made me flinch. I wracked my mind, trying to find the right words to make her understand. "We carry violence in our blood. It's part of us. It would've been part of him, too."

Her face twisted in disgust. "I'm descended from slaves, Laurel. That's intergenerational trauma. Not the shit you're dealing with. Tons of people manage to deal with their abuse without murdering their family members. That's on you, and you alone."

"I grieve for Maura every single day of my fucking life. I'm paying for what I did. If you came here to berate me, you've wasted a trip."

"This isn't just about you. That's what you don't get. After Maura... died, I fell into a depression. I tried to hide it from my mom, but she knew something was wrong. So I cracked and told her everything." She laughed softly. "This experience actually brought me and my mom closer together. I finally told her how isolated I feel in my family. Like I'm a stranger. She helped me resolve some stuff with my stepdad and half-sister. At least something good came out of this mess."

The tension in my shoulders lessened somewhat. I was relieved she'd grown closer with her mother and found the belonging and love she'd always sought from her family. Belonging that Garrett had been incapable of providing her. I only hoped it was enough to save her from our family's curse, the never-ending cycle of suffering and pain the men in our family had inflicted upon us.

"My mom told me something else. Something you need to hear." She paused for a moment, taking a deep breath. "My parents didn't have a one-night stand. They were together for a few months. When my mom got pregnant, he got scared and ran off. She was crushed. Embarrassed, too. Her family didn't know about the relationship, and she was too proud to ask him for support. So she made up a story and stuck to it. Even when I begged her to tell me more."

"So Garrett lied," I said, shrugging. "Not surprising, given his history."

"He didn't, Laurel. That's what you're not getting. Garrett wasn't my father. I'm not a Ryder. And neither are you."

33

I stared at April, struggling to process what she'd just said. Because it didn't make sense. She was a Ryder. We both were.

"You're wrong. We're cousins. My birth mother didn't have any siblings. Garrett has to be your father. It's the only plausible explanation."

"My mom knew who my father was. It wasn't him. It wasn't Garrett."

"That's impossible. The DNA test—"

April slammed her hands on the table. I stared at her in mute shock, while the guard near our table cast a concerned look in our direction.

"Just stop, Laurel. I'm sick of you force-feeding your version of the truth to whoever'll listen. It's my turn now. So shut the fuck up and just listen to me."

My mouth slammed shut, reeling from the viciousness in her voice and the malice glinting in her eyes. How could she not be a Ryder, with that rage percolating beneath her skin, prepared to boil over at the slightest provocation?

"My dad's name is Ethan Becker. My mom finally realized how important it was for me to learn where I came from. She reached out to him, and he agreed to meet me. He even took a paternity test. It... it came back positive, Laurel. He's my dad."

The room started spinning. Waves of nausea pulsed through me. Bile churned upwards from my stomach, scorching my throat. I tried to respond, but found my mouth dry, vocal chords paralyzed, forced to listen as she spun more lies.

"Finding him was so incredible. My dad. The man I'd been searching for my entire life."

April's eyes lit up and her voice filled with longing. For a moment, I saw a glimmer of the hopeful, radiant young woman I met at a Chicago café two years ago. Back when things were simple, and my life made sense.

"Despite everything that happened with Garrett, all my previous expectations and hopes about my actual father came rushing back. But then I met him, and I realized he'd spent the past few decades pretending I didn't exist." She fell silent, her face hardening. "Maura was right. We give blood too much power. I know that now. But it still matters to you."

I pressed my hands tight over my ears, fingernails digging into my scalp, determined to drown out her voice, unwilling to face what was coming next. Instead, her voice was replaced by Garrett and Brandon whispering in my ear. Their voices melded with hers, nourishing the seeds of doubt they'd planted years before.

Your mother was a flirt. A whore. A slut.

April leaned forward and rested her elbows on the table, eyes boring into mine. I struggled to wrench my gaze from hers, but found myself unable to look away, filled with morbid curiosity. Like a motorist craning their neck to view the shattered remains of a crashed car and its broken inhabitants. Defeated, my hands fell into my lap.

"Turns out Ethan has a brother. Harry. He's your dad, Laurel. Your real dad."

Even though I'd braced myself for the revelation, her words hit me like a punch to the gut. Still, I managed to choke out two words. "You're wrong."

She cocked her head to the side and smiled at me, as though I were a particularly slow child requiring extra attention.

"I met with Harry, and he told me everything. His long-term affair with your mom. Her troubles with Brandon. He was willing to leave his family to be with her, but she always refused. She thought Brandon would kill her if she tried to leave.

"One day, she ended things with him. Apparently, it was very sudden. Devastating, even. The timing was interesting, though. It happened while she was pregnant with you."

"You're wrong," I whispered. "Brandon Ryder was my father."

She continued as though she hadn't heard me. "Harry didn't learn about your birth or your mom's suicide until years later. He suspected you might be his child but chose to ignore your existence. Like his brother chose to ignore mine.

"You see, Laurel, we aren't Ryders after all. Just cousins whose fathers wanted nothing to do with us."

Each word sliced through me like a knife, leaving me weak and trembling, as though the blood had drained from my body. April leaned back, arms crossed over her chest, and stared at me with something close to hunger in her dark eyes. As if eager to devour my despair.

I refused to succumb to her lies. Her story was nothing more than a manipulation designed to punish me. Violence was embedded in my blood, a product of my family's lineage. Our bloodline was tainted, our children destined for lives of pain and despair. I couldn't allow her to convince me otherwise.

Because if she was right, and I wasn't a Ryder, it meant my violence was a choice. And I couldn't accept that.

"Do you understand now? Maura's death was meaningless. It was all for nothing. You can't use your blood as a reason for your crimes. As an excuse for your crimes. Because Brandon and Garrett's blood isn't your blood at all."

Rage coursed through my veins, as potent and deadly as venom. I burst upwards from the table, my chair screeching as it skidded across the floor. I lunged forward and grabbed her sweater, yanking her towards me. Her eyes widened with terror.

"You're wrong!" I screamed, spittle flying from my lips. "You're wrong, you're wrong, you're wrong!"

Around us, people jumped from their seats, shouting and scattering in every direction. Someone grabbed my arm and tried to pull me off her. I shrugged from their grasp, shouting those words in her face over and over like a mantra as she cowered beneath me.

Then a barb burrowed into my back, rendering me speechless. Excruciating pain radiated through my entire body. My grip on April's shirt loosened. I collapsed to the ground, muscles twitching and convulsing, my skin crawling with fire ants, struggling like a fish caught on a hook.

Someone's knee pressed into my back, pushing the air from my lungs. I heard shouting, the words garbled and meaningless. My mouth filled with the coppery tang of blood. Spittle dribbled from my mouth, pooled on the floor beside my cheek.

A muffled shriek burst from my chest. My eyes roved past the scuffed leather boots of the prison guards and the fearful, pitying eyes of nearby prisoners and visitors, before settling on April. My only remaining kin. She locked eyes with me for a calculating moment, mouth curling into a grimace.

She turned on her heel and walked away.

34

I spent the next week locked in solitary confinement, where I slowly lost my mind. For the first few days, I paced back and forth in my cage, howling like a trapped animal as the walls and ceiling pressing tight against me, unable to see the sun or sky or stars. Faceless correctional officers monitored my every waking moment to prevent me from ending my suffering. To ensure I didn't gnaw off my own leg to escape the trap.

Eventually, I fell still and nursed my wounds. The taser left a bright red circle on my shoulder. It would leave a scar, joining the ones crisscrossing my wrists and the ones carved on either side of my belly; permanent tattoos reminding me how I'd failed my sister, my nephew, my cousin, my family. Reminding me of the rottenness within me.

At night, I lay awake atop a bare mattress, unable to sleep for fear of nightmares, deluged by harsh lights that never ceased. Then the nightmares started haunting my days. During those episodes, it felt as though thorns were wrapping tighter and tighter around my heart with each shallow breath, until I was certain blood would pour from my mouth and nostrils.

I finally realized how Maura felt when confronted with reminders of her past. Caught in a hellish loop, forced to relive the most terrible moments of her life over and over. Each time we'd met, I'd grabbed her and pushed her back into that never-ending carousel of horrors.

With only my thoughts for company, I was forced to examine the beliefs and stories I'd nurtured ever since learning the truth about my heritage. I'd convinced myself that the violence and anger lurking within me had sprouted from the dark seed of my bloodline, gestated by previous generations of Ryders. I'd convinced myself that killing Maura and her unborn child was necessary to end the cycle of trauma and abuse. That violence was an inevitable expression of my genetic code; the reason I could commit horrific acts against my kin.

I'd wanted to pull our family tree up by the roots and poison the earth so nothing else could grow.

I needed our suffering to mean something. It was the only way I could make sense of my family's history; otherwise, the pain and horror were too much to bear.

But there was no greater meaning. There couldn't be, because I wasn't a Ryder. I alone was responsible for my actions, rather than some deep-seated flaw in my genes. How could I bear that truth?

Killing Brandon hadn't been self-defense. I knew that now. I hated and despised him for the torture he'd inflicted upon my sister and mothers. I wanted to avenge their suffering. Once I tasted the righteousness of violence, I allowed it to wield me, embracing it as my inevitable inheritance. Rather than challenge my motivations, I charged forward, blinded by falsehoods and a desire to end our suffering. My sister died because of it.

As I lay in that prison cell, tears streaming down my face, I realized what Maura's pregnancy had meant. What the life she'd created for herself had meant.

Hope.

For herself. For our family. For me.

A chance to be a sister. An aunt. A cousin.

A chance for our family to blossom into something wondrous and new, free from the shadow of our family's blemished history.

I'd destroyed it all.

When Maura first showed up at our parents' graveside, I'd wanted her to be the angry, desperate girl I'd grown up with. It blinded me from seeing the woman she'd become. She'd built a life for herself, brimming with color and light and love. She'd shown up for me, even when it hurt.

I'd repaid her by retraumatizing her, over and over, until there was nothing left.

Maura had been right. The only path towards healing was by moving beyond the past and focusing on the future, built on compassion and love. Our past would still haunt us, be a part of us, but it didn't have to define us. Maura had offered me a chance at sisterhood, but I was too stuck in the past to accept the chance to begin anew.

She taught me that blood matters, but it also disappoints. Sometimes it isn't enough. Other times, it's enough for a start.

I never deserved her in my life.

By the time my isolation ended, I no longer recognized myself. My body had crumbled to pieces, with old parts of me sloughing off, revealing raw, pink skin beneath. I studied the woman in the mirror with a mixture of curiosity and dispassion, wondering who she was. Where she'd come from. Who she might become.

During my absence, I received a package and a letter from April. I opened the letter first, which contained two documents. The first page displayed lines of embellished genetic code and a list of relatives I'd matched with.

April Heller, first cousin.

Ethan Becker, uncle.

Harry Becker, father.

On the second page was a letter from my father. Whatever that meant. I'd had enough fathers to fill several lifetimes. Still, I handled the letter with care, as if it would singe my fingertips.

Dear Laurel,

I'm sorry I wasn't there for you when you needed me. If I had, maybe you wouldn't be where you are now. I'm partially responsible for that. Despite all you've done, I'm not ashamed to be your father, but I am ashamed of abandoning you and your mother when you needed me the most. I loved your mother more than you will ever know. I wish you had the chance to know us both.

I forgive you. I hope you can one day forgive me. Please write.

With love and regret,

Dad

The blue ink smudged beneath my fingertips as my tears pattered across the page. My body felt numb, unable to process what this meant or decide whether it actually mattered. After so long spent obsessing about my heritage and bloodline, I found myself detached, bordering on uncaring. Perhaps the pain and longing would come later, once I allowed a glimmer of hope to pierce through the darkness.

I opened the second package, from which spilled an assortment of handwritten letters, cards, postcards, sketches, and photographs.

All from her.

My heart lurched, waves of emotion rippling through me, stirring my body from its state of inertia. Tears sprang from my eyes before my mind could fully register the package's contents. Hands trembling, I gathered up the materials into a neat stack and read the first page, written in April's handwriting. It took several attempts to comprehend the words, tears blurring my vision. I choked back a sob as realization crashed over me.

These were Maura's missing letters. Not destroyed by Joan, as we'd suspected, but squirreled away in a safety deposit box, where they'd waited patiently until Chris discovered them while executing Joan's will. Unsure whether they were a blessing or a curse, Chris contacted April, asking for her advice. April decided to share them with me, though I wasn't sure if they were meant as a punishment or kindness.

I'd spent my entire life yearning for and doubting Maura's love, when it was there all along. Hidden, obscured, and twisted until it was finally annihilated. I leafed through the pages and cards, skimming Maura's words, not quite ready to lose myself in phantom memories and dreams of what might have been.

Unable to bear these reminders of what I'd lost, I unlocked the locker beside my bunk and placed the letters inside, atop a small collection of photos of my family and a few of Maura's sketches.

Grabbing a notebook and pen, I curled atop my bunk. Beside me sat a small white stone I'd found in the prison yard, upon which I'd scrawled an image of a bird in flight. The illustration was crude. I never had Maura's artistic talents. When I lost the original stone, I lost my way. Unwilling to risk losing myself again, I picked up the stone and squeezed it tight, its jagged edges biting into my palm.

I began writing a letter.

Afterword

While The Inheritance is a work of fiction, the reality of family abuse—particularly incest—affects far too many lives. Studies indicate that incest is more pervasive than most people realize, yet it remains one of the most underreported and stigmatized forms of abuse. Survivors often carry the weight of this trauma in silence, uncertain of where to turn for help or healing.

If you or someone you know is struggling with the effects of incest or other forms of sexual abuse, know that you are not alone. There are organizations dedicated to offering support and resources to survivors:

RAINN (Rape, Abuse & Incest National Network)
Website: www.rainn.org National Sexual Assault Hotline Phone: 1-800-656-HOPE (4673)

1in6 (Support for Male Survivors of Sexual Abuse)
Website: www.1in6.org

Healing is a journey, and reaching out for support is a courageous step. There is always hope.

With care,
EV Morgan

Acknowledgments

Many people influenced the trajectory of this novel and provided invaluable support throughout the writing process. I am indebted to Shelly Stinchcomb for her early feedback on the plot and characters. Thank you for helping me understand Maura and your role in bringing her to life. I am also grateful to Emily Ohanjanians and Kieran Devaney for their feedback on later drafts of this novel. Thank you to Alexia for serving as a beta and sensitivity reader. Thank you to my early readers and dearest friends – Lindsey, India, Neal, and Ezekiel. To Melissa, thank you for stating the obvious – that I should write stories – and for helping me feel like I could. And to Neal, thank you for asking the challenging questions and showing me what it means to be creative.

About the Author

E. V. Morgan

E. V. Morgan lives in the San Francisco Bay Area with her partner, two cats, and a dog. She works in the field of environmental conservation. This is her first novel.

www.ingramcontent.com/pod-product-compliance
Lightning Source LLC
Chambersburg PA
CBHW071540110726
47908CB00007B/1948